shrug

shrug

A Novel

LISA BRAVER MOSS

SHE WRITES PRESS

Published 2019
Printed in the United States of America
ISBN: 978-1-63152-638-1
ISBN: 978-1-63152-639-8
Library of Congress Control Number: 2019933686

For information, address:
She Writes Press
1569 Solano Ave #546
Berkeley, CA 94707

She Writes Press is a division of SparkPoint Studio, LLC.

To survivors of childhood domestic violence,

And to all who aspire despite the odds

part one

1

shrug

I call it my shrug, but it's not a regular shrug. It doesn't mean I don't care about stuff, or that I don't want to talk. It doesn't mean "I don't know"—though if my story were made into a famous book, some English major would probably write about how not knowing is a big deal in the main character's life. But meanings aren't the point. The point is, sometimes, for no particular reason, my right shoulder just jumps up.

This quirk of mine does not exactly help in the coolness department. Frankly, it's a miracle I got through Cragmont Elementary, King Junior High, and now Berkeley High School, class of 1972, rah-rah, go Jackets, without ever getting hit at school. Maybe the kids have always considered me so pathetic that it's never occurred to them to clobber me. Teasing, rolling of eyes, snickering, spitballs—sure. But no hitting.

Sometimes I forget I wasn't born with the shrug. It started when I was five, right after my mother got mad at my kindergarten teacher and wound up pulling me and my older sister, Hildy, out of school for a month in protest. Even in Berkeley, where people make a point of being against the establishment, parents didn't do things like that.

I remember I couldn't wait to start kindergarten. Mainly, I think,

I wanted to show the teacher how much I already knew. For two years, since she'd started kindergarten herself, Hildy had taught me everything she learned. After school, she'd grab the little wooden step stool from our bathroom sink and drag it into the room we shared. She'd turn it backwards so the stool's bottom step was my seat and the top step the surface of my desk. I'd climb in, and then she'd stand in front of me with a little portable chalkboard. Even though she knew my mother would get mad, Hildy had taped her hairbrush to the chalkboard as a handle. She had a worn-down piece of white chalk that she'd use to write on the board. Then she'd hold the thing up to show me what she'd learned that day.

I'd sit up with a straight back and listen, my hands folded neatly in front of me on the surface of the "desk." If I wanted to ask or answer a question, I'd raise my hand just like a real student. I had to wait for Hildy to call on me—"Yes, Martha?"—and if I forgot to raise my hand and blurted something out, she'd pretend she hadn't heard.

If my mother happened to pass Hildy's room while I was being tutored, she would tell Hildy to stop being so officious, or she'd say Hildy had no concept of child development. I'm serious. To a seven-year-old.

Even at five, I knew it would hurt my mother's feelings if I defended Hildy. But sometimes I just had to, because of all the games Hildy and I played, teacher-and-student was my favorite. My mother was always reading to us, and telling us how important books were, and how important it was not to skim them, to really savor them and understand them thoroughly. You'd think she'd be happy that I wanted to learn. But that wasn't how things worked with my mother.

I hoped my mother couldn't tell how excited I was to be starting school, because she might start crying if she knew I didn't want to stay home with her anymore. Plus, she said Miss Kitchen, who had also been Hildy's kindergarten teacher, was "rigid." My mother didn't approve of Miss Kitchen's rules, her perfect tight curls, her garish coral lipstick, her ironed, pleated dresses, her long, skinny body. My mother was getting fatter because she was pregnant with our younger brother, Drew, and she said that was the natural way for a woman's body to look.

Natural: to this day, I can't stand that word, even though all the cool kids at school think natural means good. Which, obviously, they wouldn't think if they had a natural tendency to shrug.

If I liked Miss Kitchen, my mother might have a conniption—tell me I didn't have good taste, or say I didn't understand how "imperative" it was to preserve a child's natural creativity and individuality. So I was pretty anxious going in.

When I was little, I used to suck my thumb, and at the same time (this is really embarrassing) rest my other hand over my crotch. I did this outside my underwear, and I was really young, but it's still embarrassing to talk about. Anyway, my mother told me that other mothers were ignorant and got angry with their kids for that kind of thing, but that she didn't believe in squelching children's natural instincts.

The night before school started, my mother overheard Hildy telling me I was going to like Miss Kitchen, but that I shouldn't suck my thumb or reach underneath my dress at school. My mother told Hildy to stop trying to damage my self-esteem.

I woke up early. I got up and put on my very best dress, white socks, and the white patent leather shoes Hildy had grown out of. I climbed up on the step stool and looked at myself in the bathroom mirror. I brushed my teeth, and then I brushed my hair, an unruly mess of thick chin-length brown curls going who knew which way. If I left it up to my mother, my hair wouldn't look as good. When I was ready, I woke Hildy, and we went downstairs to have cereal.

Eventually, my mother got up and came downstairs. I thought she'd make me change clothes. I thought she'd say it was ridiculous to put on a party dress for school, or that dressing that way wasn't going to make the teacher like me, because clothes don't matter, it's only what's on the inside of a person that matters, blah blah blah. Instead, she just patted me on the head and smiled.

That was another thing about my mother: sometimes, she was nice. To me, at least. I can't think of a time when she was nice to Hildy or Drew, but then, neither of them made the kind of effort with my mother that I made. How was I supposed to know that all my effort wasn't going to save me?

During the walk to school with Hildy that first day, lugging a pillow under my left arm and a scratchy, faded-green army blanket under my right, I started crying. Hildy grabbed the blanket and carried it for me, and assured me that school was going to be a lot more fun than being at home. I wiped the tears away with the backs of my index fingers.

It turned out Hildy was right. Miss Kitchen's room was a spacious wonder of art supplies and books and pictures on the walls and wooden cubbyholes with all the children's names already printed on them. The wooden cubbyholes were each painted, and there were four colors: red, blue, green, and yellow, in that order. I loved being in a big class with lots of kids and the activity schedule written out neatly on the blackboard. Because of Hildy, I could read.

In the middle of the morning, it was rest time. I saw that only a few other children were sucking their thumbs. But I had that five-year-old idea that my mother knew everything; I was worried she'd find out I hadn't been natural and have a fit. So I put my thumb in my mouth and slipped my other hand under my dress. I fell right to sleep, and when Miss Kitchen came around with her magic wand to wake each of us up, my thumb was still in my mouth—and my hand was still under my dress.

I pulled my hand away quickly, even though I could tell it was too late: Miss Kitchen had already seen. My eyes filled with tears, but I managed to blink them back. Even that was something my mother

wouldn't like: she thought if you felt like crying, you should goddamned well cry, and not worry about what other people think.

I tried to do all the right things until the end of the day, when
my mother came to pick me up. Second graders weren't dismissed
early the way kindergartners were, so Hildy couldn't walk me home.
Miss Kitchen wanted to talk with my mother. My mother was too big
now to use a kindergartner's chair, so she plopped herself down on
Miss Kitchen's desk chair while Miss Kitchen sat on a kindergartner's
chair with a cheerful smile, unaware that she was defying my mother,
who said life was not all about cheerful smiles and the perfect hairdo.

Even at five I just kind of found my mother ugly and embarrassing to have as a mother. She had long honey-blond hair like Hildy's,
but she wore it in a messy asymmetrical braid whose three sections
were never equal. Sometimes she didn't even brush her hair before
braiding it. Also, she didn't shampoo often, and there was something
icky about the sour smell of my mother's hair, something burden-
some that, at its best, reminded me of the feeling I had just before
crying, and at its worst, made me gag. I never seemed to get used
to my mother's smell in general, the smell of milk that wasn't fresh,
or one of those fermented dairy products that grownups liked and
ridiculed you for being too childish to appreciate.

As she and Miss Kitchen talked, I wandered around the classroom, exploring the empty, high-ceilinged quiet. I remember wondering whether my mother was a bank robber. She'd warned me that
you never knew if someone was a criminal, so you had to be careful.
Didn't that mean she herself could be a criminal, and I wouldn't
know it? I took myself as far away from my mother and Miss Kitchen
as I could, enjoying how different the space felt without all the other
children there. I tried to fit myself into an open vertical art cubbyhole
on the far side of the classroom, but I was a little too tall, and the coat
hook jabbed me.

Suddenly my mother was pulling my arm, getting me into the car to go home. Her belly was so big, it was touching the steering wheel. She was crying, and she was angry. Miss Kitchen didn't understand the needs of children, she said.

Why hadn't I listened to Hildy instead of my mother? I'll tell you why: because I always did what my mother wanted, even though God forbid she should ever help me when it came to fitting in. Or when it came to practically anything else.

A few weeks later, after Drew was born, Hildy and I finally returned to school. I remember being worried about leaving Drew. He was tiny and adorable, and his cry sounded like the bleat of a lamb.

I didn't suck my thumb anymore, and I didn't touch my crotch either. Somehow the shrug was there instead, kind of like a reminder: being natural *wasn't* good. If I wanted to do well in school, or anywhere else, I had to be careful, because wherever I was, whatever I was doing, I might be about to make a mistake.

At first I was grateful for the signal my body gave me, but of course, I quickly grew to hate it. I spent years trying to get my mother to help me get rid of it, but she'd always say I didn't have to be perfect, and that self-esteem comes from within, not from what other people think. See, she always *sounded* like she knew what she was talking about.

As I've gotten older, I've found ways to deal with the shrug, like wearing my thick wool pea coat from the army-navy surplus store year-round and draping it over my shoulders when I'm in class. That was my best friend Stephanie Kenyon's idea. No one in my family gives me ideas like that, stuff that actually might help you solve a problem.

I've noticed that if I catch the shrug right before it happens, I can think of my whole arm as being very heavy, which sometimes delays the inevitable for a few seconds. That definitely comes in handy. Or maybe I should say shoulder-y, ha ha.

2

in France

My teachers always pretty much ignored my shrug. I'd see them notice, and I'd see them pretend not to notice, but they never asked me about it. I was always a good student, and they probably figured that was the main thing.

Well, there *was* this one time in seventh grade when we had a substitute teacher who shouted at me, "And stop that shrugging!"— mostly, I think, because I was kind of being a smart-ass. Once in a while, being a smart-ass is necessary. That's something I know from being best friends with Stephanie, who says you have to live a little.

It was a Monday, the day after my parents had a huge fight while my mother was ironing one of my father's shirts in the kitchen. My mother had been scrubbing the sink with Ajax while the iron was heating up. An ugly old pair of two-toned blue rubber gloves was draped across the counter, and the place smelled like a swimming pool. It was almost as if we were a household where stuff got done.

I can't even remember now what the fight was about. The point is, my father came at my mother with his fists and started pounding her shoulders and her head. The hot iron toppled over onto the fabric. Neither Hildy nor I had a chance to pick the iron up, or unplug it, because we were busy shouting, "Stop it! Stop it!" at my father and trying to pry him off my mother, and also, trying not to trip over the cord and trying to make sure our parents didn't, either. Drew, who had been upstairs playing in his room, came running down, crying and adding his little voice to ours: "Stop it! Stop it!" But my father kept hitting, and my mother kept shrieking and trying to hit back. The Ajax scent was eclipsed by the smell of hot cotton, then singed cotton, then burnt cotton.

All of a sudden, what flew out of my mouth was this: "You pathetic goddamned bastard! *STOP IT!*"

Hildy and Drew gasped. My father whipped around. I knew I was about to get pummeled, or at least slapped hard across the face. But then my father grabbed the hot iron. At first I thought he was just taking it off the burnt fabric to set it upright. Instead, he pushed the iron through the air toward my face, too close.

I didn't flinch—or shrug—because it was the kind of situation where you only get it afterwards, how terrifying it was. In that first split second, I just stared at my father with hatred. Then I realized Hildy and Drew and my mother were all screaming, and I had darted backwards. My mother was still in a pile on the floor, shrieking, "You son of a bitch! *STOP!*" and scrambling up.

It was Hildy who struggled with my father for the iron. My father was stronger, but luckily, all he did was yank it away and send it clattering onto the vinyl tile floor—though Hildy did have to do a little foot dance to avoid its hitting her. My mother was upright by this time, but still hysterical and completely useless. My father ran out of the house, slamming the door so hard behind him that the windows shook as if we were having an earthquake. Two of the vinyl floor tiles got ruined and, by the way, they've never gotten fixed. But at least he was done hitting for now.

Afterwards, my mother stomped upstairs and climbed into bed, crying loudly. Hildy unplugged the iron and put it on the tile kitchen counter to cool, then peeled my father's iron-shaped-black-tattooed shirt off the ironing board and took it to the garbage can at the side of the house. Drew and I cried, wiping our noses on scratchy paper napkins. I wished we had Kleenex, like other families. No doubt we needed it more than other families. But of course there was some goddamned reason why my mother didn't believe in Kleenex.

All afternoon, I kept going up to check on my mother, who was in bed, alternating between crying so we could hear, then not crying for a while, and then starting up again. In between, I called Stephanie and told her about the fight. Her parents fought, too—in fact, her father had recently moved out and her parents were on the brink of divorce—so she understood what I was going through. I left out the part about the hot iron until the very end of the conversation, because I knew Stephanie would have a spaz about it. Which she did.

Later, Hildy boiled up some wagon wheel noodles, my favorite, and put lots of margarine and salt on them for dinner. But I was jumpy, and so was my shoulder, and that's how I was the next day, too. When I got to English, and Stephanie told me we were having a sub, my eyes filled with tears because things weren't the same as they always were at school. I didn't want Stephanie to think I was a crybaby, especially about something as stupid as that, so I said I was still really upset about yesterday's fight at home.

The good news about English was that Paul Shapiro, the boy I liked, was in our class. The bad news was a kid named Logan Starch, who was friends with Paul, even though for the life of me I couldn't understand why. Paul was nice, and handsome in a kind of dreamy way, and he had the look of someone with real depth as a person. Logan, on the other hand, had already tormented me throughout elementary school and was constantly getting in trouble for using swear words. Here's what's funny: I remember that the first time I heard Logan swearing, I thought, *Gee, I didn't realize he knew Dad.* I just figured that anyone who swore had learned it from my father.

My mother knew Logan's mother from when Logan and I were

babies, and Logan always seemed to be making damned sure I understood that this history did not mean we were friends. His assigned seat was two rows behind mine, one desk over, and his latest amusement was to shoot me with a spitball whenever I shrugged. He had really good aim, because for a delivery system, he used a waxed paper straw that he'd cut a little so it would fit discreetly into the pocket of his plaid flannel shirt.

Even though Stephanie was two rows over, we were able to pass notes back and forth thanks to a girl named Paisley, who sat between us and wanted us to like her. It was only because of Stephanie's notes that I formulated an idea. *Turn the tables somehow,* she urged. *Use it against him!!!*

The class was rowdy in that substitute-teacher way, kids talking and laughing and then shushing and then talking again. Logan had already pelted me half a dozen times. Suddenly I realized I had stood up and turned around to address the enemy, my knees shaking. "Too bad you have that awful nervous *tic,* Logan," I said loudly, "where you just can't help shooting spitballs."

All the kids who heard me burst out laughing, including Paul. As Logan struggled to figure out what to say, I glanced over at Stephanie, who was flashing her huge smile, her eyes crinkling with the joy of shared mischief. The whole thing was so unlike me, it was as if I'd stepped out of myself and into someone else. But I'd had enough of bullies for a whole year, let alone twenty-four hours.

"You really should see a doctor about that, Logan," I went on, making my voice as contemptuous as I could. "A psychiatrist, that is." By this point, I had everyone's attention. More laughter, louder now. And then, as if to show I could *play* at being cool but was never actually going *be* cool, my goddamned shoulder put in its two cents' worth. Twice in a row, actually, so I guess that's four cents' worth.

"Siddown!" the sub bellowed at me. "And stop that shrugging!"

When our regular English teacher came back, she caught on to

Logan's straw shooter, confiscated it, and moved him to the very front of the classroom. Eventually, Logan wound up in reform school somewhere, which is kind of sad. Plus, his older brother nearly got killed in Vietnam and is now in a wheelchair for the rest of his life. Not that I miss Logan Starch. It's just that he was actually a smart kid. Starting in fourth grade, he'd made his way through those color-coded reading comprehension exercises more quickly than anyone else. The teacher had encouraged us to read a little above our level (I was never sure what that meant, exactly) and skip what we didn't understand. Logan was one of those kids who had dived right in. As for me, all I wanted was to read just *below* my level and have all the time in the world to slow down on what I didn't understand. But of course, I couldn't let anyone find that out. It would ruin my reputation.

Unlike the others in my class, Logan Starch seemed to notice my lagging. It was as if he saw through me, saw that there was something not quite right about my good grades. Now that I think about it, he kind of reminded me of my father. Not just the bullying part. The part that understood what a fraud I was.

I'm the exact opposite of Columbo, that bumbling detective on TV, who doesn't mind looking like an idiot, since he actually understands everything. I really, really mind looking like an idiot, because even though I've always been able to blend in with the high-achieving kids at school, secretly I don't comprehend much of anything. It takes a lot of effort for me to fit in, but I don't have a choice. Apparently, Columbo has self-assurance to spare—he doesn't even care if he's being annoying, testing the suspect's patience over and over again with his "dumb" questions until you squirm just watching—but I sure don't have that kind of confidence. Why would I want people to know how confused I am when seeming smart is the main thing I've got going for me?

You probably think I'm fishing for compliments or exaggerating, or that I need to get therapy to fix my low self-esteem. But—and this is where my father is right—you can do well in school and still be a big fat idiot. When I look on a world map, for instance, I always do a little double-take: I'm expecting South America to be where Africa is, even though that's just plain stupid. I can't keep any of the Scandinavian countries straight, or maybe it's the Norwegian countries? No, wait, the Nordic ones? Why is Australia a continent and not an island nation? Why does Brazil take up so much room while Japan, which is a much more influential country, is virtually un-findable on the map? And while we're on the topic of Brazil, how are you supposed to know the language they speak there isn't Brazilian, and it isn't Spanish, either?

And yet, I get B+'s in social studies, history, and geography. B+'s, when I should be getting F's.

I doubt I could even grasp a much-needed explanation as to why communism is so bad, or what "iron curtain" really means. There are just certain types of information my brain can't seem to absorb. Books and encyclopedias supposedly help people with things like that, but they sure as hell don't help me. When I'm reading or listening, I try really hard to concentrate, but it always turns out there's something basic I don't understand. Then I try to understand the basic thing. But just at the moment when I'm hearing or reading the part that's going to explain everything—that's when I realize my concentration has evaporated. Instead, I'm thinking about what I might've been missing the moment before, while I was trying to concentrate—unrelated things that might have needed my attention. Someone getting angry, someone getting hurt, someone disapproving of the teacher's assignment, someone not liking the way I think about things. And then I'm right back where I started.

But meanwhile, the world keeps spinning, new assignments keep coming, I keep turning them in and getting good grades, and no one ever notices how lost I am. It's like I'm in France, lugging some big suitcase around while trying to find my way from one place to another, and stopping to ask for help. I've taken some French (I got A's), so my question might be nicely phrased, and I might even have a reasonable French accent. So the French person might think, "Oh, here's a foreigner with correct French grammar and a decent accent." But then—based on my grammar and accent—the person gives me some lightning-quick, idiomatic response that I have no prayer of following. See? The problem of appearing to be competent.

My teachers seem to think of me as intellectually curious, the type that just *loooves* learning. And after fighting so hard to do well in school and apply to college, how can I possibly admit out loud that I *don't* love learning?

Here's the real question: why doesn't anyone ever talk about how humiliating it is to learn, since you're constantly finding out how dumb you were before?

3

s**m**oke and records

People connect whistling with happiness, probably because of *Snow White and the Seven Dwarfs*, where cartoon characters run around singing about how if you whistle while you work, the work gets done faster, and that makes you happy. At least, that's what I understand, never having seen *Snow White*—Disney movies had crappy plots, the ideas in them were "very Hollywood," life was not all about syrupy princesses with lily-white skin—you get the idea.

My father whistled while he worked. Literally. He owned a smoke shop and record store called Smoke and Records, which was located at the corner of Bancroft Way and Telegraph Avenue, right across the street from the UC Berkeley campus. All day long, my father could put on whatever he wanted: a Bach cantata, a Haydn string quartet, Brahms' second cello sonata, Mahler's *Des Knaben Wunderhorn*. Whenever he wasn't lecturing the customers or chewing out one of the guys who worked for him, my father was whistling along with whatever he had on the turntable. Or he was singing along. Or he was conducting.

It's funny, though—I never thought about whether my father was happy when he whistled. To me, the whistling meant *I* was happy. Everything was okay. We were all safe, for now.

I miss the store. It smelled of sweet tobacco and magazines and also, somehow, of cold, if cold has a smell. Hildy and Drew and I loved to hang around and watch students and professors buying the *New York Times*, or red boxes of Dunhills, or bright yellow packages of pipe cleaners for their pipes, or those weird miniature lozenges called Sen-Sen that tasted like a cross between licorice and charcoal.

We kids were allowed to roost on the stacks of *Look* and *Life* and other magazines that were piled on the floor against the vertical news racks facing the smoke shop counter. From our perches, we could see everything that was going on, which was probably way better than watching some dumb Disney movie anyway. We did have to be on the lookout in case a customer seemed to want a magazine—and scramble up, straighten the piles, and get out of the way if that happened. And absolutely no staring or giggling if someone was scanning for a *Playboy*—even if it was "the mooch," Hildy's nickname for this fat, balding guy who came in every month to have a long look, but always put the magazine back instead of buying it.

It's almost as if Smoke and Records existed just to show a complete opposite of how things were at home. We lived in a house with dark wood all over the place, and cottage-cheese-textured walls, and tons of boring old stuff—art objects and dusty vases and rugs, which my parents collected by dragging us around to antique stores as if that were a fun family activity. I wanted to be surrounded by cheerful things like the smooth walls, white painted cabinets, and comfy floral-patterned chairs I'd seen at other people's houses. I didn't let on, though, because then my parents would say I didn't have good taste.

At Smoke and Records, the main point seemed to be enjoyment. Across from the huge red-and-white Coke machine, the entire wall was lined with candy racks, and if my father was in the right mood, and my mother wasn't there, which she usually wasn't when we hung around the shop, we could have whatever we wanted—Junior Mints for Hildy, chocolate Necco wafers for me, and for Drew, anything from Jujubes (gummy, but good if you wanted long-lasting) to barbe-cue-flavored potato chips.

Even though the store was kind of grimy, things were so colorful in there, you didn't care. The metal displays for the Life Savers, for instance—instead of holding the candy in place with plain metal, the fronts of the little racks were rounded, and painted to look exactly like the candy rolls they contained. Cherry. Five Flavor. Butterscotch. Pep-O-Mint. The vivid metal looked so realistic.

If we were hungry for substantive food, my father would pull money from one of the two cash registers and send us next door to Joe's Ranch Burgers for cheeseburgers and French fries served in cheerful, paper-lined, red oval plastic baskets. Or we could go to the soda fountain half a block further down Telegraph, at Foley's Rexall Drugs, and get mayonnaise-y egg-and-olive sandwiches on white bread, cut into triangular quarters—we didn't even have to eat the crusts—and share a chocolate milkshake as if it were an actual drink.

All this was about as different from my mother's kitchen as you could get. If she made lamb chops, we were thrilled, but the edible part was small, and there was never enough. If she made something totally disgusting, like that cold gelatin dish with sliced hard-boiled egg and pigs' feet in it—well, there was plenty, served several nights in a row, and we couldn't even spit it out, because she checked our napkins.

My mother was always bitching about how sugar was terrible for you, deep-fried food was poison, white bread had no food value, blah, blah, blah, and even though she probably had a point, I think mostly she hated how my father always had to be "seen as the good guy." Which is another way of saying she couldn't stand the fact that my father was basically more likeable than she was. I was the only one in the family who liked my mother at all, and even I didn't really like her. I just kind of forced myself to like her because no one else did. Plus, someone had to stand up to my father and his stupid behavior.

But whatever need my father had to be "seen as the good guy" didn't extend to music. If some ditzy co-ed with puffy hair and a flowery mini-skirt breezed into the shop asking for the Beach Boys, my father, depending on his mood, might demand to know why she wanted that dreck—even though he had plenty of Beach Boys albums, filed just in front of the Beatles section. Then he'd start in about what Bach cantatas or Mozart chamber music the ditzy girl should be buying instead. It wasn't exactly an environment that made you want to ask for stuff.

"Your turn," Hildy nudged me one day when *Help!* had just come out. I was sitting next to her on the magazine stacks, Dietrich Fischer-Dieskau's voice was delivering Schubert lieder, and Drew was hanging around behind the smoke shop counter with Bob Metcalf, an architecture student with thick black glasses who'd been working for my father for years, in between the times my father got mad and fired him before hiring him back a few days later. Underneath Fischer-Dieskau's soothing baritone I could hear the percussion sounds from lower Sproul Plaza, where drummers would sit together and pound on congas for hours on end for God knows what reason, probably to give people headaches. "I've asked twice in a row," Hildy pointed out.

"Well, you're the one who wants it."

"Three times, actually! I asked for *Beatles '65*, and then *two* times for *Beatles VI*. And look, he's in a good mood." My father had cornered a half-interested guy in a tweed jacket and was waving a Schwann catalog, the monthly listing of every available classical LP recording, as he explained that if the guy liked Dvořák, he really should delve into Brahms, since Brahms had a major influence on the younger composer. Hildy elbowed me again. "*C'mon*, Marth, you know you want it too." Her warm breath smelled of Junior Mints.

"Quit it! What I want is the Strauss waltzes. Or *Eine Kleine Nachtmusik*, or maybe 'Clair de Lune.' And you know what he said about all those: *pure dreck*." For the life of me, I could never understand how Hildy was so self-assured about her own tastes that she could ask repeatedly for whatever pop music she wanted. If my father thought Johann Strauss was a crummy composer, or that *Eine Kleine Nachtmusik* was formulaic, or that "Clair de Lune" was maudlin—well, he probably had a point. I wasn't about to make him think even less of me by asking for the Beatles. And by the way, now that I'm older, I see what my father meant about the Strauss and the Mozart (I still love the Debussy, though).

"So what?" Hildy countered. "He says 'pure dreck' about everything. Doesn't mean you can't ask."

It exactly meant I couldn't ask. I wanted my father to see that I loved music the way he did—that I wasn't bored by his musical opinions like Hildy. I wanted him to be impressed that if I'd heard a record once, I always knew what note it was going to begin on, because I had perfect pitch. I wanted him to notice that if he was explaining to some professor why a particular Pablo Casals recording was superior to the one in stereo by János Starker even though the Casals was in mono, I considered it important information. But my father didn't notice things like that about me, because the simple truth was, he liked Hildy more.

I know, I know, parents love their children equally, blah blah blah, but the fact is, Hildy was Hildy, whereas I had a shrug, and somehow my father didn't care about my musical loyalty. And maybe that's good, because he just kind of ruins everything. Obviously.

Drew trotted over to us, looking like a miniature replica of my father: a head of disorderly dark curls set off by too-thick brows and big brown eyes. Why was it all so adorable on my brother, and not on me? He was clutching a Hershey's almond chocolate bar, probably because that was Bob Metcalf's favorite. "Are you sure you want that, Drewy?" I asked.

"Drew, you don't like nuts," Hildy reminded him. "That one has nuts in it."

He held the bar tightly to his flannel-shirted chest.

"Let me open it for you," Hildy offered.

"Mine."

"Just the top part, so it's easier for you to eat it. Okay?"

Reluctantly, Drew parted with his treat, hopping on one foot and then the other as Hildy tore off a small part of the foil underneath the wrapper. I watched his cute little feet in his cute little red PF Flyers as he danced on the dark vinyl flooring, waiting. The floor tiles were marbled, their original colors long gone, obscured by years of accumulated grime. How many feet had walked on that floor, altogether? Who at the vinyl tile factory had decided on that marble pattern? These were the kinds of mysteries that I liked. The kind where you could just imagine the answer and not have to look it up somewhere, because the answers to questions like that weren't in books.

Drew took his candy bar and started counting the items in the fragile, yellowed display case. He was really good with numbers for a little kid, and I could see why he was fascinated by the glass case, which was filled with all kinds of pipes and chrome accessories and tartan plaid pouches. What were those chrome gadgets used for? Who sewed the pouches? Who decided they should be green and dark blue? At the store, there was always something new to observe. Nothing was completely knowable, and for some reason, I found that comforting.

"I wish I could just go *buy* the record, like every other kid," Hildy sighed. We both had little secret stashes of money from the times when my father had given us cash for one thing or another and had waved his hand dismissively when we tried to give him his change. But how would Hildy get a Beatles album into the house? My mother didn't believe in allowances, didn't believe in piggy banks, and wouldn't let us do chores or babysitting for money.

When we got money from her parents for our birthdays, she'd put it directly into "savings," saying she'd get us anything we needed

(which we understood was really an invitation to ponder the meaning of "need"), and that we weren't old enough to have our own
spending money. So if Hildy walked in with pop music, my mother
would assume my father had given it to Hildy—exactly the type of
situation that could lead to World War III. As for my father, he'd have
a goddamned cow if we bought records anywhere else in an attempt
to hide our bad musical taste.

Hildy's candy box gave a hollow waxy rattle as she tilted it up for
more, as if to fortify herself. Then she handed me the box, got up, and
walked over to my father, her head bent in deference: she talked big
to me, but it was another thing to do the actual asking. My shoulder
put in its opinion as Hildy waited for my father to finish his sentence.
"Dad," she began, "um, I was wondering—"

"You probably want a Beatle record." My father winked at the
Dvořák customer, confident that the guy would commiserate about
the dubious musical tastes of a twelve-year-old girl.

"Well, kind of." Hildy ran the toe of her white sneaker against a
seam of the vinyl floor tiles. "It's just that, see, there's also a Beatles
movie called *Help!*, and all the other kids—"

"Pure crap," my father pronounced, turning back to the customer,
hovering a little too close, as usual, as he waved the Schwann catalog.
"Brahms wasn't all that prolific, you know. Four symphonies, the two
piano concerti, the one violin concerto, but no concerto for solo cello...."

Without even blushing, Hildy shrugged and came over, first
grabbing a copy of *Newsweek* from the vertical rack behind us before
flouncing back down. She started flipping the pages from the back
toward the front, which was for some reason how she always read
magazines. I handed her the Junior Mints. She took them but didn't
look up.

I got that left-out feeling I often had when Hildy read, especially if
it was about stuff that was hard for me to understand. Which, let's face
it, was practically everything that was in magazines. Current events,

politics, government—it all made my eyes glaze over. Or maybe my brain. Life was such a struggle already; why would I want to find out about things that would only make me feel worse once I knew about them? Wars. Famine. Torture. Disease. I could learn about all that once I grew up.

When Hildy was reading, she got into it so completely that she practically went into a trance; nothing else mattered. My mother would complain that if Hildy's nose was in a book, the house could be burning down and she wouldn't notice—which was kind of true. Take now, for instance: what was that shouting coming from over across Bancroft? Hildy's eyes stayed glued to the page as I twisted my body around and squinted through a small horizontal rectangle of filthy window in the space between the upper magazine racks. A crowd seemed to be gathering near the steps of the student union building, where some crazy preacher guy named Holy Hubert was always yelling about sin and doom and flaming hell. But today it wasn't Holy Hubert. It was these two guys with bands around their arms, and a couple of other guys shouting at them. It didn't look serious—yet. *Shrug.* I was certainly familiar with the concept that shouting could lead to hitting.

But then the men who were being shouted at turned and left. I twisted back around on my perch, still a little uneasy but mostly relieved. Hildy didn't even look up. How was she able to be so unconcerned most of the time? Also, how could she flip through the magazine pages so fast, and backwards, no less? I couldn't help thinking maybe my mother was right about Hildy being kind of a bullshit artist. "*No skimming,*" I intoned, mostly to make fun of my mother, but also partly to get Hildy's attention.

Hildy looked at me, flared her nostrils. "*Skimming is like sucking the sweet juice out of an orange and—*"

"*—throwing away the nutritious pulp!*" I finished, and both of us laughed. Then I kept laughing, until I realized I was kind of crying. "Mom still won't take me to the doctor," I lamented.

Hildy rolled her eyes, flipping to the previous page. "Bitch."

"Don't call her that," I said halfheartedly.

"Wait, let me guess. *Stop being so self-conscious, Martha! No one's looking at you.*"

Of course, my mother was right that no one was looking at me: who would look at someone with a stupid shrug? But I went along with the joke, because there were still tears in my throat, and imitating my mother while contorting my face into a mean expression would help me hide the tears from Hildy. "*You want to be beautiful? Be natural,*" I mimicked.

"*My God, your perceptions are—*"

"*—so lopsided!*" we finished together, giggling. This was my mother's comeback any time we disagreed with her.

"Just a bunch of big fat excuses for her never helping us," Hildy declared, polishing off her candy and using her index finger to fling back her silky blond hair, which she parted in the middle and wore all the way down to her waist. Sometimes she let me put her hair in braids and would keep it that way all day so that later, when she unfastened it, her hair would be transformed into this amazing cascade of wheaten waves. Besides the fact that she didn't have a shrug, Hildy had beautiful dark brown eyes and stylish granny glasses. How had she gotten my mother to buy those glasses? Maybe my mother was hoping they'd actually make Hildy look like a grandmother.

"Hey, Jules?" called Bob from behind the cash register, pushing his glasses up toward the bridge of his nose. "You know anything about a demonstration out there?"

"I don't like this," Drew whined, handing me the candy bar with one bite taken out. There were wet tooth marks in the foil. "It's stupid," he added. "Stupid-head candy!" When I got up to throw the wrappers and uneaten chocolate away, I had a clearer view of what was going on across the street. There were more people gathered, and the two men with armbands each had a megaphone.

4

speaker

Suddenly one of the two men started shouting. It was hard to be sure of his words, because his voice had that sound of someone holding the megaphone too close, but I thought I heard "mongrels!" and then "Aryan race!" Then the other man chimed in: "Enemies of the Reich!" *Shrug.*

Hildy had slipped the *Newsweek* back into its slot and stood next to me, reaching out for my hand on one side and Drew's on the other, as angry shouts began coming from the gathering crowd. I glanced around behind me. There were a few customers, including, I noticed, a handsome graduate student named Herschel who worked next door at Prufrock Books and always wore a Jewish skullcap on his head. No one was buying anything; everyone had migrated to the window and was glued in place. Everyone, that is, except my father, who was unable to hold still.

"The shop is closed," he shouted abruptly at no one in particular, and tossed the unlit pipe that had been dangling from his mouth down on a coffee-stained Schwann catalog. A few ashy flecks spilled out.

"Dad, what's going on?" Hildy asked.

He locked the register, dashed over to the Spoken Word section, and riffled through quickly, scanning records until he found what he was looking for. Then, coming over toward the turntable, he took the record from its inside paper covering and flung it on the turntable without any of his usual care, letting it spin around and around without putting the needle on.

"What's Dad doing?" Drew tugged at Hildy's sleeve.

"Gimme a hand here, wouldja?" my father yelled at Bob, as if he'd already asked half a dozen times. "Cover me," he barked at Herschel, apparently expecting Herschel to keep an eye on things even though he didn't work there. A few customers left; half a dozen stayed and looked scared but uncertain. I shrugged twice in a row.

Bob followed my father's lead, helping him untangle some wires and trailing him to the back of the store, where a giant dusty loudspeaker had sat, partly blocking the bathroom door, ever since some student with no money had traded it to my father for a stack of jazz records. The two men dragged the speaker over to the doorway, my father pivoting it so that it faced outward, near those tiny, inexplicably pinkish frosted glass panels on the sidewalk—for electricity or phone connections, I guessed.

My father adjusted the angle from outside and inched his body back inside. "They want free speech? Well, they'll get it!" my father shouted from the turntable. "I don't give a good goddamn if I blow this thing out." He put the needle on one of the tracks, listening and skipping around while the volume was low, and then cranked it way up. A powerful yet calm voice spoke about fighting on the seas and oceans.

"What *is* this?" Hildy murmured admiringly. I could tell the admiration was not so much for the orator as for my father.

"Winston Churchill," replied Herschel from behind us. I looked up at him. He was smiling out of one side of his mouth.

"Keen!" Hildy exclaimed. "See, Drewy?" She leaned down and gave Drew a big grin. "Dad is making those mean men stop saying bad things."

Sure enough, the two men now seemed disoriented. Along with the crowd, they were looking over in our direction, trying to figure out what the noise was and where it was coming from. *We shall fight on the beaches, we shall fight on the landing grounds. . . .*

The crowd roared in appreciation. Some of them clapped and cheered, or waved at us, and we waved back. There aren't that many situations I can remember where I felt proud of my father, but it was one of those times, and I realized this was the version of Jules Goldenthal that Hildy always saw: someone bold and creative and heroic.

When the speech was over, people from the crowd started pouring into Smoke and Records, and when I looked back over across the street, the two men had disappeared into the confusion.

"Dad, that was just—*boss!*" exclaimed Hildy.

"You got 'em, Jules!" Bob agreed.

I could tell my father was thrilled. "The hell with 'em, the bastards!"

People were congratulating my father, shaking his hand. After the Churchill, my father had put on Copland's *Fanfare for the Common Man* with the speaker still facing outward, and we all stood around and basked solemnly in the good feelings. Then my father lit his pipe and looked at me and Hildy and Drew as if he were seeing us for the first time all day. He winked and smiled, and we all smiled back.

The Copland was just ending as Hazel, a cute little lady with blond bangs who worked further down Telegraph at See's Candy, wandered in wearing her white uniform and hat. "Hello, good-looking," she said to Herschel, "what's going on? I sure heard a lotta commotion on my way over here."

"Well, ma'am," he replied, "you just missed seeing Jules Goldenthal singlehandedly break up a riot."

What was amazing was how quickly things returned to normal. Within ten minutes, Bob and my father had dragged the speaker back inside. Not exactly back in its place, of course, because the only thing my father put away methodically was records (well, with the exception of the chaotic tall stack of LPs next to the turntable). They angled the speaker in behind the last record case, where it only partially blocked the wooden ladder leading up to the tiny mezzanine back there. Then my father put side eight of Bach's *St. Matthew Passion* on the turntable—the Karl Münchinger recording, his favorite—and picked up his pipe, put it back in his mouth, and lit a match. The burning sulfur stung my nose.

An old man hobbled into the store. I thought for sure he was going to congratulate my father, but it turned out he didn't seem to know what had just happened. "I'm looking for a recording with Mischa Elman," he said in a thick European accent. "The Khachaturian violin concerto, do you have it?"

"The *Elman* recording?" my father snorted. "That thing is a monstrosity!"

If the man noticed my father's contempt, he didn't seem to care. "Well, do you carry it?"

My father sighed and shook his head as he retrieved the record from the section of twentieth-century Russian composers. Smoke and Records was a "full-catalogue" store, meaning that my father stocked virtually every classical and jazz LP there was, even the ones he hated. "You insist on spending your money on this abomination—fine!" my father growled. "But lookee here, Professor. This purchase is not returnable for any reason, you understand? Particularly aesthetic!"

As the professor was leaving with the record, my father couldn't resist his captive audience. "Academics," he muttered loudly, turning toward the customers and us kids. "Members of the *establishment*. Well, you know the old joke—BS stands for Bull Shit, and MS stands for More Shit. And PhD means—the shit is Piled Higher and Deeper!"

Drew beamed, delighted by my father's use of a bad word; Hildy grinned; a couple of customers giggled uncertainly. All I could do was wince and hope the professor was out of earshot. My mother hated that joke. She'd had to fight to go to college, she said, because her parents didn't understand the value of education and only wanted her to study things like bookkeeping and sewing. My mother had even majored in education in college. Which is pretty ironic, but more on that later.

Mein Jesu, gute Nacht, lamented the Stuttgart chamber chorus. My father's pipe dangled from his mouth as his arms began waving, his body swaying in broad conductor's movements, as if the music depended on it.

5

socks

The first time my mother kicked my father out of the house, I'd just started seventh grade, so I was already pretty anxious. It was hard having to run around to different rooms between classes, not to mention juggling all the homework. Plus I had to make sure not to act too worried in front of my parents, both of whom would call me "anal" if I fretted over which assignments were due on what day. *Anal!* They never ran out of ways to be completely gross. It's funny, they hated each other—well, for sure my mother hated my father—but they were so similar in how they felt about me.

By now you're probably thinking, *Wow, her parents are full of crap!* I'd love to tell you I know this, have always known it, in every fiber of my being. The trouble is, some of my fibers are weak. So in between the times when I'm thinking, *Wow, my parents are full of crap!*, I'm always wondering, *What if they're right about me, and no one else loves me enough to tell me?* I mean, couldn't that be the explanation, since they know me better than anyone else does? Even now, sometimes without even realizing it, I look for ways in which they were right, and are right. They're smart, and unlike me, they're very sure of themselves.

Right before I started seventh grade, Berkeley decided to integrate the schools. In elementary, the white kids mostly went to schools in the hills and the black kids mostly went to ones west of Shattuck Avenue, because where people live is pretty segregated, not just by race, but by what people do for a living. The working-class people live in the flats, the professors and doctors and lawyers in the hills. Stephanie's family is an exception—they live in the flats—but their house is this big old Victorian on a huge corner lot with a beautiful garden, so it kind of doesn't count as the flats.

My family is an exception, too—or at least it was. We lived in the hills, but that was because my mother's parents had bought some old warehouses in Manhattan when they were worth hardly anything, and then sold them and made piles of money. I guess if your parents are rich and you need to buy a house, they give you a bunch of money, even if you moved all the way across the country to get away from them.

Anyway, now the Berkeley schools had decided to bus all the kids so we could be integrated. Which sounds great and much more fair, but in reality it made everyone a lot more jumpy. I hate to admit this, because it makes me sound prejudiced, but I was anxious about getting beat up by the black girls, who seemed to know how to crack their chewing gum in the exact way that would be the most intimidating. I heard that in the girls' bathrooms, mean black girls pulled white girls' hair or slapped their faces or took their wallets or made them hand over their watches, all for a lot less than having a shrug. So I avoided the bathrooms.

Then in PE, I overheard two tough-looking black girls talking about me, and when they saw me standing there at the lockers, they tried so hard to be nice to me that I was scared it was part of an elaborate plot to beat me up after school. But they kept being nice, for the whole year. Which was not true of the tough white girls, with their big hair and overdone mascara and cheap frosted lipstick. All through seventh and eighth grade, a little clique of them would do these exaggerated shoulder movements when they saw me coming, laughing the whole time as if they were the first ones ever to think of ridiculing me.

So I just kept trying to avoid everything that was scary. I'd start my day in Orchestra, where I was second chair, second violin. I wasn't very good on violin, but I always knew what note we were supposed to be on, and could tell whether my violin was in tune even if the teacher, Miss Transom, didn't give us the note with her pitch pipe. The first violinist, a bossy eighth-grade girl, was supposed to lead the tuning, but I always started before we had the official pitch, and soon, everyone was following my lead, even the concertmistress.

The idea of Orchestra as a relief from scariness is kind of hilarious, though, since Miss Transom was apt to throw her conductor's baton at people who messed up the beat or didn't come in at the right measure. Frankly, it's a miracle no one ever got their eye poked out because of her temper. And here's the kicker: the next day, when Miss Transom saw the kid who had gotten her so mad the day before, she'd smile and call him or her "cookie-dunk" and act as if nothing had ever happened.

It wasn't like that at home, of course. Once my father started hitting my mother or Hildy or Drew or me, "cookie-dunk" was not in our future. Not that my father stayed angry after his shit fits, exactly. He just kind of sulked, as if he'd been wronged and everyone owed *him* an apology. And of course, my mother acted as if we all owed *her* an apology. She never remembered afterwards how hard we kids had tried to make my father stop—unless it was by way of saying, "You couldn't stop him because that's the kind of goddamned louse he is. Now you *finally* see what I'm up against."

This time, the fight started because my father had tripped on

Hildy's sneakers, which she'd taken off and carelessly left toward the middle of the staircase instead of putting them definitively to the side. "Whose are these?" he demanded. Hildy quickly moved the shoes and said over and over how sorry she was and how she'd never do that again. But he was still angry, and then my mother called him a louse for not being able to calm down like a normal man, and then he came up way too close to her and said, in a surprisingly quiet voice, "You fucking bitch." His posture was threatening, and the veins stood out in his neck.

Hildy and Drew and I tried to pull my father away, but my mother shouted right into his face that she was sick of tiptoeing around him. Then she kind of let out all the stops. It wasn't her fault that he had low self-esteem because of his not making it in the army, and not making it in college, either. It wasn't her fault that his parents had worshipped and coddled him to the point of crippling him. She was goddamned glad they'd stayed in New York instead of moving out to Berkeley, which they had wanted to do. She was goddamned glad she'd put her foot down about it, so that geographical distance prevented my father's parents from doing even more psychological damage than they already had.

My mother had wound up with a black eye and two big black and blue marks on her back. My father had elbowed Hildy pretty hard in the neck when she'd tried to intervene, and he'd pushed me away with so much force that I'd been thrown into the corner of the kitchen counter and banged the middle of my back really hard.

I know this'll make you wince, but my mother acted like she was proud of her injuries. I say this because she forced me and Hildy to look at her bruises the next day. As sorry as I felt for my mother, even I had to gag at her complete lack of dignity. Didn't she know by now that she was never going to convince Hildy what a bastard my father was? As for me, I already knew what a bastard my father was. And my mother knew that I knew it. There's only one reason she'd flaunt her bruises in front of her children: because she is a disgusting human being.

But as a twelve-year-old, I felt terrible that she was stuck with a monster who thought he could just hit anybody any time he felt like it. I understood completely why she'd kick him out of the house. I still do—even with everything about my mother that made me gag. Makes me gag.

See, my father also makes me gag. It's not only that he hits and never says he's sorry; he just kind of turns my stomach. When I was younger, he'd come home at night and kiss my eyelids wetly. I had to try not to wipe my eyes off until he left, so he wouldn't call me uptight or mean. Another thing I absolutely hated: sometimes he'd kiss the top of my head and take a deep whiff, as if my hair were a bouquet belonging only to him. But my father was the same with Hildy and Drew, and they didn't seem to mind, so it always felt like there was something mean about me that I *did* mind. Besides, if I tried to get away from my father, it made him mad. I always wound up thinking, *I don't need to get away that badly.*

Plus, my father hated it when I had assignments that made me "uptight," which, by his standards, were basically all of them. I guess he was trying to help when he brought home books for me, but they were college texts! And I had to act grateful. Get this: in fourth grade, when I had a report to do about bridges, he came home with an engineering text from Prufrock.

I still remember sitting next to him on the edge of our scratchy dark brown couch and leafing through the book. The print was small, and there were very few pictures. "*The towers serve as stabilizers, enabling the main cables to be draped across significant distances. The cables carry most of the structure's weight to the anchorages, which are imbedded. . . .*" I swallowed. "This book is kind of hard, Dad."

My father was sitting too close to me. He smelled of cherry tobacco and saliva and grown-up-man smell. Slowly, I scooted back on the couch so that it wouldn't seem like I was scooting away, exactly: my father couldn't stand my trying to put space between him and me.

"Hard?" he exclaimed. "Nah! What part of it is too hard?"

"Well, like. . . ." I hesitated. Even the *World Book* entry had made my eyes glaze over, and that was supposed to be easy for kids to understand. "It's just kind of—boring."

"Boring—are you kidding?" Surprise, disappointment. "Look, I'll give you a simple explanation of suspension bridges, okay? Take the Golden Gate. Basically, you have a deck, and the deck is suspended."

"Uh-huh," I said uncertainly.

"From cables, of course," he added, standing up in front of me and pantomiming a line with his index finger and thumb. "And then the cables are anchored at their extremities."

"Wh—what are extremities?"

"You know. The ends. The *extreme* parts. That's where we get the word *extremities*. Come on, now. You *know* that."

"But I thought extreme meant—"

"Look, basically, it's all a matter of engineering!"

"Oh." What did engineering have to do with my report, anyway? *Geez, I hope I don't have to figure that out in order to do the assignment*, thought my nine-year-old brain.

I had to find a way to make the conversation okay. "Um, Dad? You know that Prokofiev thing?" I loved the opening theme of the news program my parents watched at night, a frenzied clarinet and violin conversation that my father promised to bring home, but never did.

"I'll bring it tomorrow," he said, patting my head. "And don't worry about that report. You'll get your precious A." This was my father's version of a pep talk.

And yet, and yet. Around the same time, I had finally grown into a creamy, light beige satin dress of Hildy's that I had always loved and that was perfect for my upcoming violin recital. I had spun around the kitchen in the dress before realizing, and blurting out, that my white cotton socks wouldn't look right with it. My mother said, *No one's looking at you!* and that I shouldn't be so rigid. My father seemed angry, but didn't say anything.

After I went to bed, my father brewed some hot tea and soaked my socks in the tea until they matched the dress. When I woke up, there were two perfect beige socks for me on a wire hanger on the hook in the bathroom, each attached with a wooden clothespin.

6

isolating the spots

The first few days after my father moved out, it was quiet at home, almost echoey. I felt sorry for Drew, who was just getting used to being a first grader as I struggled to adjust to seventh.

Hildy didn't seem to be having any trouble getting used to ninth grade. She was popular, and she was always helping someone, especially boys. She'd immediately been asked to be a volunteer peer tutor, because even though she wasn't a straight-A student, the after-school study hall teacher could tell how brainy she was and loved her enthusiasm. Hildy would do things like purposely choose an unpopular boy to work with on a two-person assignment, or help some poor slob who was running for student council by making posters for his candidacy, or give her lunch money to a kid who'd forgotten his. Anyway, the point is, Hildy was hardly ever home after school, partly because when she wasn't tutoring or going over to someone's house, she'd secretly visit my father at the shop so he'd remember that someone still cared about him. That was probably how she had money for school lunches.

I didn't usually allow Drew in my room, but without Hildy around, it fell to me to take care of both my mother and him. So I let him play on my floor, or lie on my bed reading *Superman* comic books or doing math puzzles, while my mother kept crying to make sure we didn't forget how much she was suffering. The middle of my back still hurt, but of course there was no aspirin in the house. Baby aspirin had sugar in it, regular aspirin wasn't *natural*, it was better to let the body heal itself, blah blah blah. At least Drew hadn't gotten physically hurt in the latest fight.

That was another thing that was different: normally, I wouldn't have dared protect or defend Drew, because I'd be worried that my mother would see it as my taking Drew's side against her. In fact, I'd been very mean to Drew a few times in an attempt to make my mother feel more secure. Once, when she got mad at Drew for throwing his food from his high chair, I'd taken him upstairs and shut him in his closet, whose inside handle was too high up for him to reach. He wasn't even three yet. It seems ridiculous now, and horrible, of course, but I honestly thought my mother would appreciate my backing her up. Instead, when she heard his cries, she rushed upstairs, shoved me roughly aside, and rescued and comforted him. Then she told me angrily that there was such a thing as being an ugly person on the inside, and that just because I seemed nice didn't make me nice. I guess she hated me, too. Sometimes, I forget that.

Of course I'd rather have spent my after-school time with Stephanie. There were boys and classes to talk about, not to mention our home lives. A few times, I had to kick Drew out so I could drag the phone into my room to call Stephanie and pour out my heart about how horrible the latest fight had been, so the two of us could weigh the chances that my father's moving out meant my parents were for sure getting a divorce. That possibility felt to me like the end of the goddamned world, even though nothing could have made more sense.

Stephanie and I were both having a hard time dealing with the demands of school, where the home economics teacher would give us assignments like making a lemon meringue pie—just the type of "white bread" thing that both my mother and Stephanie's mom, Sylvia, disapproved of. White sugar was a poison, dessert-making was not a necessary kitchen skill, blah blah blah. But there was an important difference: whereas my mother refused to lift a finger to help me with the immoral assignment (sending me into a complete panic), Sylvia bought all the ingredients for Stephanie, despite her own personal opinions. Thank God Sylvia always had extra food around so I could make my pie over there.

Of course it never dawned on me to skip the assignment. Here's how my life would be described in a book: *She was falling apart, but she had homework.*

I couldn't really talk with Hildy about how I felt about my father, because she always defended him no matter what, even if it was against me. Actually, it was surprising how well Hildy and I got along, considering how differently we looked at things. We were both really upset about the fighting and the fact that my father wasn't living at home anymore, and we had no choice but to comfort each other. At night, Hildy would sneak into my room and climb into my bed, and we'd stay up whispering. Invariably, since we couldn't talk about what a bastard my father was, the topic would turn to what a bitch my mother was.

"But Hildy," I said, "don't all girls our age hate their mothers? Maybe it's from our being, like, immature."

"Just because we're young doesn't automatically mean we're wrong. Like, I think Mom is competing with me. I read about it in a book, how mothers sometimes hate their daughters."

I'm ashamed to admit this, but what I thought was, *Well, my mother might hate Hildy, but she doesn't hate me.* "What do you mean, competing?" I said. "Like, give me an example."

"*Duh!* Don't you remember how she washed us in the bath when we were little?"

I had forgotten the way my mother used to drag a rough washcloth back and forth across our private parts. There was something impatient, or even frantic, about the way she did it, as if she were trying to erase us down there. We dreaded baths until we managed to convince her we'd do a good job washing ourselves.

"But Dad's temper!" I pointed out, because I always wanted to convince Hildy. "Remember April Fool's Day?" We kids had replaced the contents of the sugar bowl with salt and my father had spooned it liberally into his coffee. Then he'd exploded, chasing after us and pounding each of us on the tops of our heads and on our shoulders with his hard fists.

"We should never have provoked him!" was Hildy's response.

Eventually we'd fall asleep side by side, her back to my front, her blond, tangled hair splaying out onto my half of the pillow.

I felt guilty leaving my mother in the mornings. But when it was time for my after-school violin lesson with Mrs. Cray, I was really glad for the excuse not to come straight home, even though aside from Orchestra, I hadn't touched the violin all week. I also told my mother I needed to work with Stephanie on a history assignment after my lesson. Which was true.

Mrs. Cray lived a couple of blocks from Garfield Junior High, very near Stephanie. She really *was* a relief from all the unpredictable behavior in my stupid life. Besides being the nicest person I'd ever known, Mrs. Cray was beautiful. Her skin was the color of creamy coffee, and her face reminded me of a bust of Nefertiti that Hildy had shown me in the *World Book*. Unlike other black women, who straightened their hair so it would look more "white," Mrs. Cray wore hers cropped close to her head, as short as a man's. She didn't even bother with earrings to make herself look feminine. Why was it that instead of giving her a mannish appearance, the style only made her lovelier?

Plus, her whole studio was wallpapered in this really inviting shade of pink with bright yellow and orange and red flowers on it, and there was plenty of light in there, so everything was cheerful. Mrs. Cray kept a dozen yellow pencils in a clear glass jar, all sharpened and ready to use. The pencils matched the accent colors in the wallpaper, and the eraser tips matched the pink.

Mrs. Cray would start our hour-long lessons by playing records for me that she thought I might like, just for five or ten minutes. It was like getting to eat dessert first, before we got down to technique, the pieces I was studying, and sight-reading practice. Mrs. Cray felt jazz recordings were a great way to learn music theory, which, she said, I was probably going to need, because I might want to major in music when I got to college.

One time she played "The 'In' Crowd" for me, starting with the original vocal version recorded by Dobie Gray. I didn't think much of it, since I wasn't in the "in" crowd and never would be, besides which, the song was just kind of lame. But then Mrs. Cray put on the live instrumental version by Ramsey Lewis. "They transposed it to D!" I exclaimed, unable to keep my head from nodding. The very same melody that was uninspiring when sung by Dobie Gray was provocative in Ramsey Lewis's hands, something whose honest, smoky beat you couldn't resist.

"They did indeed! I think the story is that Ramsey Lewis's bass player wanted to use his open strings, because the trio had just learned the piece the very same day they performed it. But you're right—usually the original and the cover versions of a song are in the same key."

"The styles are so different," I marveled.

"Notice the dynamics," she pointed out. "It's not just mezzo-forte all the time. They get really quiet, and then the energy picks up." She went on to give me the music theory behind the chord progressions, and the way in which the sequence was unusual. The song as performed by Ramsey Lewis revealed gospel influences, she explained: that exuberant interplay between the musicians and the audience, which could be traced back to West African rain dances, was part of what gave the track its magic.

Now that I think about it, it's weird that my parents let me take lessons with Mrs. Cray. My mother was skeptical that a teacher could be kind and gentle and also effective. My father didn't quite understand music lessons: he seemed to think great musicians were born proficient. I guess he liked Mrs. Cray because she was a customer of his and valued his opinions. If he ever warned her about how rigid a person I am, she must have ignored him.

I had to assume my parents didn't know Mrs. Cray was introducing me to jazz and telling me I was going to need to study music theory, and I could easily see them getting mad if they found out. But the truth was, Mrs. Cray and I always got down to the business of violin quickly after our fun.

"This is such a difficult section," she sympathized as we worked on the Corelli passage that I'd been mangling in Miss Transom's orchestra. She picked up her own violin and ran through it absently, experimenting with a few different fingerings. "In bar forty-two—hmm . . . try shifting into second position."

I hesitated.

"Now, Martha, don't be upset with yourself for not sounding like me. You should have heard me when I was your age! Good Lord, what a racket. Made my poor mother cover up her ears."

"Really?" Even though I knew great musicians were born talented, not proficient, it was still hard to imagine Mrs. Cray ever having been crummy on the violin. She'd gone to Juilliard, taught in the Music Department at Cal, and was part of an important local string quartet. Plus, she sometimes played jazz violin in a friend's band.

"You have to remember, Martha dear, the violin is very unforgiving. It's hard to sound good on it and easy to sound bad. And let's face it—it's a pretty awkward position in which to put your chin and left arm."

I wrote the new fingering into my music with a pencil from her jar. With Mrs. Cray, I could imagine a different life for myself, a future that made sense. I could have students, too, and be their favorite teacher. I could get rid of the shrug somehow and get married. Who knew? Maybe the shrug would go away as soon as I found the right person to fall in love with and who would fall in love with me. The shrug could be all psychological, from having psychologically sick parents, couldn't it? It could disappear with love. I could have children. I could teach violin while the children were in school.

It wasn't so much that I wanted to be a violinist. I just wanted to be good at something that would make people outside my family notice me for something other than my shrug. Also—I almost never shrugged while I was playing violin, even if I was sight-reading or didn't know the piece well yet.

"Excellent work today, Martha." Mrs. Cray smiled as the lesson ended. "Now, what's the key to good practice?"

"Isolating the spots," I answered. Mrs. Cray encouraged her students to play very slowly, start a beat or two before a problem area, play through the problem, play a couple of extra beats, and then go back and repeat the same thing a little faster, and then a little faster, until it was seamless. Often, her method meant starting and ending in very odd places (the odder the better, Mrs. Cray said), playing absolutely nothing except the "isolated" spot, and resisting the temptation to lead up to it or end it with parts I already knew well. The technique really did work—when I used it.

"Exactly," Mrs. Cray said. "Practice isolating with the new fingering, and I'll see you next Wednesday, okay?"

"Mom, where's the Nestle's Quik?" Mrs. Cray's son poked his head into the studio. When he saw me, he blushed and looked away.

Probably he was caught off guard because I'd changed lesson days now that summer was over.

Clifton Cray was a cute kid. He was a year behind me in school, and on the younger side for his grade, plus he was unusually small for his age, so it always felt kind of ridiculous that he had a crush on me. Like me, Clifton had perfect pitch. When we were younger and I'd come for lessons, he'd follow me around, maybe because he didn't know any other kid with perfect pitch. If I sat on the bench in the little waiting area just outside the studio, Clifton would sit down right next to me. If I moved over, he'd move over to be closer to me. I never paid much attention to him. He was kind of immature, and besides, it embarrassed me that he was already way better than I was on violin, since he studied and practiced with his mother.

My own mother had opinions about all this, of course: first of all, it was psychologically unhealthy, maybe even damaging, for a child to take music lessons with his own mother. Second (this was when our neighborhood babysitter had a black boyfriend), white girls who dated black boys had low self-esteem and needed therapy.

I absolutely hate admitting it, but I was always wondering if my mother was right about stuff like that. It's not as easy as you might think to reject everything about your mother, even if she's a complete bitch. You keep looking for places where she might be onto something. You think to yourself, *She's always saying not to judge someone by the color of his skin, so she can't be prejudiced.*

As for the idea that Mrs. Cray had crippled Clifton psychologically by teaching him violin—well, that's a big fat joke. Clifton is just about the nicest, most stable person who ever lived. And, of course, he became concertmaster of the whole Berkeley High School orchestra the minute he set foot on campus as a tenth grader. I'd see him whenever Concert Chorale and Orchestra did concerts together, and we'd say "isolating the spots!" to each other at the same time and laugh. Oh, and his girlfriend Giselle? She's white, and in my grade—a year older than Clifton—and she's a terrific cellist, and really pretty, and really self-confident, and completely lacking any kind of shrug. I mean, she's not a nice person, and I'll tell you more about that later, but the point is, my mother is just stupid.

"Nestle's Quik?" Mrs. Cray was saying to eleven-year-old Clifton. "Check in the cabinet above the toaster. If not, there's Ovaltine."

Clifton looked disappointed that he might have to settle for Ovaltine. He glanced at me, blushed again, and shut the door behind him.

I removed the shoulder pad and laid my violin in its case. Now was my chance. *Shrug.* "Mrs. Cray?"

"Yes, Martha dear?"

I'd never told her about my parents' fights, and I didn't want to say anything about my father having just moved out, because it was too complicated. I'd thought many times about asking her how I could get rid of the shrug, but it always felt too humiliating to bring it up. And I couldn't come right out and tell her I was desperate to get Paul Shapiro to like me, or at least notice I was alive. "Do you think—is there anything you think I could do to feel more like other girls?" I managed.

Mrs. Cray was quiet for a moment, and I busied myself rubbing the surface of my violin with the white cotton handkerchief I kept in one of the velvet compartments. As the seconds ticked by, I realized she'd probably say the same thing my mother would—that it isn't important what other people think, that a sense of well-being must come from inside oneself. "You feel different?" she asked finally.

"I don't know," I mumbled miserably, trying to ignore the faint nails-on-a-chalkboard sound as I wiped rosin off the strings. "It's not important, really."

"Well, maybe—" she hesitated, and I braced myself. It had to be the shrug, how I needed to get my mother to take me to a doctor or something. "Maybe you could get some clothes that are—more like what the other girls your age are wearing. That might make you feel a little more comfortable."

"Oh!" I nodded sagely, as if I had been expecting this piece of advice—as if my mother would ever agree to such a thing. Come to think of it, she'd probably have a conniption if she found out that Iris Cray suggested I get different clothing. She might even make me stop taking lessons with her.

How was I going to get new clothes, especially now that my mother wanted to divorce my father? She'd say I was selfish for bringing it up when she was going through so much. She'd say I had plenty of hand-me-downs from Hildy that were "perfectly good." She'd say I was ungrateful for what my grandparents sent. She'd say, *No one's looking at you!* She'd talk about how she had just taken me and Hildy to Hink's, even though that was over a year ago, and besides, it was the time my mother had insisted on getting Hildy some expensive leopard-patterned velour pants that Hildy absolutely hated and that were too big for her. "They make me look like the Hindenburg!" Hildy had complained in the dressing room.

"My God, Hildy, your perceptions are so lopsided. They're gorgeous!" my mother had responded, and took the pants to the counter to pay for them. Thank God she hadn't found anything for me that day.

"You're a lovely girl, Martha," Mrs. Cray was saying, "no matter what you're wearing. This is just an idea, that's all."

The door opened and her next student, a scrawny boy I recognized from my history class, came in, filling the room with his teenage male smell. "Thanks, Mrs. Cray. I—I'll practice more this week," I added, immediately regretting the empty promise. Maybe from my personality, and from how much I liked Mrs. Cray, you'd assume I worked hard on violin, but I barely did what she suggested between lessons. I'd start out with good intentions, but things would always come up: a fight at home, or extra homework, or discouragement about not being very good on violin. Or my mother being on the warpath with Hildy or Drew, which made me worry that if I put in too much effort, they'd look bad.

7

starch

Outside Mrs. Cray's, Stephanie was waiting for me, her text-books in a red-gingham-lined basket whose straw handles made a tiny creaky noise under the weight. I needed a basket, since I had a violin to carry besides my school stuff. But now that things were so bad at home, I knew there was no way I was getting one. "How's Clifford?" Stephanie mocked.

"Clif*ton*," I corrected, elbowing her. "And—quit it!" Teasing me about Clifton Cray was Stephanie's way of trying to shake me from my devotion to Paul Shapiro. "How was French club?"

"Boring," Stephanie reported, throwing back her long, wavy, light brown hair with a toss of the head. "Plus, the eighth graders think they're so great! Oh. Listen, Marth—I hate to break this to you, but I found out—well, Paul Shapiro is going with that Barb girl."

My heart sank. Barb Mendelsohn: how had I missed it? Probably Paul knew her from synagogue. Synagogue! Why did my parents have to be the type of people who thought organized religion was rigid? I knew they were proud of being Jewish. My father was very attached to a special silver cup that had belonged to his grandfather in the Old Country, plus a beautiful handmade silver box that you were apparently supposed to put fragrant spices in, and that gave a satisfying little *click* when you shut it. My mother was always saying how all kinds of brilliant scientists and musicians and writers are Jewish. Why couldn't we be the type of family that kept special fragrant spices at home and had a synagogue to go to? "Barb Mendelsohn? But—she's *such* a show-off!" I fumed.

"I know," Stephanie answered. "A real prima donna."

I think I asked Stephanie once what pre-Madonna meant, but I could never remember. Before women were as humble and kind as the mother of Jesus? I forget. "I need some clothes," I said, and filled her in on my conversation with Mrs. Cray. Barb Mendelsohn didn't have to worry about having crummy clothing, that was for sure. She always looked perfect, with her perfect white stretchy headband on perfect goddamned long straight brown hair.

"Well, no offense, Martha, but actually—good idea."

Shrug. "You agree?" It kind of made me mad that she hadn't said anything before, if that was her opinion.

"Hey, I know! Let's drop off our stuff at my house and take the bus to Hink's!"

"What about our history assignment?" I pointed out.

"Let's ditch it. C'mon, Martha, after the week you've had?! Live a little!"

"I can't stay out that long. Plus, I don't have money with me."

"I can lend it to you!"

"Thanks, Steph, but isn't the whole point for me to look different?"

"You're damned right."

"So then how would I hide the new stuff from my mom? Which—she'll see it and have a spaz!"

"Martha! Why do you always have to do what she says?"

Stephanie and I had a lot in common. We weren't popular, we found the same things stupid and the same things funny, and we had the fathers-moving-out experience in common. Our mothers both hated toy guns and makeup and Barbies. And we both hated our mothers.

My mother had known Sylvia Kenyon since Stephanie and I were babies, because we had the same pediatrician. Also, we were in a carpool together when my mother decided to put me and Hildy in some kids' summer day camp up at the Little Farm in Tilden Park. The carpooling part lasted one day. My mother spent the first ride lecturing Stephanie's older brother, Brett, about how he said "you know" and "I mean" too much when he talked, and about how his using "me and my sister" as the subject of a sentence was incorrect grammar.

So Stephanie knew firsthand what a bitch my mother was, and what an embarrassment. The fact that I didn't have to try to convince her of this was a lot of the reason Stephanie had quickly become my best friend when we'd met again. We'd recognized each other at the end of sixth grade at a picnic for all the kids who'd be going to Garfield Junior High in the fall, and she and I spent a lot of time hanging around together over the summer, mostly at her house, since I never knew when there was going to be an explosion at home. Stephanie understood what I was going through. But sometimes, she seemed to forget the fact that I was the one person in the family my mother could stand, or who could stand her.

"I *don't* do everything she says, Stephanie," I countered, trying to keep my voice steady, because I was kind of angry. "Don't you get it? Right now, just leaving her alone to go to school feels—"

Suddenly I felt her elbow in my ribs. "Don't look behind you!" she whispered as a group of girls passed us on their way to the corner store.

Before I could make sense of the words, I heard the sneer in Logan Starch's voice. "Well, if it isn't Miss Martha Goldenthal." I whirled around, felt my face go crimson as I saw who he was with. *Shrug*.

"C'mon, Starch," coaxed Paul Shapiro, "leave 'er alone." He was so dreamy, with his long eyelashes and faraway look, it was almost impossible not to hope his defense of me meant something.

"Why should I? Martha Goldenthal here thinks she's smarter than I am."

"I do n-not, Logan," I stammered. I could feel another shrug coming on like a sneeze I didn't have a Kleenex for. I tried to concentrate, ward it off, but it was no use.

Logan had just enough time to mock, "Hey Martha, what's ten times ten?" just as the shrug came, sending my violin case swinging, so that it seemed as if I were responding to Logan's question. "Oh, so you don't *know!*" he shouted triumphantly.

"Logan, that's just plain mean," Stephanie put in as I swallowed about a thousand times to choke down the tears. Without a word, Paul Shapiro grabbed Logan's jacket collar and dragged him toward the corner grocery. Neither of them looked back, but Logan was laughing hard, until Paul socked him.

"*Ow!*" Logan complained, the sound deadened a little by distance.

Stephanie put her hand on my shoulder, walked me quickly up to her front porch where we'd be out of view, and sat me down on the faded green cushions of a wicker couch where her white cat, Fathom, was snoozing in the afternoon sun.

"I hate myself," I said tearfully. "This stupid goddamned shrug! No one is *ever* gonna like me."

"Logan Starch is a rat fink. Just ignore him!"

"How can I ignore him when he's right?" I shrieked, then realized Sylvia might be able to hear me. "I mean, it's the truth," I said, lowering my voice.

"It's not the truth! He's right that you have a shrug, but—he's just a jerk in how he acts. So that right there, Martha? That means you should just pretend like you don't care."

I *had* pretended I didn't care that time when I told Logan Starch off in front of the whole class. Why couldn't one time be enough?

Why did I always have to keep doing things to stand up for myself? It was exhausting. *Is* exhausting.

"Act like you're above it!" Stephanie was saying. "Then he'll stop bothering you."

I had no idea how to act like I was above anything, or how that was supposed to help me. The problem was the shrug, *duh!* How was acting a certain way going to solve anything?

"Hey, I know!" she said, flashing the big smile. "Let's go to the library and see if we can find anything about a shrug!"

I reddened; the idea of doing this kind of research with Stephanie felt just too embarrassing. Besides, I'd already tried a couple of years before and hadn't found out anything, other than the fact that I hated librarians. I was maybe ten or eleven, hoping to come across information about the sickness of shrugging without anyone ever finding out that I'd looked.

I'd walked over to the North Branch of the Berkeley Public Library after a violin lesson. In the Reference Room, I was barely able to breathe as I looked through the entry on "nervous behaviors" in an illustrated medical dictionary. I'd perched myself with only half my butt in the chair, in case someone walked in. But even though there was stuff about "nervous tics," there was nothing about shrugs at all.

"And what are we reading today?" The librarian was suddenly right next to me.

Quickly, I'd slammed the book shut and pulled the volume toward my lap at a diagonal. *Shrug.* I looked up at her. She was smiling kindly. She was pretty like June Cleaver, but with wavy salt-and-pepper hair, dangling silver earrings, and a multicolored Mexican vest over a white blouse. I didn't think she'd seen what page I'd been on, but she could tell it was a medical dictionary because the cover was visible from where she was standing. I leaned forward in the chair, trying to obscure the book. Why did librarians act like it was their business what someone was trying to find out about?

"It's natural to be curious about the human body," the librarian had remarked, putting a hand on my back before walking away. *Natural*—ugh, that awful word. Of course, she assumed I was investigating something about sex.

"I've already tried," I snapped at Stephanie, trying to sound angry at life, not at her. "There's nothing!"

"Bummer," Stephanie said simply.

She was so easy to talk to that I just kind of let loose about how things were at home. The shouting, the hitting, the throwing things, the swear words. Being hated by my father and hated by my mother, for different reasons, and feeling like it was my own goddamned fault. I told Stephanie everything—well, mostly everything. I left out some of the disgusting things about my mother, like the way she used to try to "erase" our private parts in the bath. That was just *too* gross.

"Hey, Martha," she said after a while, "I have an idea! Why don't we raid my closet and find something that looks good on you?"

"Really?" It was true that both of us were about average in height and were starting to "develop" (another word I hated, because my mother used it). People sometimes even said Stephanie and I looked alike, probably because we both had kind of a full face. But her entire face lit up when she smiled. "But won't your mom care if you give me your stuff?"

Sylvia was already so generous. The very first week of school, I'd started coming home for lunch with Stephanie, bringing meager bag lunches I'd scraped together with whatever there was around the house: stale heels of rye bread, a few squishy grapes, "Precious" (what a sick joke) mozzarella that had hardened because my mother didn't believe in Saran Wrap, besides which, the stuff was pukey-bland and grainy even when it was fresh, and probably bounced like a tennis ball if you dropped it. I'd made the best of it alongside Stephanie, declining Sylvia's offer of whatever Stephanie was having. By the second week, Sylvia had come right out and insisted that I needed a hot meal, dishing out an extra bowl of the unlikely but somehow tasty combinations of Campbell's canned soups she'd heat up. Corn Chowder with Pepper Pot; Chicken Noodle with Beef Vegetable. For bread, Sylvia warmed corn tortillas in the oven, and we rolled them up with butter inside. I had never tasted anything so delicious.

"She won't notice," Stephanie assured me. "She's not here, and besides, she's too busy to care." Unlike my mother, Sylvia had her own life writing poetry and going on long hikes and listening to jazz, and also being a lesbian, which didn't seem to bother Stephanie any more, even though it had really upset her last year when she'd found out. Secretly, I thought the whole idea of homosexuality was icky, maybe because my mother had told me it was "psychologically very unhealthy." Still, Sylvia seemed to be a way happier person than my mother. My mother would say, *Well, of course she is! Because Morris Kenyon isn't a violent louse!*

Stephanie and I went upstairs. I already felt better, even though Brett had the volume cranked up so high on the record player in his room that we practically had to shout to talk. Brett was a regular customer of my father's, and since my father didn't hold him to the same standards of musical taste to which he held his own children, Brett had quite a few records in his rock and roll collection.

We looked through Stephanie's closet and found a navy blue denim mini-skirt that she said she never wore, because her legs were "pasty white," not nice and tan like mine. I let myself believe her, even though I'd seen her wear the skirt before. There was also a gauzy blue-green blouse whose sleeves were a little too long for Stephanie and that fit me perfectly. And in the back of her closet, there was a gingham-lined book basket that she'd used the previous year but that had a little tear in the gingham, so Sylvia had gotten her a new one. Stephanie said I could have it. I was pretty sure I could repair the fabric with a needle and thread.

"Now let's see how your hair looks loose," Stephanie said.

I always used a big tortoise-shell barrette to hold back my hair, which I only wore long because that's what all the other girls did (a shrug being plenty to set me apart). I didn't think of my hair as any kind of asset. "It's not great," I said, taking out the barrette. "See?"

"You're wrong," she said. "Wear it loose for now. Okay? Just try it."

We went back downstairs, and Stephanie made white popcorn in a huge Revere Ware pan with a pool of safflower oil at the bottom. I loved the reassuring *tap-tap-tap* of the kernels popping inside. Stephanie melted half a cube of butter in a little white enamel saucepan that fell over on its handle when it was empty. She put the popped kernels in a big bowl and drizzled the butter over it. The butter was still hot when she used the salt shaker, and the puffy kernels gave a tiny sizzle.

We worked on our history assignment at Stephanie's kitchen table, licking our greasy fingers so we didn't stain our textbooks. Fathom rubbed his body against my legs. I could feel the bass line of Brett's rock music in my chest.

8

the "in" crowd

"Hey, you look nice."

That was about the last thing I expected to hear when Brett, having smelled fresh popcorn, came tromping down the stairs. He left the record player on and his door open, which made the music so loud that I thought I'd probably misheard him. *Shrug.*

"See? Toldya!" said Stephanie's eyebrows as she kicked me under the table. Brett grabbed the popcorn from her and used a few kernels to sponge up the extra butter at the bottom of the bowl before tossing them in his mouth.

"Thanks, Brett," I managed. Brett was definitely cute, with curly sandy-brown hair and very white teeth and, like Stephanie, a big smile that made his eyes crinkle. He was fourteen, Hildy's age, and since Hildy had referred to Brett Kenyon as Stephanie's good-looking older brother, there were probably a thousand other girls who liked him too. Also, he was always talking about books and ideas, and I felt anxious around that type of boy. Get this: he used his allowance for magazine subscriptions so he'd have plenty to read in case he ever ran out of books. Plus, he insisted that Sylvia and Morris let him keep the encyclopedia set in his room so he could read it whenever he wanted.

"Is this the Beatles again?" Stephanie asked.

"It's The Who, dummy!" Brett answered, and then turned to me. "I'm trying to keep myself from listening too much to *Yesterday And Today* and *Revolver. Rubber Soul*, too. They're *so* cool, I don't wanna get sick of them."

"Funny, you don't seem to care if *I* get sick of them," Stephanie put in. "You've played them about a thousand times each."

"Yeah? Then why'd you mistake The Who for the Beatles? Huh?" Stephanie was practically as ignorant of pop music as I was. She had a record player in her room but used it for musical soundtracks like *Kiss Me, Kate*, which she loved to act out in front of her full-length mirror. As for me, I'd taken the portable record player at home into my bedroom, where neither Hildy nor Drew seemed to miss it, and used it primarily for the Bach unaccompanied violin sonatas and partitas, a boxed set that I'd finally gotten my father to bring home, and for Copland's *Appalachian Spring*.

Brett wiped his hands on his jeans and turned to me. "Of course *you're* familiar with the whole album cover thing."

Apparently I was being given the benefit of the doubt, coolness-wise, because of Smoke and Records. "Album cover?"

"You know! Where they had those, like, baby dolls on the front? Wait, how come—don't you get all the records you want for free?"

"Uh, I guess I'm more the classical type," I said lamely.

"Sheesh! Well anyway," he went on, "so the baby dolls are torn apart—their heads are off, and there are arms and legs and torsos all over the place, and slabs of raw meat draped over the Beatles, with blood everywhere—"

"Eeew," Stephanie and I said at the same time.

"—and the Beatles in these white coats like the ones butchers wear." He sponged up butter, crunched the kernels.

"Wait, can we see?" Stephanie asked.

"Oh, so *now* you're interested," Brett said through a mouthful. "Can't, though. Those were the copies that Capitol Records sent out before the actual release date, kind of like as a test. And Capitol got all these negative comments from the record store owners who got the test copies." He wiped his hands on his jeans again. "So they decided to take back all those records from all the stores. But some of the stores had already sold the album that first day, even though they weren't s'posed to! Wouldn't that be cool, to be one of the lucky ones who got the version with the original cover?"

"But what did they do with the records they took back?" Stephanie was confused, and so was I.

"They glued new pictures on them and then return them to the stores! And the part that's really neat is—apparently, you can peel the new picture off by, like, ironing the album, to see what's underneath!"

"But—wouldn't the record get all warped if you ironed it?" Stephanie asked, and I thought of my father's stern warnings about keeping LPs out of the sun and heat.

"You take the actual record *out* first, dodo!" Brett was exasperated. "You just do the cover!"

"Can we do that? Now?" Stephanie wanted to know. "Iron the cover?"

"It's a bummer, man. They didn't send those glued-on covers everywhere, just to some regions. The other stores got brand-new covers that don't have the butcher cover underneath. I don't know anyone who got the original." He didn't dwell on his disappointment. "Anyway the point is, is, the music is *cool.*"

I hated when people said "the point is, is." It was like they were trying to sound smarter than they actually were. Also—why didn't I know more about record stores than other kids did, instead of less? My father hadn't said anything about having to send Beatles records back to Capitol, or about *not* having gotten the ones with the original cover. But then, maybe he'd been too busy hitting people to mention it.

"So anyway, this latest album is called *Revolver.* I always get my records at your dad's store, by the way."

"Oh!" I pretended I didn't know this.

"Revolver! Get it?"

We didn't get it.

"Revolver, man! Like, the record *revolves* around the turntable! Sheesh, everyone knows that! Plus it's a type of gun, obviously." He pronounced it "*ov*-viously," like Stephanie. He turned to his sister and displayed the bowl, which was empty except for a few remaining whole kernels that weren't any fun to crunch on. "Steph. Make some more, wouldja?"

"You are the laziest person alive," Stephanie remarked as she got up and started another batch.

I looked at the kitchen clock. "Oh, God, I better go," I said. "My mom is gonna have a cow. Plus, Drew—"

"Stay for dinner!" Stephanie said.

"You can't go," Brett said. "You gotta at least hear *Revolver*. Okay?"

Blush. *Shrug.*

"Call your mom!" Stephanie urged.

Brett's room had the same high ceiling as Stephanie's, but was somehow cave-like. He had window shutters, but you had the feeling he never opened them, and that if he did, the whole room would scream and shut its eyes against the unfamiliar invasion of light. Brett had a small lighted fish tank that, in the gloom, looked like a TV that was on without the sound in an otherwise unlit space. A tall, wide bookshelf, painted olive green, was mostly stuffed with books. The encyclopedias took up the whole shelf that was one up from the bottom. On the very bottom sat Brett's record collection.

Stephanie turned on the overhead light. Brett's unmade bed was covered with books and papers and his open backpack. She gave up and flounced down on the huge beanbag chair in the corner, and a yellow flyer announcing a school football game fluttered to the floor next to her. I recognized it, because Hildy had gotten the same flyer. Stephanie snatched it up, surprised. "Brett, you're going to this?"

"*Hell,* no!" Brett answered, rolling his eyes in disgust. "Bunch of bullshit, man. *Rah-rah! Go Jackets!* School spirit—it's the hobgoblin of small minds."

I turned around and sat cross-legged on the floor in front of the records. On the far left, they went straight up and down, and then they leaned more and more diagonally, like a handwritten letter that starts out perfectly horizontal, as if with good intentions, but dips down increasingly on the right as the letter continues. "Hey, you have 'The "In" Crowd!'" I exclaimed, pulling it out. "This is so great. Did you know there was a recording before Ramsey Lewis did it?"

"Yeah, Dobie Gray wrote it and sang it, right?"

"Well, Dobie Gray was the first to record it," I said. "It was written by Billy Page."

"Really?" He grabbed the album from me and flipped it over to look on the back cover. "Hey, you're right! How did you—"

"My violin teacher. She shows me stuff about jazz sometimes."

"Wait. She teaches you how to play *jazz*?" Brett took the record out of its sleeve and put it on the turntable.

"Not to play, no. Just to learn the music theory behind it."

"What do you mean, music theory?" Stephanie asked from the bed.

I swung around on my butt to face them as the music started. Then I was worried that my new skirt was too short, so I put my legs straight out in front of me and leaned back on the shelf in the kind of modesty that Hildy had to teach me about because my mother didn't. "Isn't it great?" I said, and they both nodded and grinned. After a few bars, I started explaining. "Theory. Well, like, in this case, you have regular blues in D. What I mean is, the chords go in the standard blues sequence. But then, in the last few bars of the progression, instead of the chords being 3, 6, 2, 5, 1, which is standard, it goes up to flat 7 after the 5 chord. Wait, here—it's coming up!"

They both gaped, but didn't seem to notice the quirky flat 7 chord. Maybe I wasn't explaining it clearly.

"I mean, like, you're expecting the 5 to lead to the 1, so it's a surprise. Get it? That flat 7 chord in the turnaround is what's unusual."

Stephanie said, "Brett, Martha can tell you what any note is."

"What do you mean?" Brett asked.

"I can hear what key things are in," I explained. "It's called perfect pitch. Like, if I've heard a piece, I can sing what note it's going to start on before it starts. Or, if you ask me to sing an E-flat, or whatever note you want, I can do it."

"But—how?" The song was over, and Brett took the needle off.

I gave a real shrug. "I just hear it." This was one thing in my life that I was confident about. "Try me. Here, you have Beethoven's 8th Symphony, which is in F major. If you put it on, I'll sing it to you before it starts." I handed Brett the record and started singing before he'd put the needle down. When the first movement started, his eyes went wide, but oddly, he seemed more impressed by my voice than by my having gotten the right note. "You sing really well," he said.

Afterwards, I squished in next to Stephanie on the beanbag chair and listened to a few of Brett's favorite Beatles songs, like "Dizzy Miss Lizzie" and "I Saw Her Standing There." I hated both of them—still do. Then he played "You're Gonna Lose That Girl," which is great, even though it's horribly out of tune in a few places.

I just let myself have a break from my stupid family for a few more minutes because I'd had such a shitty day. Then I really, really had to get going.

9

al-blum

Eventually, my father did bring home a Beatles record. It was the following year, when I was in eighth grade.

He'd moved back home a few months into seventh grade, but my mother kicked him out again a couple of weeks later. The same thing happened over the summer between seventh and eighth grade. Now he and my mother were getting along again, and it looked like he might be moving back in. I guess he brought the record in a show of hope that we could be a happy family.

Believe it or not, I was constantly wishing my parents would get back together. As disruptive as it was to have my father moving out, and back in, and out, and back in again, to me this seesawing meant reconciliation was possible. Stephanie kept saying I shouldn't get my hopes up, but I figured she might be jealous because her parents were already in the middle of their divorce. Besides, I couldn't help it. I wanted my parents to change how they acted so they could be together. Maybe I wanted them to love each other so that I wouldn't have to love them.

In retrospect, it's a little strange that *Yesterday And Today* was the album my father chose to bring us. There'd been several records since then—*Revolver*, and then the new one, *Sgt. Pepper's Lonely Hearts*

Club Band. Maybe he was worried that the more recent albums were too psychedelic to be appropriate for kids. Maybe he figured that if Capitol had already sanitized the *Yesterday And Today* album cover, its contents were probably fine, too. Maybe he was overstocked with the earlier album, or maybe someone had returned this one. Or maybe he just grabbed whatever album was handy, figuring it didn't matter, dreck being dreck.

It was a Saturday afternoon, and my father was getting a ride home from Terry Lamb, who worked for my father, and Terry's wife, Trish. My mother was making dinner. She'd even invited Terry and Trish to stay. When I came downstairs to check on her, she was stirring some gamey-smelling stew with a big wooden spoon. I grimaced. No doubt there was some reason why things like roasted chicken and buttered noodles weren't good for you.

The kitchen table was barely visible, with items strewn every-where, and I quietly got to work. There was a rickety wooden fruit bowl with two sad brown bananas in it. I took it and put it next to the dish drain. I fished pieces of mail out from in between a stack of folded paper bags and newspapers. Some of the mail was opened, some wasn't. I separated out the newspapers and bags and gathered the mail into one pile, which I wedged into the crowded corner of the counter. "Mom? Is Dad moving back in with us?" I asked as casually as I could, picking up a pile of clean socks and putting them to the side on the staircase.

"I don't know yet." My mother dipped a clean stainless steel tea-spoon into the stew for a taste. She didn't believe in putting her germs on the cooking spoon.

"Well, when do you think—?"

"Martha, stop being so rigid."

"I'm not! I just—"

"Jesus, you're like a little old lady!" My mother put the lid back on and turned down the flame. "Now set the table."

"I am! I had to clear it first."

"I'm hungry," Drew whined, trotting down the stairs.

"No snacks! I'm making dinner," my mother said.

I made Drew help me finish the table and then took him into the living room, where we peeked out from behind the dusty dark brown curtains and waited for my father. Drew counted the cars as they drove by, multiplying by four each time to keep track of how many tires had rolled along the street.

Soon, a white Buick pulled up in front of our house and the driver's side door opened. Terry Lamb climbed out and opened the back door for his wife Trish, a bubbly, dimpled brunette who was as tall as her husband and expecting a baby soon. My father climbed out the passenger side. "Dad's home!" Drew squealed. "With a fat lady!"

There was a gleaming square under my father's arm, a record. I remember thinking: Prokofiev's 5th Symphony, finally? Drew and I scrambled to the door and opened it, waving from the porch. "Dad, I can multiply by four! Wanna hear?" Drew shouted. "Four, eight, twelve—"

My father was smiling broadly all the way up the stairs. He handed the record to me without a word.

". . . sixteen, twenty, twenty-four—"

"*Dad!*" I shrieked. "You *brought* it!"

"What? What is it?" Drew craned his neck.

"The Beatles! The Beatles! *Hildy!*" I shouted, running inside. *Shrug.*

Terry and Trish Lamb were grinning, and my mother appeared in the hallway, drying her hands on the bottom of her apron. Her nylon headband was a little crooked, and she looked like she was about to smile. I wondered whether she'd known beforehand about my father's surprise.

"Hildy! Hildy!" shouted Drew as Hildy came running down the stairs. "A Beatle al-blum!"

"It's Beat*les*," Hildy corrected, grabbing the LP out of my hands. "And it's *album*, not al-blum."

"I wanna see Ringo and John," Drew demanded as the adults filed into the kitchen, Trish's pointy flats sliding along the hardwood floor.

"It's John, Paul, George, and Ringo," Hildy corrected.

"Paul, John—" Drew repeated.

"Come on, let's sit down on the couch and I'll show you," Hildy said. "Here, look at the picture. See? There's John, then Paul, then George, and then Ringo."

"They have only one order?" Drew asked.

"Well, not exactly, but John is the leader. See? This is John," she pointed. "He's kind of an—iconoclast."

"Don't use sophisticated words!" Drew cried.

"You are so *cute!*" Hildy laughed, pulling Drew onto her lap. "Iconoclast means he, like, breaks the rules in a way that's really cool. Anyway, Ringo is the last one, 'cause he's the drummer, plus, he's not as cute as the others. Paul is second, I guess," she said, tapping at the picture of the one sitting inside the open trunk. "Yes. Definitely. So that's why George is third."

Brett had never said anything that definitive about the Beatles' "order," even though he'd been tutoring me and Stephanie for months by playing songs for us, saying he wanted to make sure we weren't the least "in" girls in junior high. Whenever he'd introduce a new song, he'd make me say what key it was in. Brett never seemed to get tired of that trick, even though I could tell he didn't quite understand my odd ability—maybe because he himself couldn't hold a tune.

I kind of knew what Hildy meant about the order of the Beatles. It was like red, blue, green, and yellow: ever since I first saw the line of wooden cubbyholes in my kindergarten classroom, those four colors seemed to demand being thought of only in that sequence. It holds true for the Beatles too. Red really *is* the color of John Lennon. Paul is sky-blue. George is green, and Ringo is yellow. I'd have to tell that to Brett and see if he agreed, even though lately, he was always burning incense in his room, which Stephanie was pretty sure he did to mask the smell of grass. One thing Stephanie and I both knew for sure was that we didn't want to get hung up on drugs.

"Dad?" I shouted. "Can we put this on?" The living room turntable and speakers sounded a lot better than the children's portable record player, but we weren't allowed to use it ourselves.

My father came back into the living room, his eyes twinkling. "Let's do it!"

The three of us gathered around my father as he slid the disc from the inside cover, extending his hand so that the middle fingers reached the papered inner circle while his thumb stayed at the edge. "Never put your fingers in the grooves," he reminded us—then used the sleeve of his shirt in a round elbow motion to remove any dust from the factory.

I didn't say anything, but because of Brett, I was already familiar with *Yesterday And Today*, along with all the other albums. I'd figured out that when I responded deeply to a song, it was often written by George Harrison. "You Like Me Too Much," "If I Needed Someone," "Think for Yourself"—I loved all of them. There were plenty of great Lennon-McCartney ones too, like "Ticket to Ride."

So when my father laid the record on the turntable and put the needle down, I was surprised to hear the dazzling guitar opener of "And Your Bird Can Sing." My father had started with side two. As soon as he went back into the kitchen, Hildy went over and cranked the volume up. By now Hildy had also heard Beatles records at parties and friends' houses, and I wondered if she also noticed we were listening to the second side first.

"I'll be John, you be Paul," Hildy shouted to me over the music. I did what came naturally from playing violin, and Hildy corrected me, explaining that Paul was left-handed, so I had to "strum" with my left hand and pretend to hold the neck of the guitar with my right. "Is this good?" I asked Hildy, and she nodded to the beat. Drew, having chosen drums, was tapping his hands on the coffee table as my father came back into the room.

My father clapped and danced around, acting as if he liked the music. The clapping sounded forced and heavy, being on the downbeat, but I was so happy I didn't care. He patted Drew's curly head.

"Don't!" Drew jerked his head away and resumed his drumming.

"Okay, Beatle boy," my father chuckled. He resumed his clapping, an unlit pipe hanging out of his mouth. As the song wound down, he made his way back into the kitchen, twirling one end of his mustache. I heard my mother talking to Trish about how important it was to breastfeed.

Next came the mysterious beauty of "If I Needed Someone." I imagined a dark wood panel next to one of the Beatles' beds, a telephone nearby. But wouldn't you get in trouble for carving your number on someone's wall? My father was back, clapping on the downbeat again. I tried not to wince. Not only was he ruining the syncopation; he seemed to expect credit for it. But Hildy didn't seem bothered. She never seemed bothered by him.

"Beatle boy," my father said affectionately, patting Drew's head. Drew grimaced, and then my father scooped him up like a baby, grinning and cradling him. He danced around the room with Drew, his pipe dangling from his mouth.

"*No!* Put me *down!* I'm Ringo!" Drew shouted, but my father was smiling, laughing, swaying Drew's body in rhythm to the song. "Dad, *stop!* I'm *six!*" Drew shrieked now, kicking his legs. "I'm Ringo! Put me *down!*"

"Dad, put him down!" I called. I remember the music was starting to sound silly to me. The way it probably sounded all along to my father.

Hildy chimed in. "C'mon, Dad, he wants to be with *us!*"

We had only an instant to absorb the transformation of my father's face as he put Drew down, the absoluteness of that change and the complete attention it commanded. A moment before, my father had been an irritation to us—well, to me and Drew, at least. Now veins stood out in his neck and his forehead, and his face was red with rage. His pipe clattered to the floor as he began pummeling the top of Drew's head with his fists. When Drew tried to turn away, one of the blows landed above his left eye.

Panic gripped the insides of my wrists, my intestines, my bottom. "*DAD!*" Hildy and I screamed, and Drew howled as we desperately tried to pull my father off him. My voice was an underwater echo in slow motion. My legs felt as if I were in a dream: I had to run, but I was waist-deep in wet sand. "*DAD!* It was *my* fault!" Hildy shouted.

Screams, chaos. The clang of a Revere Ware lid in the kitchen as my mother dropped what she was doing and came running. Terry and Trish following behind. Terror, yes, but also shame: we should have known. We all should have known. *Carve your number on my wall*—stupid! stupid! The Beatles were stupid idiots.

No! No. My father—*he* was the stupid idiot. "You big fat shithead! Stop it! Just stop it!" I screamed, and my father whirled around and slapped me across the face, hard. The blow—I say blow because it felt more like a punch than a slap—didn't land right on my cheek. It was more on my left ear.

Whenever I got hit, whether it was a face slap or fists pounding on top of my head or on my back, there was always a moment before my body seemed to understand that it should hurt. It was like a grace period before the pain started, and the tears. This time was no different. What I felt first was really a sound, the sound of ear cartilage crunching against my skull. By the time the pain in my ear and face set in, I was crying, holding my face, glaring at him. "Just because you hit people doesn't make you right!" I shrieked. Weirdly, I could hear my own voice in the room, and separately, I could also hear it from inside my head. My father raised his hand to me again, glowering.

"*Jules!*" Terry yelled.

My mother was shrieking, "What are you *doing*, you son of a *bitch!*" and running toward us. Hildy was crying and dragging Drew away. Slightly behind them, I was trying to escape, but my father lunged after me and managed to fist-thump me in the back, the blow softened by my flight, before my mother got there and began screaming right into his face. "*Stop* it, you son of a *bitch!*"

"I'll do it to *you!*" He leaped at my mother and began attacking her now, punching downward on the back of her head, her back, her shoulders, with both fists. "I'll *slam* you, Willa! I'll fucking *slam* you!"

For just a moment, everything was slow. Maybe I kind of left my body. Or maybe it was the opposite, that I was more *in* my body, because suddenly I realized I wasn't hearing anything with my left ear. Instead, there was a kind of ringing, on a note somewhere between E-flat and E-natural.

A second later, I snapped back into the frenzy. "Stop it! Stop it!" I screamed at my father, trying to pull him off my mother. "You are just *pathetic!*"

"*JULES!*" Terry roared, finally pulling him off. My mother collapsed onto the living room floor, sobbing and somehow alone, her arms still flailing away in self-protection even after my father flew out the front door.

Slam!

"Are you all right? Willa?" Terry asked, drawing a handkerchief out of the back pocket of his slacks and wiping his brow. "Kids?" he asked, turning to us.

My teeth ached, and there was too much saliva in my mouth. I could hear myself wailing. I could hear it from inside my head, and I could hear it from outside my head. It seemed impossible that I had ever loved my father. I had hated him all along; I'd just forgotten it for a while here and there. I tried to fix the hatred in my mind permanently now, so I wouldn't be swayed ever again. Never, even if he dyed a hundred pairs of white cotton socks with hot tea.

Incredibly, the record was still on. "We Can Work It Out" blasted through the living room, and it seemed almost criminal that we'd so confidently cranked up the volume only minutes ago. "Turn it *off*," Hildy moaned, grasping the side of her face. Drew was in her lap on the floor. My mother needed me, but dizzily, noisily, wiping my nose on the sleeve of my shirt, I veered past her, back toward the record player, because I couldn't stand the music for one more second, either. I forced my shaky wrists to hold still and removed the needle from *Yesterday And Today*. Somehow, I was unable to be careless about it.

Every detail was clear. The searing ear pain. The secondary pain on the right side of my upper back. The whitish lump standing out just above Drew's left eye. Hildy rocking him back and forth. My mother's belly rising and falling as she sobbed. My father's pipe on its side on the floor, with little flecks of tobacco and ash nearby. Terry looking bulky and inept; Trish looking similarly ill-equipped. The fan-shaped gleams of light on the record. The putting on of side two instead of side one—the bastard must have assumed the sides were interchangeable. Dreck being dreck.

Stupid! What a stupid idiot I was. It would never matter that we had heard side two first. We'd never listen to the record again. We'd never brag to our friends that we could get Beatles albums for free. I wouldn't even tell Brett, ever.

I left the disc exactly as it was and then switched the turntable to the "off" position so we Goldenthals could cry without the intrusion of ignorant songs.

"I'm okay," Drew insisted over and over, sitting on the closed lid of the toilet with Hildy and me gathered around him on the tile floor, taking turns holding an ice-filled dish towel over his left eye. My mother didn't believe in putting ice on a wound. She said it was too cold for the human body. But Drew liked the ice, and I knew my mother was too upset to give a damn.

Hildy's cheek was still red, and Drew's eye was swollen. It had taken him a long time to stop counting by fours. Now that I had a moment, it occurred to me I could put my finger in my right ear to see whether I could hear out of my left ear. I could—but not very well. What I could hear was a ringing, somewhere between an E-flat and an E-natural.

"Let's try to clean it now," Hildy said to Drew, running warm water over a washcloth which she wrung out and spread tenderly across his puffy, smeared face. "Sorry, Drewy," she said as he grimaced. "How 'bout another M&M?" She fished one out of the packet, and Drew opened his little mouth like a bird and crunched down on the cheery green pillow. His nose was shiny.

Terry and Trish had stayed with us for a little while. Terry tried to help my mother settle down while Trish tried to comfort us kids, but she didn't seem to have any idea what to do. For some reason, I thought of an airplane-crash movie Stephanie and I had seen on TV at her house. Trish was like that one dumb stewardess whose crisp uniform and matching hat couldn't begin to mask her personal terror.

Then Terry and Trish slipped out. They liked us; they wished us well, but they couldn't really fix things for us. I knew my mother would hold it against them.

Now, an hour later, she was in bed, and we kids were in our customary huddle, trying to learn, and teach one another, what had happened. We all touched pinkies, our way of comforting each other without saying anything. But it was hard to ignore my mother's sounds. She'd left her door open: *people shouldn't be ashamed of their emotions!* Hildy closed the bathroom door to shut out the noise. My mother was too busy suffering to get on our case about how children didn't need privacy and how we should never close our bedroom doors, or the bathroom door either, because there was nothing to hide—and besides, what if there was an emergency?

"We shouldn't've tried to pretend we're the Beatles," Drew said.

"I'm the one who wanted the goddamned record," Hildy said. "If anything, he should have come after *me*."

"He did," I reminded her.

"Maybe he was mad because we cranked it up too loud," said Hildy.

"That doesn't mean he can just start hitting us for no reason," I said. "He is just *pathetic*. No one else has such a pathetic father."

"Don't say that, Martha!"

"You guys—" Drew begged.

"Why not? He doesn't have any self-control whatsoever. It's an embarrassment just to have him as a father. Anyway, why are you defending him? He slapped you across the face."

"Which Mom does, too!" Hildy pointed out. "Dad just lost his temper."

"Lost his temper? Had a *cow* is more like it." *Lost his temper* was for other fathers, the kind who felt bad afterward just for raising their voices. The kind who said they were sorry. The kind whose wives apologized, too, when they did something mean, and who didn't think it was phony-baloney to think about other people's feelings.

"Don't fight!" Drew cried.

"Okay, okay," Hildy and I both soothed.

Hildy pulled out another M&M for him. "Drewy, should I go downstairs and get you fresh ice? I'll wrap it up in a towel and come right back up, okay?" She opened the bathroom door.

My mother was still crying and blowing her nose. Drew and I looked at each other. We both knew what needed to happen. I took care of my mother; Hildy took care of everything else. Red, blue, green, yellow. In the quiet, I could still hear the E-flat/E-natural ringing in my ear, but it seemed to have lessened. Drew nodded at me, and I patted his curly head before turning to go.

"Mom?" I knocked on the open door and came in at the same time. "Are you all right?"

"How could I be all right?" she shouted. "That *louse*. He's like a bomb about to go off any minute. How can anyone live with that? You kids have no *idea* how hard it is."

If I said, "We do *so*, Mom! He hits us, too, haven't you noticed?" my mother would tell me I didn't understand. Or she'd argue that it was proof of my immaturity, thinking my own suffering was more important than it really was.

"He can drop *dead*, for all I care," she went on. I could hear Hildy wrestling with the ice tray downstairs as I perched on the edge of the bed and straightened my mother's headband. She pulled away from me; the side of her head was hurt. A roll of toilet paper that she'd taken from the bathroom was lying on its side next to her. I put my finger in my right ear again just as Hildy dropped an ice cube on the kitchen floor. My hearing was better already.

Even with the door open, the room felt airless, as if my mother's misery were a solid. The smell of her and the stale bedding and the already-worn clothing draped carelessly over chairs—it all made me want to gag, or weep.

Or hit. I wanted to hit my mother, I suddenly realized. Was that my actual nature? My father's nature? *Shrug*.

No. No. Even if I felt like it, I would never do it. That was the difference.

"I'm kicking him *out* of here. Once and for all."

"I don't blame you, Mom," I said, adding, "I hate him, too, you know."

My mother looked at me and started crying again. "You know, you're the only one of the *lot* of them with any *insight!*"

10

headache

Now that my father was out of the house for good, my mother spent most of her time in bed, cycling through talk shows and KQED programs on the television set she'd recently bought with money her parents had sent her. My mother was always talking about how intellectually "limited" her parents were, how lacking in insight. They'd named her Gladys because of a character called Gladys on some God-awful radio melodrama that my grandmother just loved. (My mother found the name so repugnant that she'd changed her name to Willa when, as a young teenager, she picked up a book by Willa Cather in the library. Not sure if she ever read the book.) Also, my mother would talk about how sick her parents' relationship was, since my grandmother was rarely sober, and my grandfather never did anything about it. My mother said her *natural* instincts had told her to move as far away from that pathetic situation as she could. When her parents sent her money, she'd spend it on stupid things like a "gorgeous" antique chair that, even if it had been comfy, was too rickety to sit on. Then she'd complain about her parents some more, so we kids would understand that her love couldn't be bought.

The TV was black-and-white, like the small one in the kitchen, but it included a gadget called a remote control which my mother could aim at the television, her flannel arm extended, changing channels and turning the set on and off without having to get up. A brown hardback with a faded woven cloth cover sat on the bedside table, but I don't think my mother ever opened it. Wads of toilet tissue were strewn across the bed, because she didn't believe in wastebaskets. Sometimes she'd stick used toilet paper clumps into the lacy elastic wristbands of her nightgown and, when she started crying, pull the wads out and unfurl the congealed paper to look for an unused spot, sending tiny white particles into the dead air.

My mother didn't believe in keeping a lot of canned food in the house, because it wasn't good for you. But she didn't seem to believe in fresh food either. Hildy put meals together for me and Drew from whatever cans were lying around—Heinz baked beans, Riviera mine-strone soup, Dole pineapple chunks—and figured out how to un-stale Triscuits by heating them in the oven for a few minutes on a cookie sheet, and then cooling them to crisp them up. But there were limits to Hildy's creativity.

Often Hildy would go to Smoke and Records after school and my father would give her money to go down Telegraph to Hunan Village, which Hildy and I always called Human Village, or next door to Joe's for a burger and fries. Drew became a fixture at one of our neighbors' in the afternoons and, often, for dinner.

I was anxious about how frequently I was eating dinner at Stephanie and Brett's, even though Sylvia didn't bring up the fact that my mother basically never invited Stephanie to eat at my house—or that during school, Sylvia had been supplying me with lunches for the past two years. My mother didn't respect Sylvia anymore, since Sylvia's divorce hadn't been a "necessary divorce" like hers: Morris wasn't a louse, and this business of playing around sexually with other women went against nature. Real sex, between a man and a woman, was *natural*, and it was a very beautiful thing. I shouldn't let myself get confused about the beauty of sex just because my father was a goddamned bastard.

Fortunately, Sylvia seemed too busy with her women's poetry workshops and women's drumming circles and women's hiking groups to track my meals at her house, and Stephanie kept assuring me it was okay for me to eat there. So did Brett. The three of us spent a lot of time listening to records and talking about music, and we all got along great.

One of the things my mother cried about was the way my father sent home money for child support after our every-other-weekend visits. More than once, he'd given Drew the cash and told him to fold it up and put it in his shoe for safekeeping during the cab ride home. My mother was furious that my father was using Drew for this task, though I wasn't sure what she would have preferred, since she didn't allow my father in the house and certainly wasn't going to go pick up the money—or us. Maybe she was insulted that the cash had been sitting in Drew's sour-smelling PF Flyers. Maybe she was mad that my father put us in a cab when money was tight and we could've taken the bus. I didn't ask.

One day, my mother put her long wool coat on over her night-gown and drove to Smoke and Records to confront my father about all this. She came home fuming. "Guess who was at the store!" she demanded, standing in the doorway to my room.

"I don't know, Mom—"

"Just guess!"

I was sitting at my desk, trying to finish a math assignment. I twisted around to face her. "Mom, I have no—"

"Iris Cray, that's who! Buying some jazz album—"

For a second, I thought my mother was going to start bitching about how shocking it was that a Juilliard-trained musician and teacher would be buying a lowly jazz record. Then I realized— *shrug*—she'd probably gotten wind of the fact that Mrs. Cray played jazz tunes for me during our lessons.

"—as if it's perfectly fine to shop at Smoke and Records! Martha, haven't you made it clear to your teacher just how sick your father is? How destructive?"

"What? Mom, she and I have other—"

"What could possibly be more important than your father's behaving like a psychopathic madman?"

"But Mom, if I used lesson time to talk about that, you'd be mad at me for not working hard on violin!"

"Frankly, Martha, Iris Cray has never struck me as being all that insightful."

"Mom, that's not fair! Just because—"

"Look, Martha, you're old enough to learn that life is about standing up for what's right, even if it's inconvenient. I thought for sure that with your insight, you'd see through your father's bullshit. His seductive charm. His phony—"

"I do see through all that!" *Shrug.*

"And yet you don't think it's important to mention that to your favorite teacher?"

I tried again. "Then you'd be mad because—"

"*The hottest seats in hell*," my mother intoned, "*are reserved for those who cannot take a stand in a time of crisis.* That's a quote, Martha. From Dante!"

Of course it fell to me to tell Mrs. Cray that I couldn't study with her any more. I let her think it was because of money problems. She said I should feel free to come over any time I wanted, especially on Saturdays, because she could use my help teaching her younger students, and she'd be happy to keep giving me lessons in exchange. I did a regular shrug and looked down at my white canvas Keds.

I know, I know: I should've fought harder. I should've found a way. But that's not how I was. My outrage faded, and I began to see things from my mother's perspective: maybe it *had* been immature of me not to tell Mrs. Cray that my father hit us. Wasn't it possible my mother had a point?

Being a complete bitch and being wrong about everything—those are two different things, aren't they?

This is stupid in retrospect, but I assumed my mother would want me to keep playing the violin, just with a different teacher. She didn't care, though. Since the whole reason I liked violin was Mrs. Cray anyway, what was the point of continuing? I finished out the semester in Miss Transom's orchestra, and then I switched to Chorus. Which turned out to be a good thing.

I wouldn't have thought of singing in Chorus except for Paisley and Philip, the Gorman twins, who were in my homeroom all through junior high. They both sang and had seen me with my violin. I must've said something about not signing up for Orchestra on the day we were enrolling in classes for the following semester, because they both started trying to convince me I should be in Chorus.

Paisley Gorman acted a lot more grown-up than other thirteen-year-olds, but it was genuine. It wasn't so much a case of her seeming like an older teenager; it was more as if she'd skipped through childhood and adolescence altogether and was already a grown-up. She had this tedious kind of maturity—niceness and wisdom and goody-goody-ness—where you could just tell she'd been like that since she was four or five. Paisley was passionate about the art and music of the Renaissance, whose palettes I found depressing. One time her mother took me and Paisley to the Renaissance Faire, and Paisley just wouldn't stop with all the *prithee*s and *fie*s and *huzzah*s, which made me roll my eyes when she wasn't looking. Actually I kind of felt sorry for Paisley, because even though she had pretty features, it all added up to something bland and unnoticeable, and also, she was more interested in being friends than I was. But there was something so earnest about her affection for me that I couldn't just ignore her.

Philip had always liked me, too, and he had his good points. Midway through second semester of eighth grade, when Dr. Martin Luther King was assassinated, a group of mostly black eighth-grade students from Garfield, plus some seventh graders like Clifton Cray and his friend Ben, marched up the hill to the Berkeley Unified School District building and demanded that Garfield be renamed in memory of the slain leader. The students won. It was a very important statement, and I was proud that students had made it happen, but thanks to Philip Gorman, it was also funny. Philip insisted on calling our newly renamed school "The Reverend Doctor Martin Luther King Junior Junior High School," pausing in between the two "Junior"s for emphasis. I was the only one who laughed, so he kept finding reasons to say our school's "full name" in front of me. Which was kind of annoying, but I kept laughing. Funny is funny.

In Chorus, Paisley planted herself next to me in the alto section and kept telling me what a nice voice I had. At first I thought it was just her usual thing of trying to get me to like her, but soon she pointed out that other altos were trying to sit as close to me as they could. It turned out that because of my violin training, I was a good sight-singer, meaning I could follow the music and look up at Mrs. Finkelstein, the conductor, basically at the same time, which is exactly what Mrs. Finkelstein said you should do. You were also supposed to keep going even if the others in your section were lost, so I did that too, and the other altos started using me for orientation whenever we were doing something unfamiliar.

Most of the other kids were shaky and noncommittal while sight-singing, but new music was fun for me. In fact, I kept myself from studying the music in advance, or listening to a recording of whatever piece it was, so that I could enjoy the challenge—and also, not get completely sick of the music.

The third week of the semester, we read through the first movement of Bach's Cantata #140, *Wachet Auf*. I wasn't familiar with
Wachet Auf—it wasn't one of my father's favored cantatas. There's
a tricky syncopated sub-theme that the altos are supposed to sing at
Letter I, until the tenors come in four bars later, but it didn't throw
me. I came in and sang even though the other altos were lost and only
straggled in because I sounded sure of myself, I guess.

Mrs. Finkelstein started tapping her baton against the podium.
Tik tik tik tik tik. "Altos!" she exclaimed. "Where were the rest of you
at Letter I?" It was a rhetorical question. "Let's try that again. Along
with Martha, this time?"

I knew I was being complimented, and it was inevitable that I
would shrug in that moment. But for the first time, I didn't mind
the shrug, because it made me realize something. Whenever I was
sight-singing, or doing any kind of singing, I *didn't* shrug. The same
thing had happened with violin—when I was really lost in the music
and could forget about everything else in my stupid life, it was as if
my body forgot about the shrug and just floated along.

At the end of class, Mrs. Finkelstein asked me to come speak with
her. Did I want to be leader of the whole alto section?

I kept having a dream where I was about to slap someone across the
face, hard, but then their hair would get in the way, or their arms.
When I woke up, my hand would be tingling with the frustration of
having been unable to get in a good whack.

School was getting harder. I could never seem to concentrate. It
was tiring, having to remember not to look confused or blurt out
something stupid while I was orienting myself with what the teacher
and other kids were saying in English or Social Studies. *Shrug.* I would
grab onto certain bits of information as if they were placeholders,

without actual comprehension, as if I were borrowing something that I would pay back in the future, once I understood. But the future never seemed to come. I had this gut feeling I was falling more and more deeply into a kind of debt that would eventually get me in big trouble.

My eighth grade history textbook was full of baffling sentences. *"The general determined that the most effective course of action was to cut through and subdue the rebellion."* Cut through and subdue: Stephanie and I laughed endlessly about that rhyming phrase, and I didn't want to ruin the joke by telling her that I didn't get the point and was terrified of the upcoming test. *Cut through*: trample, like Jules Goldenthal, on whoever was in your way. *Most effective course of action*: divorce the son-of-a-bitch! *Subdue the rebellion*: Hildy. Drew.

I knew the term "suicide mission" had to do with bravery in war, but I couldn't seem to hold onto that meaning. Suicide, my mother said, was something other people didn't have as much reason as she did to think about, let alone commit, because they didn't have to deal with a psychopath like Jules Goldenthal.

There were protests going on all the time on the Cal campus. A lot of my classmates had started hanging around Sproul Plaza and going on marches. So had Brett. They didn't care about shallow things like homework. They cared about free speech and the war and women's lib and racism. *Free speech*: having the right to tell my father he was a bastard. *The war*: my family, obviously. *Women's lib*: a way to free people like my mother from having to put up with people like my father.

It took forever for my parents' divorce to go through, partly because my mother kept getting hysterical and switching lawyers. She didn't see why my father should have visitation rights at all, and she was constantly trying to find a lawyer who would agree with her. She said if the judge really understood the situation, he wouldn't have allowed any visitation with my father at all. Still, it was a relief that I didn't have to figure out for myself what was fair. My mother couldn't get that mad at me for seeing my father if the court said that was the deal.

My mother was panicked about how close Hildy and my father were. How "incestuous." Whereas she used to call Hildy "the little mother," now it was "the little wife." My father was deeply seductive, my mother told me, and even though it was only psychological seduction, it was still very damaging to a young girl. The court didn't understand things like that, because they were completely lacking in basic psychological insight.

On most of the allotted weekends, I went along with Hildy and Drew to the studio apartment my father had rented on Bancroft, just a few doors down from Smoke and Records. If I had a ton of homework, or if my mother was crying a lot and talking about swallowing a bottle of aspirin, I skipped the overnight and just came for a while on Sunday. My father didn't like that, but at least I didn't have to worry about him killing himself over it: he still had Hildy and Drew.

It wasn't that my father had never mentioned suicide. One time, during a fight with my mother, he shouted that he was going to hang himself from the flagpole at Cragmont Elementary. As horrible as it was to hear him yell that at the top of his lungs, it was way worse when he threatened the same thing quietly. That had happened just recently, while Drew was watching TV in the kitchen of my father's apartment. In a muffled, eerily calm voice, my father told me and Hildy that when he'd shaved that morning, he'd thought of taking the blade out of the shaver and using it to slit his wrists "to just be done with it."

When I came home after that visit, I was so shaken up that even my mother noticed. "What's wrong?" she asked as I stood at the foot of her bed, and I realized it had been a long time since she'd asked me anything like that. "Martha, what happened?"

I wanted to ask her for more details about my father's "emotional instability reaction," the thing that had happened when he enlisted during the war, and for which the army had apparently dismissed him early on. I also wanted to know more about my father's parents, whom my mother had referred to as "very old-country, neurotic, superstitious people," even though the few times they'd visited, they seemed nice, and Hildy told me our New York cousins loved having them around. They had come to America penniless from Eastern Europe and eventually opened up a smoke shop in Brooklyn, which had always seemed really brave to me, but my mother said they had a compulsive need to overprotect their precious darling and cripple him emotionally to the point where he couldn't achieve anything in life despite all his talents. Plus, they'd wanted him to stay in New York, which my mother felt was manipulative and selfish. But if I asked about any of this, I realized, it'd only give my mother a green light for bitching about my father. So I just kind of stalled.

"Oh my God! Oh my *God*. They were all talking about me, weren't they! Your father, Hildy, Drew—" my mother filled in the scenario with wild certainty— "and you—you were the only one who defended me!"

"Mom, that's—"

"Martha, you're way too young to be put in that position. The pressure you're under! You see what I'm up against? Do you?" She was crying now, of course.

Afterwards, all I felt toward my father was anger: he was too selfish to protect us kids from threats of slitting his wrists or hanging himself. Maybe I didn't really believe him. Maybe I couldn't afford to. Or maybe I kind of figured my father was Hildy's headache. I already had mine.

11

helvetica

By the time we started ninth grade, Fathom was old and sick and had to be put to sleep. Stephanie was pretty upset about it, even though she was still flying high from having gotten a boyfriend over the summer at the camp she'd attended back East.

Soon after the school year started, Stephanie noticed a grey striped cat without any tags that was wandering around scavenging for food way down on University Avenue near West Campus, which was where all we ninth graders went for a year before starting tenth grade on the main Berkeley High School campus. The main campus was in downtown Berkeley just a few blocks from the Cal campus—a much cooler location. At West Campus, on the other hand, the big attraction was a run-down Foster's Freeze right across the street that was so crowded with other kids that I never went to it. Oh, and a vertical neon sign on one of the nearby store fronts that spelled out "L-I-Q-U-O-R" a letter at a time, pausing a beat after the "Q" and again after the "R" so it was in 4/4 rhythm, before lighting up the full word "LIQUOR" for two beats and then starting over again with the "L." Stephanie and I kind of made a song out of it, because it cracked us up.

Anyway, Stephanie kept seeing the stray cat and giving it little bits of food, and eventually, she and I brought it to her house on the bus. It was Brett who suggested the name Helvetica.

"Hel—what? Why?" Stephanie asked.

"Helvetica! It means Swiss," Brett said. "We don't know if it's a he or a she, right? So it's, like, neutral. Like the Swiss. Get it?" He'd been reading a lot lately about World War II.

Stephanie and Brett and I continued to hang around together when I came over. Sometimes Brett's door was closed, but usually not for long. The three of us would listen to records, and Brett would talk about how terrible the war was and tell us about all the ways people were finding to avoid the draft. Plus he'd do a lot of philosophizing, most of which I couldn't follow. I assumed it was because of his bookishness, but Stephanie thought he sounded more and more like a stoner.

When Stephanie and Sylvia took the cat to the vet for shots and neutering, the sex mystery was solved: Helvetica was pregnant. Stephanie filled me in on what was going to happen. When Helvetica was about to have the kittens, she'd lose all interest in food and start licking her belly and vaginal opening like crazy. If we were very observant, we might notice the cat breathing more quickly right before she was ready to give birth.

Stephanie said we should get a dark, quiet place ready, since the gestation period was only a little over two months and Helvetica was getting very fat. We decided to empty out the bottom drawer of Stephanie's bureau, which was in her closet, and put the drawer on the floor in there. We made a nice bed with some old blankets that Sylvia let us launder so the spot would be fresh and clean. We put Helvetica's food and water dishes into the closet and let her get used to it.

All this was suggested by Stephanie's father, Morris, a psychiatrist who taught at the medical school at UC San Francisco and had a private therapy practice in Berkeley. He'd had pets as a kid and knew a lot about cats and dogs. Stephanie was always making a point of asking Morris about things they were both interested in. She'd ask him about how he diagnosed patients, and learned about how various mental conditions were categorized in some book called "the DSM." Mainly, I think, Stephanie did this so Morris wouldn't feel as bad about the divorce from Sylvia, and about the fact that he only got to see Stephanie and Brett on Sundays.

I wished I could be like that: looking for ways to make my father feel better. It seemed like a more mature attitude than the way I felt. The problem, of course, was my particular father, but it was easy to forget all that and be mad at myself for not being a nicer person. I'd long since stopped asking my father musical questions. I didn't let on that I loved a lot of the same records that he did. I never told him I admired his ability to add up numbers practically as fast as the adding machine could. These small things I did just to be mean—they were my form of what everyone calls "nonviolent resistance." Nonviolent doesn't necessarily mean nice.

My father wasn't as angry now that he was out of the house. Come to think of it, he hadn't thrown any violent shit fits lately. But he was always saying nasty things to me. Sometimes he called me judgmental, and it was all I could do not to say, *Well,* duh *now, why* shouldn't *I judge you for your pathetic lack of self-control?* Sometimes he said I was a *provocateur,* and I would roll my eyes right in front of him, disgusted by how he threw the word around as if he knew French. If he was being a shithead, I was going to let him know it, unlike Hildy. And if he hit me—well, too goddamned bad. I had my own personal Vietnam War to protest.

Not that I could stand my mother. These days I talked to her as little as I could. I didn't bug her about my shrug. I didn't tell her Helvetica was pregnant. I hadn't even told her I'd gotten my first period. When Hildy had started menstruating, my mother had explained that in traditional Jewish families, there was a very sick custom of slapping a girl across the face when she got her first period. I guess my mother was expecting credit for only slapping Hildy across the face for reasons *other* than menstruation.

Now that I'd started, I couldn't stand the thought of my mother talking about how *natural* it was, nothing to be ashamed of, blah blah blah. If it was so goddamned natural, how come she wouldn't buy Kotex pads for me and Hildy? I guess she thought we were supposed to use toilet paper to catch the flow—as if there were plenty of extra toilet paper lying around. Luckily, all Hildy had to do was tell my father she needed money "to go to Rexall," and he'd hand her a five from the cash register. Then she'd sneak the Kotex or the toilet paper into the house for both of us.

One day, Stephanie called me before school to tell me Helvetica had been licking her belly a lot that morning, which meant we had to get over to her house right after school. I had a sore throat and felt a cold coming on, but didn't feel I could miss school because I had a math test, and besides, my mother had figured out that I sometimes skipped wearing cotton undershirts. If I told her I didn't feel well enough to go to school, she'd start bitching about how my not "layering" was the reason—that is, it was my own goddamned fault I'd gotten sick.

My mother wasn't in bed all the time anymore. In fact, she'd started cooking again, so now she was always on the warpath about our not being appreciative enough. We tried to explain that we wanted things like spaghetti and meat sauce for dinner, not for breakfast, even though the truth was that morning or night, there was something about my mother's cooking that always seemed sour or smelly or the wrong temperature or an icky texture, whether I was hungry or not. But my mother insisted that morning was the best time for a big meal, that she'd seen a program about this on KQED. She said she could tell by our attitude that Jules was "fomenting aggression" against her, besides being unreliable about child support. Really, she said, she should just farm us all out and move back to New York.

It was easier to try to gag down the food than to deal with her threats, which weren't serious anyway.

When Stephanie and I got to her house after school, *The White Album* was blaring from Brett's room. I wasn't crazy about the album, mainly because of "Martha My Dear." Brett had been excited to introduce me to the song, and it was flattering that he was excited about it. But at school, Logan Starch must have caught me looking happy about the attention I was getting. "It's about a *dog*, stupid," he said, before shrugging a few times with a sneer on his face. I quickly became sick of kids at school calling me "Martha My Dear," or singing it in front of me as if they were being so goddamn original.

Sylvia told us there were five kittens, born a few hours earlier. "Damn it!" Stephanie said, wishing she'd stayed home so she could've seen the births. We ran up the stairs and went straight to Stephanie's closet, Stephanie first. I crouched in the doorway next to her, trying not to be too obvious about glancing at Brett's door. "Hi there, little sweeties!" Stephanie exclaimed to the adorable creatures. The kittens' eyes were all closed, their *mews* tiny and high-pitched. They moved their heads upward over and over, as if sniffing in the air for the definitive answer to some eternal kitty question.

"They're *so* cute!" I couldn't wait to have a closer look.

Stephanie scooped two of the kittens up to move them closer to Helvetica's nipples. She stroked Helvetica's head over and over and told her what a good girl she was.

"Can I hold one?" I reached over.

"Sure. Just, not by the scruff of the neck. And not too much handling, my dad says. I mean, it's a balance. If you don't handle them at all, they won't connect with humans later."

"Oh." But what was too much and what was too little? I wiped my nose on my sleeve so I wouldn't get snot on my fingers.

"I gotta get my dad over here!" Stephanie climbed over me and went into the hallway. "Mom?" she shouted down the stairs. "Can I talk to you?" Thanks to the loud music, Sylvia couldn't hear, so Stephanie tromped down the stairs, leaving me alone with the kittens.

"C'm'ere, sweetie," I said to one of them. It was stripey grey like Helvetica, the tiniest one of all of them, and had detached from Helvetica's nipple. The pink nose and paws reminded me of a little pig, or maybe a guinea pig, and it looked lost. I was guiding the kitten back to the nipple just as I heard the faint scrape of Brett's bedroom door against the carpet.

"Cute, huh?" he said, from Stephanie's doorway.

Shrug. "They're so tiny!" I gushed.

"So Martha, what key are they mewing in?"

"Um—" I listened.

"I'm just kidding, man!" Brett said. "You take everything so seriously!"

"Oh." I sniffled.

"You allergic?"

"I don't think so." Helvetica had never bothered me before. "Just maybe getting a cold, I guess."

"Well, you better not touch them, then," Brett said. "You might be contagious."

"Oh! But Stephanie said—" I jumped up and tried to keep my face from burning. *Shrug.*

"She doesn't know everything, ov-viously."

I looked down at the floor. What if I'd hurt that one kitten?

Stephanie came stomping back up the stairs. "Damn it!" she

complained, turning to Brett. "Mom won't let me invite Dad over to see the kittens."

"That's not cool, man," Brett sympathized. "Want me to work on her?"

Stephanie nodded. Brett might have a better chance with Sylvia than Stephanie did.

12

the note

When I got home from Stephanie's, my mother was making a salad: a big bowl of butter lettuce (by the way, could someone explain to me the point of lettuce that isn't crunchy?), with Kraft Parmesan cheese, alfalfa sprouts, and raw sunflower seeds on top for the protein. That, with Wishbone Italian salad dressing, was dinner. I didn't care that it was a crappy dinner, because by now my throat was really sore, and I was sniffling and sneezing, so I couldn't hide my cold from my mother. I rolled my eyes at Drew while she bitched at me about my having gotten myself sick.

I wished Hildy were around, but she had a Student Council meeting. She was doing everything she could to avoid spending time at home. If she didn't have an after-school activity, she'd go to Smoke and Records and see what my father needed: a run to the bank for rolls of dimes or quarters; help re-stocking things; straightening out the candy bars, which were always getting messy. My father would give Hildy money for a bite on Telegraph, or at one of the food stands that had started appearing just east of Holy Hubert's steps across the street.

"That goes for you, too, Drew," my mother was saying. "You dress poorly, your body is more susceptible to germs. *Layering* is the answer."

Hildy was at the front door. "I'm home!" she announced, something she never did. It turned out Greg Gold was with her. He was a good-looking boy who was also on the Student Council and who had liked Hildy for years. They'd sat right next to each other in homeroom since seventh grade.

Lately, Hildy told me, she kind of liked him back, even though he sometimes monopolized the conversation in Student Council and said stuff like, "Come *on*, people!" to his fellow council members when they took too long to decide on something that seemed obvious to him. Greg Gold had also made a poster saying "Fuck the UC Regents!" to take to a rally about People's Park, which Hildy hadn't known about when she went with him to the rally, and was kind of embarrassed by. I guessed Hildy felt the word "fuck" should be reserved for my father's use only.

Secretly I had no idea why everyone was so angry about People's Park in the first place. It was Cal's land, wasn't it? It didn't make sense to me that they should be forced to give it up just so people would be able to gather for free speech somewhere besides the campus. Getting another place besides Sproul Plaza—that wasn't a real crisis like the Vietnam War, or racism, was it? But everyone acted as if it were completely obvious that the university was mean for keeping the land. I didn't want anyone to know I had no idea what the moral outrage was about.

I expected my mother to dislike Greg Gold on principle—he liked Hildy. But when he extended his hand and flashed a nervous, toothy smile, my mother's face lit up. "Hello!" she said.

"Nice to meet you, Mrs.—do you go by Goldenthal?" I winced, sure my mother was going to tear his head off for mentioning "Goldenthal."

"Oh, please, call me Willa!" she said breezily. "We don't stand on ceremony around here."

"Nice to meet you, Willa!" Greg Gold said, with a little too much enthusiasm. "Wow, Hildy looks just like you!"

Hildy made me some hot chamomile tea, which I hated but which was the only tea in the house, and put a bunch of honey in it while my mother wasn't watching because she was too busy grilling Greg. *Oh, your father teaches in the Political Science Department? Oh, your mother is writing her second children's book? Oh, your family goes to Congregation Beth Emmet? Oh, you're planning to go to college on the East Coast?*

My mother even offered Greg Gold some salted cashews that we didn't know were in the house. They were in a can, and my mother got them out of a drawer in the dining room. The can went *pfft!* as she opened the vacuum seal. I stuffed as many cashews into me as I could before my mother said, "That's enough, Martha. You'll ruin your appetite," as if there were an actual meal waiting. I finished my tea, sipping up the thick sweet liquid gathered at the bottom of the cup.

After Greg left, I went upstairs to bed without so-called dinner, not even waiting to talk with Hildy about Greg. I knew she hadn't made up her mind about him anyway. There was another boy on Student Council, Matt Baskit, who Hildy thought was really cute. When Hildy had found out Matt was in Math Club, which met before school on Friday mornings, she'd signed up for that, too.

I missed the next two days of school because of my cold, but I talked to Stephanie both days to get homework assignments and ask about the kittens. She was happy; Sylvia had relented and let Morris come over to meet them. Stephanie had already named them all: Portico, Trivia, Gumby, Orbit, and Salmonella.

By Friday morning, I felt better. Hildy had already gone to Math Club. When I came downstairs, dressed and ready, my mother was washing the frying pan that she'd used the previous night to brown some meat before putting it into her new gadget, something called a crock pot, to cook overnight. "I presume you're wearing an under-shirt, young lady?" she asked.

I pulled the thick white strap toward my neck from underneath my blouse and sat down to a lukewarm bowl of congealed, bland, beef-barley stew from the crock pot. I flared my nostrils at Drew, and when I thought my mother wasn't looking, I reached for the salt shaker.

"It doesn't need salt, Martha. I already salted it."

I took a bite, trying not to gag. Drew wasn't having much luck with his, either. "Mom, could you write me a note for school? I've got binder paper."

She didn't answer.

"I need a note, Mom," I repeated. "I've been out for two days."

"Write your own note, Miss Rules-and-Regulations."

"And then you'll sign it?"

"You got yourself sick, Martha. Now you deal with it."

"Okay," I sighed, and Drew and I glanced at each other. In my binder for school, I had a plastic pouch with a few things in it: pen, protractor, pencil, eraser, emergency dime. It'd be easier than trying to find a working pen in the house, let alone blank paper. "I need you to sign it, though."

My mother was putting the pan in the dish drain.

"Mom?"

"Martha, I'm not signing anything." She looked straight at me. Maybe she wanted to see how I'd react.

"But Mom—an unexcused absence will go on my record!" *Shrug.*

"And stop that uptightness of yours."

"What?" I wasn't sure whether she meant the note for school, or the shrug.

"That neurotic affectation! Just stop that shrugging. It's as if you're claiming you don't know. But you goddamned well *do* know. You know perfectly well."

"Mom, that's mean," Drew said in a small voice.

I tried to sound calm. "Mom, if I don't have a note, it'll make my grades go down. I mean, it's one thing if I skipped school to go to a peace rally or something. Then I could understand—"

"You made your bed, Martha," my mother snarled, "now you're going to lie in it."

Before I knew it, I was standing up, jiggling the chair just as my father did when he was angry. "Jesus Christ! I comfort you whenever you cry, which is, like, practically every minute!" I shouted. "About how much better your life would have been if you'd never met Dad! Which is completely—a very ugly thing to say to your own child!"

"Oh yes," my mother said, "how the truth hurts."

Drew said, "Mom, that's not fair to Martha." He had gotten up from the table, his skinny body next to the kitchen wall, his white socks showing under his too-short jeans.

My mother kept looking at me with contempt. I paused a moment, just to make absolutely sure this wasn't a mistake. A misunderstanding. Then I started shrieking. "Well, if you're going to be like this, you can just go *fuck!*"

The next instant, I saw the frying pan coming toward me.

There was infinite time to think: *she's not throwing the frying pan; she's just getting ready to hit me with it. This isn't like a scene with Dad. Dad would have thrown the pan while it was hot, with hot food in it. He would've meant it for Mom, but the hot food would've gotten on me and Hildy and Drew if we happened to be in the way. Mom isn't doing what Dad would do. This pan is still wet, but it's clean, and it's not hot. She's holding on to it, getting ready to hit my head. This isn't like Dad. . . .*

I jumped out of the kitchen and grabbed my books, binder and Concert Chorale music, then made a leap toward the front door. I squeezed the front door latch, opened the door and slammed it behind me. The brass knocker echoed my slam as I pounded down the wooden steps.

I didn't have a sweater, and I'd left without money for the bus, and the handle of Stephanie's old gingham-lined basket had long since broken, so I was carrying my books in my arms. But I started to run down the path behind the Bakers' across the street, past the Bernards' house where a camellia bush was growing up out of a huge wooden planter with a metal band running around it. The metal band had gotten so old that it matched the Bernards' leaded glass windows. My sandals flapped loudly on the sidewalk, then quietly against my socks, over and over. I ran clear down to Spruce and saw that a bus had just left—not that I had money for it anyway. Even if I found a dime on the sidewalk now, I'd be late for English. I thought about running all the way to West Campus, but it was a couple of miles away. I felt like crying. *Shrug. Shrug.*

I started to get a cramp in my side and slowed down, trying to calm myself. I thought of Drew, at home alone with my mother. I hoped he'd gotten out of the kitchen and was putting on his high-top PF Flyers by now, getting ready to walk to school, and that my mother was so mad at me that she didn't notice Drew leaving his barley stew uneaten.

Suddenly I remembered the emergency-phone-call dime I'd seen only a few minutes earlier in the plastic three-ring pouch in my binder. Bus money! At the beginning of the school year, I'd put it in there from the loose change I had in my desk drawer, knowing that if I asked my mother for it, I'd get a lecture about not spending it on something sweet after school and ruining my appetite for dinner. I took the dime out now and held it in my palm, thinking of the children's book *Half Magic* and its magic nickel. *Life is not all about magic nickels, young lady. . . .*

I perched myself on a fire hydrant to wait for the next bus. I got off downtown, transferred to the 51, got to campus, and went straight to the principal's. The hallway was dark, but the door was open, and it was bright inside the office.

13

h⊙bgoblin

A boy named Declan with shoulder-length fine blond hair had just met with the principal and stopped in front of Mrs. Worth, the plump, frosted-haired secretary with fake eyelashes, who evidently needed to type something up before Declan could leave. The principal's name was Mr. Scranton, but the boys all called him Mr. Scrotum. He was on the phone and kept talking as he walked over and closed the door to his office. The curly black telephone cord stretched as he moved.

Declan wore a black leather jacket and black tennis shoes, and I recognized him from History, though he was rarely in class. Not wanting him to notice my shrug, I decided to stay clear of Mrs. Worth's desk until he left. But a moment later, Declan spun around and saw me, flashing brilliant blue eyes. "And what might bring you to this corner of the world?" he demanded.

I took a breath. "Need a pass," I said.

"Ah," he said, raising one eyebrow.

Something about this one syllable made me want to talk to him more. His profile reminded me of John Lennon's, and he seemed mature for his age, not at all concerned about what people thought. "Aren't you in Smith?" I asked. "Seventh period?" *Shrug.* Damn it! *Shrug.*

He looked at me narrowly, and his leather jacket made a creaking sound as he dug his hands deep into his pockets. I could tell he was thinking of asking me why I'd shrugged, then decided not to. Instead, he answered coldly, "Yeah, what about it?"

I knew how to win him over. "Are you feeling better?"

"What?"

"Are you better now?" I repeated. "I mean, you've missed a lot of class. You've been sick a lot."

He gaped at me.

"What?" I started to blush.

"You think I miss class because I'm *sick*?" He broke into a grin. One of his top front teeth was layered the slightest amount over the other, giving his smile an intriguing imperfection.

Shrug. I knew I had committed some huge act of stupidity, but I couldn't imagine what it was. I glanced over and saw that Mrs. Worth looked as if she were trying not to laugh. And then suddenly I understood.

"Mr. Wilder?" Mrs. Worth said sternly, clearing her throat. She took her glasses off and let them dangle asymmetrically against her bosom from a metal chain.

"Yes, fair damsel," replied Declan airily.

"Here's the letter. And we're sending a copy home to your parents."

"You mean, to my dear mother."

"To your mother, yes."

"Because I don't have a father. I'm a *bastard*, you see." He was enjoying himself.

"Mr. Wilder, go directly to class. And we don't want to see you in here again. Is that clear?"

Declan Wilder grabbed the paper and made an extravagant bow. "*Goodnight, ladies.*" He kissed his fingers and spread them out toward me and Mrs. Worth. As he turned to leave the office, I saw a paperback jammed into his back pocket. *Tropic of Cancer*, it was called.

Mrs. Worth turned to me. "And you are—?"

"Martha Goldenthal." *Shrug.* "I need to see Mr. Scranton right away, because—"

"Goldenthal," she repeated. I shrugged again, and I could see her deciding not to ask me about it. "Well, you're going to have to wait a little. He's on a long-distance telephone call."

Jesus Christ, didn't Mrs. Worth understand that I needed to get to class? I put my binder and books down on a wooden bench and hoped she didn't notice me watching Declan Wilder through the open door as he went down the dark corridor, past the first classroom, then past the second and the third. Why was it that when someone was walking at a distance in a dark hallway, sometimes you couldn't tell if they were coming toward you or going away from you?

I sat down on the bench. The noisy wall clock read 8:46, then 8:49. My mother would say it was "about a quarter to nine" or "about ten 'til." She felt it was ridiculous that people were so precise in how they told the time. Then I thought about that saying, how even a broken clock is right twice a day. It's a weird saying because really, a broken clock is *precisely* right twice a day—way more accurate than practically any regular clock.

I looked over at the wall of locked wooden cabinets next to me. At school, there were always intriguing little forbidden broom closets and shelves that only the janitor knew about. And underneath the finished walls, sheet rock and studs and nails, hidden order. Without my having had to be involved in any of those things, they had gotten done. Plans had been made, decisions carried out—even mistakes, cast in concrete—all entirely without my participation.

Mr. Scranton opened the door. "Go on in, Martha," Mrs. Worth said.

I put my books down on Mr. Scranton's desk and saw him glance at them: *Latin for Beginners, Advanced Algebra, English Composition*, Concert Chorale music. Also *The Lilies of the Field,* which I'd checked out one day when Stephanie was home with a cold, and I had decided to eat lunch alone in the school library. There was a huge window in there with a nice view of the eastern hills, and if I looked out the window and forgot about all the books around me that I hadn't read, it was peaceful. Paisley Gorman had come in with her bag lunch and eaten with me. She was getting ready to return a couple of books of Renaissance poetry, plus *The Lilies of the Field*, which she told me she'd really liked. So I checked it out, took it home, and tried to read it. I didn't finish. It was about nice people who didn't have to deal with anyone like my mother or my father.

I sat down. Mr. Scranton closed the door, came around the desk and sat down across from me. "What can I do for you?"

The lack of accusation almost made me want to cry. "I'm Martha Goldenthal," I began.

"Goldenthal," he repeated, just as Mrs. Worth had done. Did his eyes flicker? "You're Hildy Goldenthal's sister?"

"Yes. My mother—" I couldn't help it, I started weeping. Wordlessly, Mr. Scranton handed me a shallow box of Kleenex like the kind I'd seen in the pediatrician's office. "I was sick for two days. And my mother wouldn't write me a note, because she said it was my fault I got sick."

"Oh!" Mr. Scranton said.

"Plus, I think maybe she was mad because I didn't want to eat barley stew for breakfast. Which, I mean, she worked hard on it, I guess, plus she had to go to the store for all the ingredients. But it just made me gag, I couldn't help it—" I swallowed, trying to focus. "Mr. Scranton, I tried to explain the rule to her, that if I didn't get a note, I'd get an unexcused absence. But she just—"

"I understand."

"Maybe you could try calling her at home—" Wait, he understood? *Shrug.* I glanced vaguely in his direction, but he wasn't looking at me anymore and didn't even seem to be listening. He was scribbling something on a small notepad.

"The last two days, you say? Wednesday and Thursday?"

"Right, but—"

"Take this to your first period teacher," Mr. Scranton said as he finished the note and tore off the little sheet. He got up and crossed the room, opening the door for me. Then he patted me on the shoulder—*run along, now*, with a little comfort mixed in.

I wasn't happy with Mr. Scranton's solution. I wanted to be in trouble for having two days' worth of unexcused absences and half a period of lateness. I wanted him to call my mother and see for himself how crazy she was, what a horrible person, someone who hated her own children. I wanted to tell him that when I read things, I didn't understand them—that the good grades were a kind of parlor trick I could do, like knowing what key a piece was in, and that I was worried to death someone was going to find out I had no substance. Most of all, I wanted to ask why Mr. Scranton had let me off the hook.

But I was late, and now wasn't the time to be curious. Now was hardly ever the time to be curious.

I ran down to the girls' bathroom, grateful that it was the middle of first period. Probably those two awful big-haired girls, the ones who always shrugged exaggeratedly and laughed when they saw me in the halls, were already in class. Or maybe they weren't in class. Maybe, like Declan Wilder, they were cutting. The water was cold against my hands and face, the pink powdered soap scratchy, the rough brown paper towel strangely sweet-smelling as I dried off. I wondered what people did when they cut class. Smoke grass, I guessed.

At lunch, I told Stephanie that Mr. Scranton had excused my absences without even checking with my mother. Her eyes went wide. Then I told her how while I was waiting, I'd talked with this guy who was in trouble for cutting class.

"Finally over Paul Shapiro, huh?"

"Shut *up!*"

"So what guy?"

"Declan Wilder," I said, trying not to blush. "He's in Smith with me—"

Stephanie saw right through me. "Dummy! Don't you know all the girls have crushes on him?"

"Shhh!" I whispered fiercely as Philip Gorman was coming up to us. He didn't look like a wisecracker today. In fact, he seemed kind of jumpy. "Hi, Martha," he said, his voice wavering a little.

"Oh hi, Philip."

"Hey, um, I have a question—"

"Well, I missed most of English today, so I don't really—"

"—would you go to a school dance?"

"Eeew, *no!*" I answered. I felt a kick from Stephanie under the table.

Philip looked surprised. Then he seemed to be on the verge of saying something but deciding not to. "Oh, okay," he said softly, and hesitated a little before turning around to leave.

"*Martha!*" Stephanie glared at me. "That wasn't very nice!"

"What? Everyone knows it's not cool to go to school dances and sports. School spirit is, like, you know—a hobgoblin!" Or wait, was it a hemoglobin? *Shrug.* I blushed, sure that Stephanie was going to start teasing me about how I sounded just like Brett. The cafeteria doors closed behind Philip.

"Dodo! He was *asking* you!"

"He *was*?" I thought a minute. "No! He said, *would* you go to a school dance. Like, did I think events like that were worth going to! I mean, in general."

"*The.* He said *the* school dance."

"Oh, no! He said *the*? Are you sure?"

She nodded. I managed to shriek "Oh, God!" before Stephanie and I went completely out of control laughing, rolling side to side, putting our heads down on the table, pounding our fists, laughing some more. We tried to calm down, because even in the din of the cafeteria other kids could see we were having a spaz, but we couldn't help it. Every time we looked at each other, it started all over again.

When we'd finally gotten ourselves to stop, the muscles in my face ached from trying to force myself to be serious. Stephanie avoided looking right at me and tried to change the subject to Helvetica's kittens, but her voice wobbled with the effort.

We looked for Philip after school, but we couldn't find him. "God, I feel so bad for him," Stephanie said, kind of lording it over me that she understood boys better than I did. I felt bad for Philip, too, but the more I thought about it, the more I realized I was also kind of angry about the whole thing. If I apologized, I'd have to say, *Yes, I'll go to the dance with you*, because if I said *Sorry, I misunderstood you, but I still don't want to go to the dance*, that was just too mean. Besides, I wasn't sure whether I wanted to go or not, and I didn't feel like asking Stephanie to help me figure it out, because she already thought I was an idiot. Thank God it was Friday, and I wouldn't have to think about Philip Gorman again until English on Monday.

We knew something was wrong the minute we walked into Stephanie's house. There was no music blaring from Brett's room, and it sounded like Morris was upstairs. We plunked our stuff down on the kitchen table. "Dad?" Stephanie climbed the steps two at a time, and I scrambled up behind her.

Morris and Sylvia were sitting on Stephanie's bed. Brett was sitting on her floor. "It's not unheard of," Morris was saying.

"What's going on?" Stephanie's voice was shrill as she rushed into the room. How was it that a divorced mother and father sat side by side on their daughter's bed, talking? It could only mean something bad had happened.

I peered into the closet, where Helvetica was asleep. There were three kittens, not five. I looked over at Morris and Sylvia, but they weren't holding any kittens. I looked back at the cat bed. Wait, were those bloody body parts lying next to Helvetica? A tiny grey tail, a whole white furry leg, what looked like a miniature grey ear—had Morris brought over some cat toys?

Then I saw that one of the three remaining kittens was missing both of its back legs and a front leg. It wasn't moving.

"What happened to Gumby?" Stephanie's voice was shrill. "And where's the little white one? Orbit?" She seemed to have forgotten Portico—the one I'd touched while I had a cold.

Morris was standing up. "Stephanie, sweetheart, once in a while— it's rare, but—there are instances where a mother—well, she eats her own kittens. It doesn't happen often—"

"*What?*" Stephanie said.

"Sometimes the kittens don't smell quite right to the mother," Morris explained. "Or there can be other reasons, like they have an illness that only the mother can detect."

Why had I touched the kittens? Why? *Shrug.*

"Dad, you told me not to over-handle the kittens, and I didn't! We didn't!"

"I didn't," I echoed.

"Gumby is all chewed up!" Stephanie cried. "I should never have used that name—it's like a chew toy!"

"You did everything just fine, Stephanie," Morris assured her.

"But then, *why*—?"

"Sometimes the mother doesn't feel she has enough strength to feed them," Morris explained. "Or there are too many kittens for her to care for. Mother cats sometimes perceive that there aren't enough resources to sustain the lives of the kittens. Other times—"

"It's like '*done because we were too menny,*' Brett remarked.

"Brett—*what?*" Stephanie demanded.

"*Jude the Obscure,* man," Brett answered. "We're reading it in English. At one point, the older boy hangs the two younger—"

"Shut *up,* Brett!" Stephanie shrieked. She was crying. "What are we going to do?"

"We should call the vet," Sylvia said.

"Absolutely," Morris agreed. "At the very least, we need to have the half-eaten one put to sleep. And we should probably remove the surviving kittens."

"But—?" Stephanie persisted.

"Sweetheart," Morris said patiently. "There are cats that just aren't cut out to be mothers. It happens."

Brett peered at me. It looked like his expression said, *It's okay, Martha, you didn't do anything wrong,* but I wasn't sure. He was the one who'd told me not to touch the kittens. *Shrug.*

"Look, this is all my fault!" I shouted. "I was getting sick the other day, and I touched Portico! The germs must have rubbed off on the other kittens!"

Sylvia said, "Don't be silly, Martha. It could've happened for any reason."

Then Morris got up off the bed. He came over to me and looked straight into my face. My bowels were roiling; all I could think was that I was in big trouble. *Shrug.* "Martha," he said slowly, as if about to deliver a message of grave importance. "This is not your fault."

Stephanie said she thought the two surviving kittens should be put up for adoption right away at the Humane Society, for their own safety. Morris said Helvetica should be spayed, for real this time, so that she'd never become pregnant again. Sylvia put a call in to the vet, and everyone was waiting to hear back, even Morris.

Brett offered to walk me to the bus stop. He'd never done that before, and I figured he didn't want to chew me out in front of everyone else. I said yes, just wanting to get it over with. But instead, Brett put his arm around my right shoulder as soon as we left the house. "Give yourself a break," he said as we walked slowly up the street. "Usually when bad shit happens, it's for more than one reason."

Was that true? But it still meant I could be *one* of the reasons. Let's face it, the main one. I was miserable, but at the same time, my heart was beating fast, and I hoped like hell I didn't shrug and knock Brett's hand off my shoulder. *Why can't Logan Starch see me now, walking along with a cute eleventh-grade guy? Why can't Barb Mendelsohn? Why can't those mean girls who make fun of me?* "But I was getting a cold! I should've—"

"You blame yourself for stuff too much, man!" Brett said. "Why do you think everything's your fault?"

Well, isn't it? I wanted to say. *Shrug*, went my shoulder, but Brett's hand weathered the jump and stayed right there. He waited with me at the bus stop, and we kept talking. And then, just as the bus was nosing in, Brett turned me toward him and kissed me on the forehead.

It had been the world's shittiest day, but I grinned off and on all the way home. I couldn't wait to call Stephanie and tell her, even though she'd probably give me at least a mild lecture on not getting attached. But given that Morris was still at the house when I left, my guess was that all four Kenyons would be having dinner together. Stephanie would be busy. Besides, I had my mother to face.

Usually when my mother was mad at me, she stayed mad for days. But she seemed to have forgotten all about the note for school and the frying pan and my telling her to go fuck. She was just sitting in her bed, crying and watching TV, as if everything were normal.

14

tree house

Everyone talked about war being wrong. It wasn't healthy for children and other living things—Brett had the poster in his room. That made sense about Vietnam; of course it did. But then why were so many American men in World War II considered heroes even though they killed innocent people? Morris Kenyon, for one, who had been a bombardier in the Pacific, and whose service was something Stephanie and Brett were really proud of? It was like "everything happens for a reason," except when it doesn't. It was like "parents want the best for their kids," except when they don't.

The windows at Smoke and Records had been shattered twice in riots in the last few months alone. Broken glass had become so common on Telegraph that the insurance companies had stopped reimbursing store owners when their windows got smashed. My father's sales had dropped, the rent had gone up twice over the last year, and Hildy said he might even lose his lease. Plus my father had gotten tear-gassed at least three times. None of it made me feel sorry for him.

I didn't even care that across Telegraph and down a few doors, there was a new store idiotically called *RECORDS—AT A DISCOUNT!* My main response to the unexpected competition was to joke around with Stephanie and Brett about how stupid the name was and how stupid the punctuation was.

"Just think," Brett said, getting it immediately. "Some guys had a meeting to figure out what to call the new store. They prob'ly argued about it! And *this* is what they come up with? Sheesh!"

"Can't you just see it?" Stephanie added. "Prob'ly one of 'em said, 'Hey, I've got a great idea! Let's have all three! Caps, and italics, *and* exclamation!'"

"Right, like people wouldn't notice the store otherwise!" I could barely get the words out because I was laughing so hard, maybe too hard. I'd been feeling awkward since Brett had kissed me on the forehead, partly because I kept waiting for the right moment to tell Stephanie, if only to show her I didn't care that much about Declan Wilder. But the opportunity never seemed to come up. The more days went by, the more I worried that if I brought it up now, Stephanie would think I thought it was a bigger deal than it was.

It was a week after Helvetica's surgery, and the cat was sleeping in a carpeted triangle of sun in the upstairs hallway, dark stitches across her shaven belly. Stephanie had an orthodontist appointment, and I decided to stay at the house to get a head start on our Latin translation. But then, Brett's door was open.

He was feeding his fish, and when I came in and stood next to him to watch, he put his arm around me, and I put my head on his shoulder, and then he put down the little shaker of fish food and he asked me if I'd ever been kissed before, and I said no, and then he turned me toward him and kissed my forehead again, and then my cheeks, and then, tentatively, my lips. Then we looked at each other, and then we kissed again on the mouth, harder this time. He tasted like warm milk and honey, but with a smoky undertone. I could feel the faintest brush of his tongue on the inside of my lips, which made me breathless, but the smoky taste made me pull back.

"You okay?" Brett smiled, and his eyes crinkled.

Was it tobacco I tasted? Grass? I didn't want to sound like an idiot, so I didn't ask.

He stroked my hair, which I now wore loose. "You don't even realize how cute you are," he observed, looking amused. It was kind of condescending, actually, but I felt my private parts growing warm.

We heard the front door just then, and Stephanie came tromping up the stairs. Later, I made her walk me to the bus stop so I could tell her everything, because even though she was always warning me not to get my hopes up about stuff, she'd still listen and help me sort things out. She was happy for me, but she told me that Brett was seeing a lot of this other girl, Cornelia Wang, whose name I recognized from Hildy.

Sure enough, a week later, when I was coming over, Brett was sitting on the front porch with four other kids. He had his arm around a beautiful girl, and the whole group was laughing and laughing. You could smell pot all the way up the stairs. Brett waved at me and smiled his crinkly-eyed smile.

Just then I heard someone calling my name from across the street. "Martha!" It was Clifton Cray, on his way home from King Jr. High, his violin in tow. He was walking with his buddy Ben, who seemed to be his only black friend and, come to think of it, the only kid I ever saw him hang around with. I smiled and waved.

When I was in eighth grade and Clifton was in seventh, I'd seen other black kids acting like he didn't exist. One time, a group of noontime basketball players pretended not to even see or hear him when he asked to join in the game. But if the black kids considered Clifton too puny to bother with, that protection didn't extend to the white kids, who would call Clifton a shrimp, a peanut, a 99-pound weakling, "Crayon," a weirdo, an egghead, or a spaz—and would take turns pummeling him after school. I felt terrible about this, but didn't know what to do, so I did nothing. I was glad to see no one was following him today or giving him any crap.

The girl Brett was with had shiny black hair that was so long, it looked like she'd had to push it aside (no, probably fling it aside) to sit down. She was wearing faded cutoff jeans, a gauzy blouse, Mexican *huaraches*, and silver dangling earrings. "This is Martha," Brett said to her, "remember? The girl I was telling you about who has perfect pitch, and who knows all about music theory? Martha, this is Cornelia. My girlfriend."

"Wow, nice to meet you!" Cornelia enthused. She was a little overly impressed, in that way people are about stuff they don't know anything about but want to seem like they appreciate.

Shoulder, be heavy. "I think you know my sister Hildy," I said. "From Chem class?"

"Hildy Goldenthal! Sure, I know her. Whoa, you don't look anything alike."

It wasn't exactly jealousy I felt. It was more a combination of feeling stupid and knowing I'd lost the game. It would be too exhausting to fight the way things were: Brett was sixteen and I was fourteen. Cornelia was beautiful and self-confident, and I wasn't either one. But why had Brett kissed me and told me I was cute just when he was getting serious about Cornelia Wang? It was baffling, and kind of infuriating.

I thought of all the things I didn't like about Brett. He loved that awful, preachy Youngbloods song urging everybody to "get together and love one another right now." His favorite Beatles songs were invariably the ones I found the most tedious and annoying, like "For the Benefit of Mr. Kite" and "Strawberry Fields Forever" and "Lucy in the Sky with Diamonds." I hate to admit this, but I even found myself using my mother's criticism of Brett's grammar when he was little to bolster my case.

Then I realized Brett had introduced me to Cornelia without mentioning the fact that my father owned Smoke and Records. Or that Hildy was my sister. Or even that I was Stephanie's best friend. He introduced me as *me*. Goddamn it! It was impossible to be mad at Brett Kenyon.

A cool thing happened a few days later, though: Declan Wilder stopped me in the hall to talk. Apparently he had just realized that the ridiculous girl who'd been too thickheaded to figure out he was cutting class to smoke pot was Martha Goldenthal, daughter of Jules Goldenthal, proprietor of Smoke and Records. Declan had become interested in Richard Strauss after seeing *2001: A Space Odyssey*. My father had reluctantly sold him the obvious, *Thus Spake Zarathustra*, with the understanding that Declan then also had an intellectual obligation to purchase *Don Quixote* with Pierre Fournier on cello. Declan had been getting musical advice from my father ever since. (Why hadn't I seen him at the shop? *Duh*, he probably went during school hours.)

I told Declan that Strauss was one of my favorite composers, too, especially the *Rosenkavalier* suite, and that it was nice there was one good composer in that family, since (and here I pretended I'd never liked Johann Strauss waltzes) Richard Strauss's uncle's music was so syrupy, it made your tongue curl. Declan smiled. He didn't know *Rosenkavalier* but said he'd check it out.

I did what I could to pretend I didn't like Declan. At least he wasn't mean about it. He called me "Miss Martha" and told me I took everything too seriously. I kept trying to figure out what it meant to take things too seriously. I even risked Stephanie's eye-rolling by asking her to decode it for me. I couldn't quite absorb her explanation, and you know what? I still can't remember what she said. The whole business was like my trying to understand history or news articles. Just when I think I'm going to hear the thing that'll enable me to crack the secret code, I suddenly realize I've stopped paying attention at the exact wrong moment, and once again I'm too late. It's like being trapped in some awful Greek myth.

Hildy fretted that some of the LPs at *RECORDS—AT A DISCOUNT!*
were cheaper than they were at Smoke and Records, but my father
shrugged the new store off. "They're a bunch of ignoramuses over
there," he reported to me and Hildy after going over to have a peek. "A
few Mozart symphonies, but no string quartets!—goddamned idiots.
And not only that—" he shook his head in disgust, mostly address-
ing Hildy even though I was the one who cared about music—"they
shoved George Gershwin into the classical section. In between Elgar
and Haydn! Can you imagine?" Was there any question Gershwin
belonged in the jazz section, alongside Cole Porter?

I agreed with my father about how music should be organized.
And I had to admit that when he thought a record was great, it really
was great. Mahler's *Des Knaben Wunderhorn* with soprano Janet
Baker and the London Philharmonic. The first movement of the
Brahms E-minor cello sonata, Opus 38, with André Navarra on cello.
More Brahms: in the piano quintet, Opus 34, that scherzo that you
couldn't help bobbing your head to. César Franck's Prelude, Fugue
and Variations, Opus 18. Practically any Schubert lieder performed
by Dietrich Fischer-Dieskau. More Schubert: that funereal cello solo
from the piano trio, Opus 100.

In other words, I believed in my father. In a way, I believed in him
more than anyone else in the family did, because the thing he was
best at—finding great music—was deeply important to me, too. But
somehow, that wasn't the same as being on his side.

Hildy more than compensated. Without my father's having asked
her to, she'd started working the smoke shop cash register after
school. "What, he can afford to pay you?" my mother demanded,
because he wasn't giving my mother enough money for the mortgage
anymore.

Hildy said no, she wasn't being paid.

"Oh, so he's exploiting you."

"No! I'm learning, and I'm helping," Hildy said. Eleventh grade was supposedly a heavily academic year, but Hildy didn't seem to have homework, and my mother was always bitching at her for not being productive, or constructive, or self-disciplined, or blah blah blah. Why wasn't my mother happy that Hildy was trying to save the family some money by taking over shifts for a paid worker?

It wasn't that long ago that I was sure my mother would be nicer to Hildy if she just took school more seriously, the way I did. Lately, I had to admit that no matter what Hildy did, my mother didn't like it. But it was as if my brain couldn't deal with that idea, because I still wished Hildy would try harder to make my mother happy. I kept trying harder, didn't I?

"If Jules were any kind of responsible parent," my mother told Hildy, "he'd find a way to cover his expenses. And he'd want you out of there! You think he can protect you from riots and tear gas?"

Of course my mother didn't know that Hildy had already gotten tear-gassed last year; she happened to be at the store when "all hell broke loose," as my father put it, during a campus protest of the My Lai massacre. In fact, Hildy had only narrowly escaped being tear-gassed recently during the People's Park protest that Greg Gold had taken her to, along with the rude sign he was carrying. They had left just before "all hell broke loose." Brett, unfortunately, had stayed, and had wound up being shoved around and elbowed hard in the nose, besides getting gassed.

Drew, too, tried to help my father out. It started because he loved to climb the wooden ladder up to the tiny mezzanine at the back of the record shop, squeezing in behind that big speaker my father had used to break up the Nazi riot years before. Then Drew would read comic books, or play solitaire with a greasy deck of cards that someone had left on a shelf underneath the cash register. The plywood floor up in the "tree house," as we called it, was littered with dirt-black pennies and little tubes of industrial-strength colored construction paper that lay flat until the coins were put in. Drew would sit cross-legged on top of the coins and paper tubes, shuffling the cards like an expert, arranging them in Klondike formation over and over again, making stacks of pennies to bet against himself. Hildy and I would climb the ladder and peek in every now and then to check on him. Sometimes from the main part of the store, we could hear him swearing "Shitballs!"—presumably because he wasn't doing well at cards.

The coins were the runoff of heavy canvas bags that were filled to bursting and not securely tied. My father didn't have the patience to deal with the pennies from the two cash registers, so he shoved fistfuls of them into the bags and lugged them upstairs every now and then until he could make rolls out of them—something he never got around to.

It was only a matter of time before Drew had taught himself to make five stacks of ten pennies each from the supply on the floor, hold a finger inside a paper tube, and slide the grimy coins gently inside the wrapper, making sure they all went in at the same angle so they'd lie flat against each other. Then he'd correct the diagonal so the coins were straight, and expertly fold both ends of the tube. "Extra money, Dad," he'd shout proudly, jumping down the last rung of the ladder and presenting a stack of pink cylinders in a filthy open palm. "For the rent."

When Drew had finished with all the pennies on the floor and started tackling the contents of the canvas bags themselves, Hildy and I decided to help. It was cramped with all three of us up there, but it was also kind of fun. The tree house had no air or light, just a rectangular hole about the size of two record albums cut out of the plywood, so you could see what was going on downstairs if you didn't stand up all the way. There was a dim light bulb that had to be tightened or loosened by hand every time because there was no switch or even a string you could pull. It kind of gave me the creeps to be the first one to get up there, and since Drew didn't seem freaked out by it, I always let him go ahead of me.

One time in the middle of December, with Holy Hubert's preaching and the drummers in lower Sproul Plaza still audible underneath side five of the *St. Matthew's Passion*, the three of us wound up making so many rolls of pennies that the empty canvas bag we put them back into was too heavy to lift up. We had to spill out all the pennies from another bag onto the floor so we could distribute the load into two sacks that could be carried down the ladder. I was worried my father would get mad at us for making another mess up there, even though Drew was the one who had cleared the floor in the first place. But all Hildy and Drew could think about was the $25.50 we'd wrapped.

I let them lug the sacks to my father. "Dad! See all the money we made?" Drew enthused, clunking his sack of wrapped pennies down in front of the glass display case. I ducked into the tiny bathroom to wash my hands, which were black with grime. There was no good soap in there, just a small dry piece of Ivory with gray gouges in it from all the dirt. There was no towel, either, and virtually no toilet paper. The water barely came out of the faucet. I did the best I could and blotted my hands on the sides of my jeans (Stephanie's jeans, actually) on the way out.

"Jules, uh, I hate to bother you—" Bob Metcalf was saying.

"I know, I know, payday," my father answered with irritation. "Just take it out of the register, wouldja? I'm busy here!" He was squatting in back of the glass display case taking inventory, a yellow order pad in one hand and a Lindy ballpoint pen in the other. A Sherman cigarette dangled from his mouth, unlit. It was only recently that he smoked anything besides his pipe and cigars, which he'd always said were healthier than cigarettes because you didn't inhale. Now he was never without his Shermans, long dark-brown cylinders that came in a white box with dark red swirls on it.

There were a couple of *thunks* as Bob snapped down the spring-loaded metal pieces that secured the bills in their respective compartments in the cash register. He was keeping track, I was sure. He had to be.

"Hildy! Marthy! Let's take the sacks to the bank!" Drew said.

Just then, a heavily made-up woman in a bright yellow knit suit made her way into the store. She had too much gold jewelry on, and poofy, fake-looking hair. She was probably some student's mom, or maybe a professor's wife. "Excuse me," she said, her voice raised over the music, "do you carry *White Christmas* here?"

"Uh-oh," Hildy breathed. My father routinely ignored petty theft, like the kid who'd come in earlier today and stuck an Almond Joy in his back pocket before sauntering out. But when it came to bad taste—well, all hell might break loose. My heart raced as my father rose and put the Lindy pen behind his ear, set the order pad on top of the counter, and came out from behind the display counter.

"*White Christmas*," he repeated slowly, having taken the unlit Sherman from his mouth.

"Yes! The Bing Crosby," the woman said. "Oh no, you're out of it?"

I knew my father wasn't out of it. "Madam," he said loudly. "*White Christmas* is available only in our—*Turlock* location."

Bob Metcalf tried to stifle a laugh. Of course Smoke and Records didn't have a branch in the Central Valley town of Turlock, which my father called the armpit of the cosmos.

The woman looked confused, and Hildy took pity on her, leading her toward the Telegraph Avenue doorway. "Try Mr. Lucas at On Record. Down in the next block," she advised, pointing southward on Telegraph.

"*White Christmas*," my father muttered. "Jesus Christ."

"Isn't that the whole point? Jesus Christ?" I tittered. My stomach was still churning, not having caught up with the relieving fact that the woman had left without realizing she'd been publicly humiliated.

"You guys!" Drew complained. "The bank!"

"Okay, Drewy, we're going," Hildy said, hoisting her canvas bag as my father pulled out his heavy chrome lighter and lit the Sherman. When he shut the lighter, it made a nice, substantial *click*. There was something reassuring about that sound.

"Fifty-one rolls are too heavy for girls," Drew declared, slinging his own bag over his bony shoulder with effort and reaching for Hildy's, but she kept the second bag, and the three of us walked down Telegraph.

There was no line at the bank. It was decorated for Christmas, with jars of cellophane-wrapped candy canes all over the place. Even though it was kind of redundant, given that we could have whatever we wanted at the store, I grabbed three candy canes.

Drew went right up to the merchant window, getting on tiptoes to deliver the goods, which Hildy helped him lift up to the counter while putting her own bag up there, too. "I'm from Smoke and Records," Drew told the bemused teller, and explained how he wanted the $25.50—"I'd like two tens, a five, and two quarters, please"—before she'd even had a chance to open the bags.

15

aVoiding cody's

The Berkeley schools were closed for two days for some kind of "sensitivity training" for the teachers, whatever that meant, and Drew needed to go to the pediatrician for a booster shot. But it turned out to be one of those weeks when my mother didn't get out of bed and acted like it was our fault. She was mad that we had time off school so soon after spring break—which had also been our fault. But she wanted the shot for Drew, of course, because shots involved a needle. Seriously—if we got a splinter, she'd make us hold still while she tried to take it out with a straight pin doused in rubbing alcohol, acting as if this were the only way a responsible parent would do it. We begged her to get some tweezers, but—good luck.

"I can take Drew to the doctor," I offered, "on the bus."

"That suits me fine," my mother sniffed.

If she was going to be a bitch about it, and not even say thank you, I figured there was no reason we shouldn't go to Smoke and Records afterwards. The pediatrician was only a mile down Telegraph, and Drew would deserve some consolation after getting stabbed in the arm with a needle. Besides, my father would give us money for burgers or let us go down to the fountain at Rexall for milkshakes, and then we wouldn't have to worry about there not being dinner later.

After the doctor's visit, Drew and I started toward the store. I was glad my mother had been in such a nasty mood that she'd forgotten to force us to bring sweaters, because it was a lovely, warm day. But as we walked north I started to feel uneasy. I thought I heard helicopters in the distance, and it looked like traffic might be closed off further up Telegraph. There could be trouble again on campus—a peace rally gone un-peaceful, or anti-ROTC protests, or maybe another showdown over People's Park.

We crossed Dwight along the east side of Telegraph, taking in the thick smells of incense and grass. Street vendors offered beaded jewelry, leather barrettes with peace signs on them, hand-carved wooden boxes. There were multicolored candles the very same colors as tie-dyed T-shirts: what if they sold candles that were shaped like torsos instead of cylinders?

A skinny guy with a filthy yellow dog was walking toward us, muttering to no one in particular. In between the mutters, he was taking aggressive bites out of a piece of fruit whose green skin was strangely dark, and it was only as he came closer that I realized he was eating an avocado, rind and all, as if he didn't realize "alligator pear" wasn't actually a type of pear. I thought of nudging Drew, who was looking at leather bracelets at a table in front of Caffé Med. Instead, I just grimaced and scanned the street for Declan Wilder.

Next to the bracelet table, a young woman with an Afro was selling 1969 wall calendars for half off. The wrinkled, tanned lady next to her, with a bandana and cowboy boots and a table covered with a black velvet cloth and handmade silver earrings on top, seemed edgy and kept looking north. "The fuzz are already up there. But they must've called out the National Guard," she said to the calendar lady.

"Fucking Reagan," the calendar lady said.

At the next table, a man with a long beard and flowing brown hair with a little bald spot seemed perfectly serene—maybe because he was smoking a joint right out in public. He was selling plants. "Hey, take a look at this, kids," he said. "It's called sensitive mimosa."

"Pretty," I said.

"No, I mean touch it. Like this," he demonstrated. "Go ahead, don't be afraid. You won't hurt it."

I hesitated, but Drew ran his finger over one of the fronds, and it immediately closed up, like a cat arching its back to his stroke. For some reason, I could only think of what my mother would say. *Life is not all about gimmicks of nature, young lady.* That made me shrug twice in a row, and the stoner guy eyed me narrowly and said, "Hey, relax!"—which only made me shrug again. I glared at him hotly, but he didn't seem to notice.

I glanced across Telegraph: Moe's Books, the Éclair Bakery, and then Cody's Books on the corner. Cody's! Smart people seem to view the place as a holy sanctuary, and now that I think about it, with its two-story-high atrium, Cody's *is* kind of chapel-like. But I don't feel God in there, or calm, or whatever it is that people feel in chapels. Those books, covering every wall from floor to ceiling and displayed on every available horizontal surface—they've always felt to me like an approaching tidal wave, ready to rip through a little town that's supposedly built on high ground. I'm the town, bracing for the flood, hoping I'll survive somehow simply because I do the best I can on the high ground known as school. People like Hildy and Declan and Brett—they're surfers. They don't feel reproached by the tide or mocked or accused of ignorance. No, they find the tide exhilarating.

I guess Cody's is sort of the opposite of "isolating the spots." In Cody's, there's no way I can list, let alone make an exercise of, the things that trip me up; there are just too many of them. "Isolating the spots" means you *know* you'll improve, that your future will be better. It's a kind of belief.

Drew and I crossed Haste and kept going. I thought I saw Declan coming out of Mario's La Fiesta, but it was someone else. Why did

I even want to run into him? Unless the topic was music, conversations with him only made me feel stupid. Declan Wilder was the kind of person who knew all about Proust, and could quote stanza after stanza of Irish poetry, and couldn't imagine why you would want to miss out on such cool things. Which was worse than if he came right out and called you an idiot.

The helicopters were louder now. I wanted to hurry to the store, but Drew was sniffing different kinds of incense at one of the tables, and I was trying not to rush him. Actually, maybe it was more that I was trying to know my brother. What made him tick? I knew he was popular at school, but he never seemed to want to bring friends home (neither had Hildy or I), so I had little sense of what he was like with his peers. What was Drew thinking all the time? I could never quite imagine, aside from things like multiplication tables and playing cards and marbles and army men and comic books and *Tintin*. Drew was good at making himself small, at saying very little. At disappearing. It was as if he were trying to slip through the cracks so no one would bother him.

A woman vendor was chatting with the guy at the next table. "Just more bullshit, brought to you by the purveyors of the bullshit rhetoric of—"

"—the bullshit military-industrial complex," the guy finished for her. He was selling models of bones that were made of plastic but that looked real: thigh bones and arm bones and jawbones.

"Right on, brother," the lady agreed.

Drew picked up a half-size replica of a human skull. "Neato!" he exclaimed. "This is *so* cool. Isn't it, Marth?" He looked so happy as he dug into his pocket that I smiled and tousled his curls. Drew always seemed to have money. Recently, a classmate of Hildy's at Berkeley

High had commented about the "nice little business" Drew had. *What business?* Hildy wanted to know. It turned out the classmate had a younger cousin who was in Drew's class. Drew was letting other kids copy off his math papers for a quarter, and the cousin was one of his customers. Hildy thought Drew might be playing cards for money, too.

By the time Drew and I passed Larry Blake's, we could see some army-type trucks parked on the north side of Bancroft, along the edge of the campus. Traffic was closed off between Durant and Bancroft. I was feeling some urgency about getting to the store, and without talking about it, Drew and I both picked up the pace. We were practically race-walking when I saw Clifton Cray walking up the west side of Telegraph, carrying a skateboard and looking uncertain. "Clifton!" I shouted, but there was too much helicopter noise.

"Martha, let's *go*," Drew urged.

"We *are* going. *Clifton!*" I kept shouting, grabbing Drew's hand and trotting across the eerily traffic-free last block of Telegraph. Finally, Clifton turned around and waved back, looking relieved and happy. "This's my brother, Drew," I told him, panting. "You gotta come with us!"

Bancroft, too, was completely closed to traffic. In a row that stretched way down the block below Telegraph, there were a bunch of policemen in helmets, one next to the other, all facing the campus. Other cops had batons and gas masks and guns across their bodies all at the same diagonal angle, and it looked like the ones in the line did, too. As if in opposition to the row of police, people were lined up on the Student Union balcony, facing them, or maybe just watching, I couldn't tell. There was also a huge crowd milling around across the street. I craned my neck and could see there were tons of people further into the campus, too, all the way to Sather Gate and past it. Black flatbed trucks, each one with a white five-pointed star on it, were lined up behind the row of police. Then police started crossing into Holy Hubert's area.

Over the din of the helicopters, I heard a voice: "I'm request-ing you all to leave the plaza!" I squinted up at the balcony of the Student Union building, where a police officer, or maybe a National Guardsman, was using a bullhorn. All I caught was that something was "going to be dropped in the next five minutes."

Clifton looked up at me as there was a roar from the crowd. "What're chemical reagents?" He'd heard better than I had.

Whatever the hell chemical reagents were, they didn't sound healthy for children and other living things.

16

helicopters

I shoved Drew inside first, then Clifton.

"Martha! Drew!" Hildy greeted us with a furrowed brow, coming out from behind the counter, where Bob Metcalf was poking at his own eyes with his thumb and middle finger. He'd just recently started wearing contact lenses, and it looked like he was trying to get them out.

"What are all those trucks for?" I asked, not even taking the time to introduce Clifton.

"They called out the National Guard," Hildy said breathlessly. "The helicopters are so they can shoot off tear gas. Dad says all hell's gonna break loose! The point is—you shouldn't've come!"

"Shitballs," Drew said.

"Well, how were we supposed to know," I said lamely. Of course I should have known. It seemed so obvious in retrospect: I should never have brought Drew, and now Clifton, into a dangerous situation. Everyone said *trust your instincts*. No one ever explained what to do if your instincts were stupid.

My father ran up from the record area, practically jumping out of his skin. "What are you doing here?" he demanded, as Clifton shrunk back with his skateboard. Half an hour ago, I had actually thought my father might be happy to see me; I never came to the store unless it was scheduled.

"We just—Drew needed a shot at the doctor, and Mom wasn't—and then Clifton—"

We heard the bullhorn-amplified voice again. *Vacate the area! Please cooperate!*

"We wanted to surprise you, Dad!" Drew said. "See what I got?" He showed my father the skull.

"Jesus Christ—get the hell out of the way! All of you!" At first I thought he was telling Hildy, Drew, Clifton and me to go up to the tree house, but my father reached in his pocket for the keys to the apartment just as we heard two loud *pops* that sounded like guns. *Shrug.* We were going to be shot. We could hear people screaming across the street, police shouting with bullhorns.

Clifton read my panic. "Don't worry, Martha," he said, putting a hand on my shoulder. "We'll be okay."

Three more *pops*, and some hissing.

"*NOW!*" my father yelled at Hildy, throwing her the keys.

But it was too late, because suddenly, a huge, thick white cloud of tear gas was whooshing our way.

"Get behind the counter! Down! Down!" my father shouted at us. All of us kids squished behind the cash register alongside Bob, who had managed to get out one contact lens but not the other. Clifton was somehow able to lodge his skateboard under the counter. I didn't see so much as hear a stampede of shouting people, louder as it thundered toward the store. I wanted to know what was going on, but now it hurt too much to open my eyes.

Hildy had grabbed Drew's hand, and without even thinking, I grabbed Clifton's. He gave back a comforting squeeze. An unexpected warmth spread through my body. Sexual warmth. Jesus Christ—Clifton was thirteen, and a goody-goody! Just one more example of *trust your instincts* not applying to people like me.

Meanwhile, stabbing pain attacked my tightly shut eyes, and tears coursed down my cheeks. A bunch of people—twelve? twenty? thirty?—were now in the shop. I opened my eyes to a squint and immediately slammed them shut again. My father had locked down the Telegraph door against the stampede and the cloud of noxious fumes, and was now securing the Bancroft door. It didn't make sense; why would he want to trap the tear gas inside our store? But as another wave of people rolled toward us, I realized he felt that the crowd was more of a danger than the chemicals.

In between coughs into the crook of his arm, my father was barking orders. He'd taken some ratty old towel from behind the cash register to stuff under one of the doors. Then he grabbed a stack of small brown paper bags and started crumpling them up one at a time and tossing them at the people in the store. I was confused until I realized he was having everyone shove the bags under the doors in the space where more gas was getting in.

I heard coughing, crying, gasping, whimpering. Bodies were jammed up right next to the glass display case that my father always worried was fragile. There were so many people squished into the narrow space that I was sure the magazine stacks on the floor were being scuffed and creased, the vertical metal racks bent. I huddled next to Clifton, my hand still in his. Outside, someone was vomiting, and that made me gag, too.

"Are you kids all right?" Bob kept asking, in between coughs. "I can't see a damned thing!"

Finally, with the gas outside mostly dissipated, my father re-opened the doors and shoved the filthy towel aside with his foot. "Who needs the bathroom?" he shouted, grabbing a handful of dimes out of the cash register so that anyone who wanted soda could use the Coke machine.

"Bob does!" Hildy shouted, guiding Bob in to wash his hands, get the other lens out, and flush his eyes out with the pathetic little stream of water. Hildy pulled Drew in there next, and I told her to take her turn too. My throat hurt as much as my eyes did, and as soon as Drew was done, Clifton insisted I go. I washed my eyes and slurped as much water as I could as it piddled onto the rusted drain at the bottom of the sink. Clifton went in next.

My eyes were still tearing and my stomach was churning. I was grateful for the Coke, and so were the bystanders. My father shouted at people to go ahead and use the bathroom. When everyone started to clear out, my father went in himself.

Crumpled paper bags and the towel were still strewn on the floor and outside on the sidewalk, and Clifton, Drew and I assured Bob we'd pick everything up while he ran over to his apartment for his glasses and Hildy went next door to get us all burgers. While we were gathering the bags, Clifton told me he was worried about his friend Ben. The two had planned to meet on Telegraph, have milkshakes at Rexall, do some skateboarding on campus, and then maybe pick up a copy of the latest *Popular Mechanics* so he and Ben could work on some projects with Mr. Cray in the Crays' garage. But Ben hadn't shown up.

"Dad, Clifton needs to use the phone," I told my father. "I mean, this is Clifton, by the way. My old violin teacher, Mrs. Cray? This is her son."

My father looked at Clifton, smiled slightly and reached out to shake his hand. Then he looked at me, then back at Clifton. *Shrug.*

When Clifton reached Ben, he found out that Ben's grandmother had made him stay home because she'd gotten wind of the trouble brewing on campus. Then Clifton phoned Mrs. Cray, who said to skateboard up to her office in the music building. Drew and I both told Clifton to stay for a few more minutes so he could eat.

The truth was, I didn't want Clifton to leave at all. Or, if he did,

I wanted him to take me with him. I wanted to hang around in his garage, work with him and his dad as they tinkered with their car, or did some carpentry project, or repaired something that was broken. Or maybe I'd just watch them, with Mrs. Cray's violin lessons as the soundtrack.

After Clifton was gone, my father put *Petrushka* on, and people started trickling in again, looking for gum, Camels, the *Berkeley Barb*, Beethoven's *Archduke* trio. My father encouraged us to call my mother, but Hildy, Drew and I all begged him not to make us.

Drew trotted behind the counter to retrieve the skull replica he'd left there. "Look, you guys," he said, waving it at my father and Hildy. "Isn't it neat?"

"It's really neat, Drew," Hildy said.

"*Alas, poor Yorick, I knew him well*," my father intoned.

"You mean, *I knew him, Horatio*," I corrected.

"It's *I knew him well*," Hildy put in.

"No it's not, Hildy. My English teacher—"

"*My English teacher*," my father mimicked.

"You guys are both wrong," I said flatly. Sometimes I let Hildy keep the bullshit going, because I felt guilty that my mother was so much meaner to Hildy than she was to me. But then sometimes I was just sick of it. I hated how it turned out that the Haydn string quartet my father was always whistling didn't actually have those two extra beats—he added them in, for no reason. I hated the way he misquoted things, the way he mispronounced words, the way he botched people's names. And I hated how Hildy automatically assumed this was because everyone else in the world was getting it all wrong.

Plus, now that my father had shown that he knew what to do in a tear gas situation, Hildy would probably act even more like he was the bravest person who ever lived. Jesus Christ! Just because someone isn't afraid to hit people doesn't make him some kind of goddamned World War II hero, does it?

17

rebellious

"There's nothing wrong with sex," my mother said to Hildy one evening a few months later. The doors were all open, as usual, because *children don't need privacy!* My mother was lecturing Hildy from the doorway, not even making an attempt to keep her voice down so that Drew and I wouldn't hear. "You don't want to be one of those uptight girls, playing games," she went on. "Depriving their boyfriends of intercourse when it's only *natural* that's what the boyfriends want."

"*Mom!*" Hildy said.

"You can't string him along indefinitely, you know, Hildy. That would be cruel."

Afterwards, Hildy came into my room. Her voice wobbled as she tried not to cry. "Mom wants me to go to her gynecologist so I can get birth control," she said, as if I hadn't heard the whole conversation. "She wants me to have sex with Greg."

Have sex: that was not what my mother had said. She'd said "intercourse," and Hildy had automatically corrected it, just as I would've done, maybe without even noticing, putting as much distance as possible from my mother's repulsive way of saying things. *Intercourse.* Only my mother could make something nice sound clinical and disgusting at the same time.

"Hildy, what do *you* want?" I knew she didn't want to have sex with Greg Gold. Maybe if she said it aloud, she'd have more of a chance of listening to herself.

"You know, Greg thinks I'm exaggerating about how mean Mom is. He doesn't believe me."

"I *hate* when people are like that!"

"Plus, he acts like he owns me or something," she went on. "I asked Dad what he thought. He said if I'm not having fun with Greg, or if he isn't being nice to me, that's a good enough reason to stop dating him."

"Oh." Was it?

"And I said, 'But Dad, it'll hurt Greg's feelings if I break it off.' I told him I thought I should just gradually spend less time with him. But Dad said that was a bad idea. He said breaking up with someone was kind of like an amputation. He goes, 'Do you really think it's better if you do it an inch at a time?' And I can see Dad's point."

"So—you need to tell Greg. Right?"

"I know. I'm trying to get up the nerve."

Hildy had been getting horrible stomachaches lately. I told her she should make my mother take her to a stomach doctor, not a gynecologist, but we both knew that if Hildy let on, there'd be some reason why the situation was Hildy's fault. Or Jules's fault, for being such a psychopath, it was no wonder Hildy had developed physical symptoms to mirror the psychological damage, blah blah blah. . . .

Not that Hildy could get help from my father, either. If she told him she wanted to go see a doctor, he'd open up the register and say, "What do you need?" as if the problem were cash. What Hildy really needed, of course, was help finding a doctor and making an appointment. As for our pediatrician, Hildy would no more confide in him about her stomach than I would about my shrug.

One Friday, Greg Gold's parents were letting him have a party as a reward for how hard he'd been working to fill out his college applications. That was when I realized Hildy hadn't been working on hers. At one point she'd talked about UC Santa Cruz, but she hadn't mentioned it lately.

My mother didn't seem to care, because, she told me, she didn't think Hildy was "college material." I said Hildy was as smart as anyone I knew. Smarter. And a lot more well-read. But my mother insisted Hildy's so-called intellectual life was all bullshit and that deep down inside, Hildy knew it was bullshit: that was why her unconscious mind kept her from filling out any college applications.

I was surprised when Hildy came home early from Greg Gold's party, around ten. Drew was already asleep, and my mother was in her room. Hildy closed my door quietly behind her and plunked down on my bed. She smelled strange—not bad, just not familiar. Or maybe familiar, but strange at the same time.

"What's going on? And what's that weird—"

Hildy ran her tongue over her front teeth. She spoke softly. "Okay, so, like, I was with Dad, and—wait, first, what happened was, I got my period at school and I started having cramps, and I told Greg I didn't feel well enough to go home with him after school to help him set up for the party. I just wanted to sit on the steps of the Community Theater. And then Greg left, and Matt Baskit was there, and he, like, sneaked me a joint, but then—"

"Wait! A joint of *grass*?"

"Don't have a conniption, Martha. Yes, of grass—*duh*! That's what joint *means*!"

Now that Hildy and I were finally at the same school again, I was more aware of the kids she hung around with. Most of them were fine, but there was something about Matt Baskit that didn't sit right with me. Maybe it was because Hildy was always giving him money. He'd forgotten his lunch, or coins must've fallen out of his pocket, or he'd given all his spare change to a street person on his way to school because the street person seemed like they needed the money more than he did. Matt always said he was going to pay Hildy back, but this was the first I'd ever heard of him giving her anything—and it was marijuana. "So what did you *do*? Did you smoke the joint with him?"

"Well—the thing is, Dad says you shouldn't ever smoke grass that someone gives you unless you know for *sure* where it comes from. It could be laced with something really dangerous. So I wasn't sure if it was safe or not. So what I did was, I talked to Matt for a while, and said I didn't feel like smoking right then, because I didn't want him to know I'd never done it before. Then I went to see Dad at the store and showed it to him."

"What did he *say*?" I gasped. "Hildy, did he hit you?"

"*No*, dummy! He took it and flushed it down the toilet."

"Oh."

"And then—"

"What?"

"Well, I never went to Greg's. Because Dad took me upstairs to his apartment and—let me smoke some of his own pot."

"*What*?"

"Shhh! I told you, Martha, don't have a spaz!"

"Are you *kidding*? Dad has *pot*? From *where*?"

"I don't know, but it's safe. And this girl was there, too, Shalimar. She's really nice."

"*Shalimar*? Like the perfume?"

"Not a girl, really, a graduate student, I think. She likes Dad. Which is really weird, because she's not that much older than I am. God, I'm thirsty."

"I never even heard of her."

Hildy moistened her lips, but they still looked a little shrunken. "Dad says the first time you try grass, you don't feel much, but I'm not sure."

I just sat there, my mouth hanging open.

"Don't you understand, Martha? Twelfth grade is *old* to be trying pot for the first time."

"But Hildy—"

"You know, you're really gonna like Shalimar. She's smart, and tall, kind of skinny, and she wears these billowy clothes and has this great laugh and really white teeth and this long, flowing hair. And she's nice! I needed a Kotex, and she gave me three of them."

I had a feeling that even if she never found out about the pot, my mother would think of a reason to hate Shalimar. "So what happened with Greg? Was he mad that you didn't show up?"

Hildy shrugged. "I called from the store and said I had really bad cramps and had to lie down. I mean, that part was true. Then Dad called him and said I still wasn't feeling well enough to go to the party."

"Wow." I let it all sink in. "How'd you get home?"

"Dad and Shalimar put me in a cab."

"But Hildy—*why*? Why would Dad give you pot?"

"I told you, dummy! My period. Shalimar said she used to get these really bad cramps, and it helped her. Plus, Dad said all kids are curious, so they're gonna experiment. He said it's the human condition, and it's better if I try it with him."

"Man, Hildy, Mom's gonna have a *cow*."

"She's not gonna find *out*, dummy!"

But that was the thing Hildy didn't understand about my father: he assumed that everyone, even my mother, thought of him as a basically good person and a caring parent. No matter what he did, he figured people would say, *Isn't it refreshing how honest Jules is about things? Why can't more people be that way?* So when Hildy was in the bathroom a few minutes later, sipping at the faucet, because there was never a cup in there, and the phone rang, and it was my father, probably explaining to my mother that all kids experiment, that this was the human condition, that he was just trying to protect Hildy

from something worse, he probably really believed my mother would
see things his way.

After screaming for a few minutes into the phone, my mother
slammed down the receiver and came running out of her room in
her flannel nightgown. She wasn't wearing a bathrobe, and I could
see her saggy breasts. It was hard not to be disgusted as her nipples
jiggled with anger. I was always fighting the urge to hate her.

For a minute, I actually thought she was going to check and make
sure Hildy was okay. I thought she'd feel bad about waking Drew up
with all the shouting. Afterwards, of course, the echoey slaps across
Hildy's face next to the bathroom sink, the stinging smack across
my own face when I shrieked at my mother to stop slapping Hildy,
the terror of Drew, his running out to see what was going on and
then running back into his room and crawling into his closet in the
dark to multiply numbers—all this seemed like the only possible
outcome.

Normally, Hildy wouldn't even cry in a situation like this. She
always said she didn't want to give my mother the satisfaction. Of
course I was crying, because when I got hit, I cried whether I wanted
to give my parents the satisfaction or not.

This time, though, Hildy did cry. I guess she couldn't help it; there
had just been too many slaps. The tears streamed down, but she was
quiet and held her head high. She went into Drew's room to try to get
him to come out of the closet. "How touching," my mother sneered.
"The protective older sister." Then she turned to me. "I expected
better from you, Martha. I thought you, of all people, would grasp
the need to take a stand here."

"Take a stand?" I shrieked, my palm at the side of my face. "This
isn't Hildy's fault! It's Dad's fault!"

My mother shook her head. "You know, I've come to the conclu-
sion that I just *hate* that girl."

"Wh-what girl?" *Shrug.*

"You know perfectly well what girl! Hildy!"

"*What?*"

My mother was a bitch. That was a fact. But I'm telling you, I never thought she was *this* much of a bitch. Had Hildy heard what my mother had said? She must've, with all the stupid goddamned open doors in our house. "Mom, how can you say that about your own daughter?"

"Martha, I want you to call your father right now! I want you to tell him that Hildy came home with a marijuana cigarette, and that she gave it to Drew, and forced him to smoke it."

"*What?*"

"You do it!"

"Mom, I can't just make up some bullshit story—"

"Don't you *dare* talk to me like that!"

"You're the one who supposedly hates bullshit!" I shouted.

She grabbed my arm, trying to drag me into her room and over to the phone. "You do it, Martha! You tell your head-pot father about that marijuana cigarette!"

"It's called a *joint*, for your information," I countered. I decided not to correct her about my father's being a pot-*head*, not a head-pot.

"I don't care *what* it's called. You call that son of a bitch and humiliate him, right now!"

"No! *Hildy!*"

"What did you say to me?" my mother demanded. Hildy and Drew were in the hallway now. Their mouths were open.

"I said *no*, Mom. I'm not doing it." There was no *shrug* now. Maybe I did have some control over the stupid thing, if only I'd ever get over being stupid.

"Doing what?" Hildy took a step forward, pushed Drew back. "Mom, what are you telling Martha to do?" Her voice was calm.

My mother glared at me, her jaw shaking with rage. "You rebellious little *bitch!*"

"*I am not rebellious!*" I screamed into my mother's face, and she slapped me, again, across mine.

18

best judgment

"**M**r. Lucas? Should I put Leonard Bernstein in the jazz section? Or classical?"

"Isn't *West Side Story* a musical?" he puffed from the back, where he was moving around heavy cartons of LPs that had been delivered to On Record that morning.

It wasn't busy, and, keeping my eye on the cash register, I walked toward the inventory room, choosing my words carefully so I didn't come across the way my father would've. "Um, the thing is, right now *all* the Bernstein is sitting in the musicals section. But *Chichester Psalms* is choral, and I think *The Age of Anxiety* is a symphony. The back of *Trouble in Tahiti* says it's an opera—"

Mr. Lucas gave the slight groan of an overweight man turning himself around on leather soles while remaining in a squatting position. His beefy face was red, especially the nose, and his scalp was pink under the thinning fine blond hair. "Use your best judgment. There's a stack of those white separators under the counter. Find a marker and create a new category, if you need to."

"Uh—okay." I was pretty sure my father put *West Side Story* in musicals and the rest under jazz. Or wait, did he file Bernstein with other contemporary American composers, like Copland? I'd have to check. For now, I decided on jazz for everything besides *West Side Story*, mostly because in Mr. Lucas's classical section, the composers were arranged alphabetically, and the idea of putting Leonard Bernstein somewhere between Albinoni and Chopin made me wince. It wasn't that I thought of either Albinoni or Chopin as being superior to Bernstein—if anything, I preferred Bernstein to both. But at Smoke and Records, composers were organized chronologically, not alphabetically, and let's face it, when my father is right, he's right. How could anyone think Bartok belongs near Bach, or Mahler near Monteverdi? Albinoni should be near Vivaldi, not Brahms! Obviously.

Mr. Lucas and I were reorganizing and consolidating the records to make room for a new section he'd designated for cassette tapes, which people had started using to listen to music while driving around in their cars. My father didn't sell cassettes, but then, Mr. Lucas had more room in his store, plus a more open mind about things that were becoming popular. He liked all kinds of music, from Gregorian chant to Jefferson Airplane, and he didn't seem to experience the world of recorded music as a struggle between true art and the fall of civilization or something. Sometimes Mr. Lucas played Verdi operas, sometimes Frank Sinatra, sometimes Creedence Clearwater Revival. The shop was decorated with posters of Glenn Gould and Pablo Casals, but also the Carpenters, the Jackson Five and, of course, the Beatles.

Probably Hildy thought, *How could you help Mr. Lucas out for money when I've been working for Dad for free? If you were a nice person, you'd work for Dad for free, too.* At least she had the decency not to say it out loud. My father, too, kept quiet instead of stating the obvious. *Sure, go ahead, spend time in Lucas's Emporium of Mediocrity—maybe then you'll finally appreciate how great I am.*

My mother was more up-front in her disapproval. Of all the places I could work, I'd chosen one just a block away from my destructive father. Besides, she said, if he were a decent provider, I wouldn't have to waste my time at a menial job while still in high school. Oh, and my mother didn't like my "compulsive need to hoard money." I guess she failed to notice that I spent my first paycheck on a pea coat from the army-navy surplus store, a pair of corduroy jeans from Hink's, and a couple of blouses from Dharma Bums, an imports shop on Telegraph.

I often felt anxious when Mr. Lucas expected me to make decisions, but he seemed to appreciate my efforts, and overall, I really enjoyed my job. I liked helping the customers choose records that, based on their taste, I could be pretty sure they'd want. When people liked crappy music, I bit my tongue and let them buy crap. When people had good taste, I'd chat with them about what they chose, and often wound up selling them another record or two. I saw what my father liked about having a shop and running the register: the world came to you.

One day, for example, while I was squatting behind the cash register to straighten out the bags, a young black teenager came into view.

"Hey, that *is* you!" he said, grinning. "Knew it!" He leaned his skateboard against the front window.

"Clifton!" I hadn't seen him since the tear gas incident a year earlier. He was still short, but he'd grown a medium Afro instead of wearing his hair close-cropped, and I had to admit he was pretty good-looking, for an undeveloped ninth-grader. He had this impish smile where his upper gums showed above big white teeth, and his eyebrows made a kind of jaunty tepee over his eyes when he wrinkled his forehead. "Didn't that tear gas scare you off Telegraph?"

"Nah. Just hangin' around with my friend Ben." Clifton gestured outside, where the tall, beanpole-skinny black kid with a baseball cap was playing with his skateboard, the tires loud and gravelly against the sidewalk, like one of those washboards in a jug band.

"How's your mom?" I asked.

Clifton shrugged. "You know. She's my mom."

"You're still playing violin, right?"

"Ha! Like she'd let me quit."

"You're probably really good by now."

Clifton shrugged again. "I got into Youth Orchestra."

I rolled my eyes. "First chair, right?"

He hung his head, nodded. "Everyone thinks I'm a goody-goody."

Well, he *was*. "Come on," I managed. "You're really talented, Clifton." I realized I was looking forward to next year, when Clifton would be a tenth grader, and we'd be on the same campus, and I'd get to see him when Concert Chorale and Orchestra did rehearsals and concerts together. "Plus you work really hard," I went on. "You should feel proud!"

Clifton blushed—but it was worse than that. Just at the moment I saw the bulge in his pants, Ben started tapping on the window. "Hey Clifton! C'mon!"

Shrug. I was blushing too now, but luckily, Clifton had already turned away to pick up his skateboard, anchoring it diagonally across his body. "I—better go," he stammered. "'Bye, Martha!"

"Isolating the spots!" I blurted, to make him feel better, but then I worried that it sounded like I was referring to the spot in his pants. "Say hi to your mom, okay?" I added hastily. Poor kid. Or maybe poor stupid me.

Hildy couldn't wait to get out of the house, of course, and since she had the credits she needed, she decided to graduate from Berkeley High a semester early. She hadn't figured out the whole college thing yet. Or maybe it'd be more accurate to say she made the decision about graduating early *instead* of thinking about college, kind of like eloping with a new guy to get out of marrying the fiancé you didn't really love.

Hildy was a B student. That is, she was the type who could get the only A+ in her entire grade in history, and then get a C in algebra. Hildy could've gotten an A+ in English, too. She was always coming up with these great analogies about whatever she read, and loved delving into things like symbolism and metaphor in the senior honors English class of Dr. Riggs, a former college professor who'd wound up teaching at Berkeley High after refusing to sign the loyalty oath during the McCarthy era. The problem was, Hildy would start a writing assignment about a book, and then not finish the essay on time because she'd still be trying to tie the book to current events, or to another book by the same author, or to a Japanese fairy tale. She'd go talk to Dr. Riggs about her ideas and ask for an extension, which you weren't supposed to do at all, let alone adopt as a habit. But Dr. Riggs would always give her the extension. Then she'd get an A or an A+ on the essay, but at most a B in the class.

Matt Baskit was graduating a semester early, too. He was moving to some big commune down on San Pablo Avenue in Emeryville where a cousin of his was living, and where the residents did a lot of meditating. Matt told Hildy she was welcome to move there, too. Though I'm sure Hildy would've preferred an invitation more personal than "you're welcome to," she took Matt up on his offer. Maybe she thought the invitation was warmer than it really was, but mostly I think Hildy was just desperate to leave. Besides the obvious, she was convinced the stomachaches would go away once she was out of the house.

Whenever my father sent Hildy out for burgers or some other errand, he let her keep the change, so even though she wasn't being paid by the hour, she'd been able to sock away some money. She didn't seem bothered by the fact that Matt didn't have the $25 deposit that the commune required. She fronted Matt his $25 as well as coughing up her own $25.

Partly, I think, Hildy was assuming Matt would help her find a job. He had an uncle who worked on the Cal campus at a sociology research center where they administered questionnaires about things like health and political beliefs. The research center needed workers to go through the pages of each completed questionnaire, key in all the information using a keypunch machine, and then feed the accumulated batches of computer cards into a tabulating machine. The uncle had said he could get Matt a job there, and Matt had told Hildy he thought his uncle could get her one, too. But it turned out that once Matt started, they didn't need anyone else.

As if that weren't shitty enough, Matt took up with some other girl at the commune and stopped paying attention to Hildy pretty much as soon as she moved in. I'm still not sure she ever got her $25 back from him.

I would've felt devastated by all this, but Hildy acted as if she'd understood from the start that things would work out the way they did, as if she'd known she'd have to leave shortly after moving in. She didn't like meditating, she told me, and people at the commune weren't as friendly as you'd think. Plus the stomachaches hadn't stopped.

But Hildy, as always, kept going. She got herself a job at Gabel, a big bookstore down on University Avenue, and answered a want ad: some girl named Ann was looking for a housemate in a big, sunny brown-shingle with several other housemates and a shared kitchen. The place was in Oakland, but close to the 51 bus line into Berkeley.

All through school, Hildy had been the type with a lot of friends, especially boys. She didn't usually have a female best friend. But Ann quickly became just that. Ann was older than Hildy and had a really difficult family herself, with a severely disabled brother and no father, just a crazy mother who barely noticed Ann because everything revolved around the brother's needs. Ann was finishing up her classes at Cal and applying to nursing school. She encouraged Hildy to sign up for courses at Berkeley Learning Pavilion, the community college where Ann had spent her first two years before transferring to Cal. Hildy started taking literature and psychology classes, and since the manager at Gabel let her do homework when it was quiet, Hildy had built-in blocks of time to study, read, and write. She started getting straight A's, which made me really proud, but I didn't say so because I didn't want to sound condescending.

As much as I missed Hildy, my life was easier with her out of the house; my mother had less to bitch about. I still saw Hildy at Smoke and Records, where she continued to help out whenever she wasn't at Gabel or in class. Also, she joined me and Drew whenever it was our weekend to be with my father. We were still a family—just without my mother. Maybe that should've given me a clue.

Ann insisted that Hildy needed to see a doctor about the stomachaches, helped her figure out who to go to, and stayed on her case until she made the appointment and went. Hildy found out she had stomach ulcers. She started taking medicine, which helped, but the doctor warned her that the ulcers could come back, so she should stick with bland foods if she could.

Spring came, and Brett got accepted at Humboldt State. Cornelia was going to UC Santa Cruz, and Greg Gold was off to Princeton. If everything went the way I hoped, I'd be at Cal in a couple of years— and so would Hildy.

part two

19

the list

It's a mystery how my mother found a working ballpoint in the house. Whenever I tried using a pen at home, I'd wind up with a bunch of furious spiral dents—or, as I lost patience, ugly rips in a piece of newsprint or a paper bag or whatever else was lying around to test a pen on. My mother's not throwing the pens away—her acting as if she were ever actually going to buy ink refills at the stationery store—was another reason I hated her. Not that the pencils were any better, with their chewed bodies, blunt points, too-light lead, and that setting-my-teeth-on-edge noise they made when I tried to use the mostly worn-down erasers at the end. It was as if all the writing implements in the house were mocking me for ever wanting to get anything done in life.

Somehow, though, while I was at school—senior year had just started a few weeks earlier—a blue ballpoint made contact with a jagged sheet of scratch paper that my mother must have found lying around in the kitchen. When I got home, she was on the phone. "Yes, that would be fine. I can have him there by noon," she was saying, as she glanced up and handed me the piece of paper.

"What's this?" I looked down at a list of eight or nine names and phone numbers. *Dottie and Phil Starch—LAndscape 6-1944. Harriet and Stuart Minter—OLympia 5-8684. Helen and Manny Korngold—THornwall 8-2232.* I understood that the list meant something, but I couldn't remember what. It felt like trying to think of a word in a foreign language I had once studied.

"Yes, perfect," my mother told whoever she was talking to. "Right. I'll see you then." She hung up the phone and turned to me impatiently. "It's your list," she said. "Of families that I'm sure would love to have you. I'd say you should start with the Starches. They've always had a soft spot for you, especially Dottie. And now that Logan is at that special school and the older brother is housebound, they'd probably love to have some company."

I imagined my mother, aware of the pen situation, reaching first for a pencil. Maybe she took out that sharpener that lay on its side in one of the desk drawers, a clunky contraption whose handle looked like a skinny green olive. Maybe she decided it was too much trouble to clamp the sharpener to the table. Maybe she tried to hold the sharpener together with one hand while turning the crank with the other, and then realized she didn't have enough hands to push the pencil in at the same time. Or maybe she had just decided it was too much trouble to deal with pencil shavings. She would have riffled through the pens, delighted, finally, to find one with ink in it.

I looked at the paper again. The handwriting was rushed but confident; there was no apology to it. In fact, I suddenly realized my mother was dressed. Her hair was washed, held back neatly with a black stretchy headband.

"Mom, what—are you expecting me to *live* with these people?"

"Well, Martha, you gotta go somewhere." Now she was putting some papers into overstuffed manila folders and throwing others in a paper bag filled with what she called "burnables." No one else called them burnables, and I felt a wave of hatred of her just for that, just for her having so much in common with my father, the two of them making up their own words and definitions, making up their own rules, and acting like the rest of the world was stupid for not doing things their way.

"Mom! I can't just call these people and ask if I can live with them. That's just—this is ridiculous!"

"*You're* being ridiculous. These are all people I know for a fact would be delighted to have you. I *chose* them for you! You know, ever since the Minters' younger son died, they've been just devastated. They have that daughter Sarah, right? Isn't she about your age?"

"Mom—"

"Stop it, now!" She was losing patience. "So *don't* start with the Minters. Start with the Starches."

"The Starches? How do you—" I had forgotten that even before kindergarten, Logan's mother and my mother had known each other because there was some drop-off morning play group in the Berkeley hills where mothers could take their toddlers when they had errands or shopping to do.

"Martha, just start making calls. The sooner you start, the sooner you'll have a place."

"Mom, I don't even know these people!"

"Of course you do! The Minters have known you since you were a baby. And the Starches—you and Logan were in a play group together, don't you remember? And Helen Korngold babysat you a few times when you were a toddler. She adored you!"

My throat ached with the effort of not crying and not screaming. "What am I supposed to say to them? 'My mom is kicking me out of our house, so could you please take me in? They'll think I'm crazy!"

"Martha, stop being so self-conscious. What do *you* care what they think?" She adjusted her headband. "Now either make your calls, or start helping me. God knows there's plenty to do to get this house ready for the Cal students."

"But, Mom—" She hadn't thought this through, that was all. She didn't realize. "Don't all the Cal students already have places to live? I mean, it's September. School's already going."

"No, Cal starts at the end of next week. You think I didn't check on that with the housing office?"

"But—"

She let out a sigh. "Martha, what *is* it?"

"Why can't we just stay here and let the Cal students live with us? We could double up. Drew and I could share a room."

"What, so you two can stay up talking half the night?"

"No! To save money."

"My God, Martha, your perceptions are so lopsided! You have no comprehension of child development. Children of the opposite sex need their own rooms. Sharing a room like that would be damaging."

"But—"

"I've rented the house out *unoccupied*. We can leave our furniture and kitchen things, and the books and records. But we need to be out. Now hurry up and get started!"

"Mom, why can't Grandma and Grandpa help? I'm sure they'd send us money if you asked."

"Oh, come *on*! I can't have them rescuing us from Jules's irresponsibility every time we need something."

"Irresponsibility—what do you mean?"

"I mean the slipshod way he runs the store, what do you think I mean? He doesn't know what hard work *is*." I knew my father wasn't normal, doing things like letting Bob and Terry and the other guys help themselves to their pay out of the cash register, which my mother said was a symptom of my father's sick need to be seen as the good guy. But she acted as if my father never showed up to work. "Why do you think the store is failing?" she went on.

"The store isn't failing!"

"—Because I stopped using my own money to pay his rent in the shop, that's why! He can't even make payroll."

"But Mom, it's not his fault! It's just what's happening on Telegraph, plus those, like, discount record places! And besides—your parents send you money all the time, and you just spend it on stupid stuff like antiques!"

"You watch your tongue, young lady!"

"Mom," I cried desperately, "then why can't we all move to an apartment? All of us together?"

"A crappy apartment? Children need homes, Martha."

"Homes—but—where's Drew going?" *Shrug*: a new level of panic. I hadn't even thought of what she had planned for him. Wait, was she talking about Drew on the phone when I'd come in?

"I found a school for Drew down in Fresno—Plowshares. It's like a boarding school, and it's also a working farm. The kids have chores. Discipline."

"A farm?" Farm the kid out, to a farm. Had that language coincidence somehow made a farm in Fresno sound right to my mother? Was she that far off her rocker? *Fat farm. Funny farm.* Why didn't she turn it on herself, for once?

"Yes, a farm. In fact, Dottie Starch told me about it. You know, she had to look into these schools for Logan, and that's how she heard about—"

"But Mom, Drew isn't *anything* like—wait, *when?*"

"I'm driving him there this Saturday morning."

"But Mom—" I didn't even know where to start. "Where are *you* going?"

"Home to New York!" she answered, as if nothing could be more obvious.

"But your home is here, Mom! And *we're* here, don't you *care?* Plus, I have to apply to college soon. I need your—"

"Martha, don't you understand what I'm up against? Drew has no chance when he's around a psychopath like Jules, not to mention—"

"Mom, I thought you cared about family! And college!"

"What, has Jules brainwashed you, too? You don't recognize his destructiveness? The black and blue marks all over me? And that seductive crap he pulls with Hildy?"

"Mom, you can't put Drew in a boarding school! He's just a little kid! And besides," I added hopefully, "isn't it too expensive?"

"That's the whole point of renting out the house, Martha. Money. For what's really important."

My mother had recently discovered Drew's stash of army men under his bed. I was worried she'd think they were shoplifted, but that didn't seem to cross her mind. Instead, she was furious that after all she'd taught him about army men symbolizing everything that was wrong with our society, Drew still showed lousy judgment. Violence and war and Hollywood standards of masculinity—Drew had swallowed the whole establishment package, hook, line and sinker. It was all because of his sick identification with Jules, whose approval he was obviously trying to get by liking symbols of violence, which Drew unhealthily equated with masculinity since Jules, the only male role model Drew had, was a violent louse.

"It's natural for boys to identify with their fathers," she was saying. "The problem is when the father is sick in the head. The way things are going, Drew'll be a juvenile delinquent by the time he's twenty."

"*Twenty*? Mom, *juvenile* means—" I hated my mother. She was stupid, she didn't smell good, and she was a bitch—the biggest bitch I knew. Let's face it, the biggest bitch I'd ever heard of.

"A boy needs a father," she went on. "A healthy role model, in a healthy family situation. Otherwise—well, I can see the handwriting on the wall." She was like Cassandra in Greek mythology, she said. Cassandra could perceive the future, but no one would believe her. . . .

I staggered upstairs to the bathroom, clutching the list and panting with rage. Bitch! Bitch! I'd done everything for her, and it was all for nothing. I yanked open the top drawer of the bathroom linen chest, hating her even more for what was in there: faded puke-green towels with holes in them, alongside a dried up old piece of steel wool. I slammed the drawer shut and opened the second one, then the third, as if I didn't know there was nothing comforting in there. No little heart-shaped rosewater soaps or fluffy pastel washcloths or scented candles or Kleenex. Not even a cup for drinking water. Of course not. Just the opposite: more shitty towels and, in the very bottom drawer, an old extension cord that probably didn't work, alongside some jars of screws and nails that I remembered my mother being proud of having "organized." The nails weren't even new; half of them were rusty or bent. And she thought she was so great for collecting them in a jar and storing them in a stupid place.

I let the list flutter to the floor, leaving the bottom drawer open. I was getting lightheaded from panting, and the back of my neck was hot. I let my body slide down onto the cold tile. I grabbed the jar of nails, took one out and twisted it between my fingers. I chose a straight, new-looking one, thinking of tetanus. Which was a completely stupid thought, since I knew I was up to date on tetanus shots. Shots were the type of parental duty my mother took seriously, because they hurt.

Dizzily, my heart still racing, I pulled up the left sleeve of my turtleneck. I quickly dragged the nail across the inside of my wrist. But it was pathetic, kind of like I was trying to light a match and falling flat because I was too scared to give it the force it required. *"Ouch!"* I said aloud, my eyes stinging with tears. I watched the scratch as it formed, white, and then pink. It didn't bleed at first, but it stung really badly. I threw the nail in the bottom drawer, not bothering to put it back where it "belonged." *Shrug. Shrug.* Some suicide attempt! All I'd done was add more pain to the enormous pile of shit called my life.

I wiped the tears away and glanced down at the list next to me on the floor. I'd grasped it so hard that it didn't lie flat; it went up at the edges. How had my mother managed to keep her handwriting so straight on an unlined piece of paper?

Suddenly I saw the omission. "That *bitch!*" I said loudly. I would have enjoyed living with Stephanie if I couldn't have a home, but of course Sylvia wasn't on the list.

That *bitch.*

20

the human condition

I folded the paper in quarters and put it in my back pocket. My wrist was a little bloody now and stuck to my sleeve, and my heart was still racing. I could hear my mother puttering around downstairs. Quietly, I sneaked the upstairs phone into my room and shut the door behind me. I sat on the edge of the bed, took a breath, and dialed.

"Smoke and Records," my father answered. He didn't sound at all perky, and the music in the background was slow and sad. Did he already know?

"Dad? It's Martha."

"Hi, honey."

"Is Hildy there?"

"She's right here, but—" He could tell I wasn't okay, and I realized I hardly ever let him see it when I wasn't okay. "What is it, honey?"

Before I knew it, I was sobbing. "Mom is renting out the house," I wailed. "She said we have to get out. Drew is going to some boarding school in Fresno this weekend. It's some place for rebellious—"

"Wait! Slow down, honey." I heard him cover the receiver and the muffled, "Turn that *down*, will ya?" as if whoever it was should've known he was on an important conversation. He must be behind the smoke shop counter next to Hildy, away from the turntable. I could imagine him stretching the phone cord so he could get a little quiet in the nook where the imported cigars and pipes were stored, behind the glass counter. Drew was probably up in the tree house. I heard Hildy saying, "What is it, Dad? What's going on?"

"Dad, she just gave me a piece of paper with a list of names on it," I went on.

"What do you mean, a list?" He covered the receiver. "*I said turn that down!*" His angry shout was muffled.

"She gave me these names. Of families. I'm supposed to go down the list and find a family to live with. I don't even *know* any of the people."

I remembered something else. Throughout junior high school, my mother had never asked me if Sylvia wanted my mother to pay for my lunches or buy groceries to replace what I'd eaten. Maybe she'd made arrangements with Sylvia without my knowing it, but I didn't think so. "She didn't say anything about who's going to give the family money for my rent or anything like that," I told my father. "Like, she didn't explain about my food. Or maybe you're supposed to do that? Or I guess I could use my—" my voice trailed off.

For a long, uncharacteristic moment, my father didn't say anything. I could hear a bus passing in front of the store, voices in the background. "We'll be right over," he said finally. "You wait out front."

I cried.

"Okay? Honey? You just come down to the front of the house and wait for us, and we'll go sit in the park. I see a couple cabs waiting across the street. We'll get one right now."

I nodded, then realized he couldn't see me. "Okay," I managed. "But what if Mom finds out you came over? She'll have a conniption! It's not a weekend."

"Don't you worry about that. Now you go outside and wait."

"Okay, but Dad? Can you let me talk to Hildy, just for a sec?"

He handed the phone to Hildy. "Martha?"

"Mom is renting out the house. Drew and I have to move out. She's taking him to some school in Fresno!"

"What? What school?"

I heard my father shouting for Drew to come down from the tree house. "Wrap it up, now!" he told Hildy.

"See you in a few." Hildy hung up.

I called Stephanie and told her everything. She barely let me finish. "You can stay here, Martha. You can use Brett's room—he says he's not coming home from Humboldt State until Thanksgiving. We can fill out our college applications together!"

"That's so nice—"

"Seriously! You gotta live a little! And then you can double up with me whenever Brett's here. I just know my mom'll say yes! She really likes you, Martha."

"I appreciate it, Steph, really." I didn't want to live with Stephanie. I wanted my mother. I wanted those stupid disgusting morning stews. I wanted to know her stupid body was in her stupid toilet-paper-strewn bed in the room right next to mine.

"Jesus H. Christ," Stephanie agreed. "You, of all people, don't deserve it. You're such a good kid! Plus, mothers don't kick out their own children! Even *my* mom knows that."

"But I mean, my dad—" I couldn't stand the idea that Stephanie had forgotten even for a minute about my father hitting my mother. Hitting all of us. Threatening me with a hot iron! Being mad at me for wanting to do well in school. Smoking pot with Hildy and calling it the human condition. Boring everyone practically to death with his long-winded explanations about things no one else knew about—that I was pretty sure he didn't know about, either—and mixing it all in with things he *did* know about, so that people would be so confused, they'd assume he was a genius. "My dad is the one who's crazy," I said finally.

"Fine, Martha, great—so your dad is crazy. What the *hell* is wrong with your mother?"

I went downstairs. "What about the car?" I asked my mother coldly. "Are you giving it to Hildy, at least?"

"What, so your father can use it?"

"Mom, you're not even going to need it in New York!"

"I told the Cal students it comes with the house."

I went outside to wait, slamming the front door hard behind me. I sat on the curb, pulled the shirt away from the drying blood. It didn't show through the shirt. When the cab arrived, it let my father and Hildy and Drew out a little way down the street. I was glad it was just them and not anyone called Shalimar or Mallomar or whatever the hell her name was.

I couldn't remember the last time we kids were in the corner park with a parent. It was a place defined by the absence of parents, where Hildy and I, and later, Drew, had climbed rocks, pretended to be Indians, played kickball, tried to sell crafts we'd made, and joined with neighborhood kids to form clubs with complicated premises for membership, clubs that fizzled as soon as we'd set them up.

We all sat together on a bench, with me at the end next to Drew. I let Hildy and Drew sandwich my father, because even in this moment, as grateful as I was that he'd come over so quickly, I preferred not to sit next to him.

My father lit one of his Shermans. Hildy and Drew wouldn't look at me, and thinking about it from their point of view, I knew they had every right to be mad that I'd found out what was going on before they did. I leaned across Drew to give my father the list with my right hand, keeping my left forearm covered. He unfolded the list, looked at it, folded it again, and put in his shirt pocket, and still no one said anything.

"Look, I'm sorry, you guys!" I blurted, twisting my body to face all of them. "I had nothing to do with the decision! I tried to talk her out of it!"

"Martha," Hildy began, "the thing is—"

"Drew," I began, "I think you have a right to know that Mom has some boarding school planned for you. Like, a farm or something."

"Shitballs," Drew said.

"I told her I thought we should just double up and rent out a room or two! Or get an apartment."

"Martha, we're losing our lease," Hildy blurted.

"What lease?" Wasn't that for renters, not home owners?

"To Smoke and Records!"

"*What?* Why?"

"The store is closing, end of the month. The landlord wants us out." *Us.* Why did Hildy always have to act so grown-up?

"But Dad! Why can't you just—?" I wanted my father to fix it with the landlord, explain the situation we were in, tell the landlord he just had to stay. "When did you find out?"

"A few days ago," my father said, his head bent.

"But he didn't tell us until this afternoon," Hildy said.

"Well, can't you start another store?" I didn't care that Hildy and Drew knew before I did.

Hildy said, "We can't. Because of business debt."

"Oh." I didn't even want to understand what this all meant. My father had to help us. He just had to.

"Don't you worry, kids," my father said, as if on cue. "Just sit tight. It'll all work out." We sat on the bench for a long time. He lit another Sherman, and then another, until I felt dizzy from the smoke. He said nothing about the human condition.

I missed the bus for school the next morning, mainly because I'd been up really late. Homework didn't magically get done just because you were having a hard time at home, or wouldn't even have a home pretty soon. Mrs. Fry had assigned an extra-long passage of the *Aeneid* to translate, we were having a test in Trig, and the outline for the semester-long project for my Independent Study class was due by the end of the week.

I was kind of glad to have a pile of work, since I couldn't sleep anyway, but it was hard to concentrate. I could hear my mother snoring, not a care in the world, with these occasional stupid weird throat noises that made me hate her even more. Why couldn't there be anything about my mother that was admirable or nice or appealing? Just one thing?

Somehow I could tell Drew was still awake, so I went in. He was reading his comic books under the covers with a heavy chrome flashlight, out of habit I guess, as if he'd forgotten that it no longer mattered if my mother had a cow over his staying up late on a school night. What was she going to do, put him in a reform school?

I sat down on the side of Drew's bed and asked if he wanted to talk. He didn't. Instead, he showed me the latest *Superman* with his flashlight, starting with the cover. *ACTION COMICS*, the top banner screamed. At the bottom, you were urged to guess the secret identity of the President's killer, which was guaranteed to shock you.

I'd never paid much attention to comic books, because the ones Hildy used to read, with Archie and Veronica and Jughead and Betty, made no sense to me. Cars, dating, bikinis, milkshakes, button-down cardigans with letters sewn on them to signify athletic talent? The characters were supposedly my age, but they might as well be sailors on a whaling ship for how easy it was to relate to them.

But when Drew read *Superman* to me, adding sound effects (*Boom! Bam! Kapow!*) and explaining past plot elements as he went along—it was surprisingly soothing. I lay next to him on top of the blanket, sharing his pillow. I guess this was comforting to him, too, because it wasn't long before there was a pause, and then the flashlight gave a little *clunk* against the wall and was suddenly shining up onto the ceiling. Gently, I pried it out of Drew's hand and turned it off, straightened the blanket, patted his head, and crept back to my room. I finally got to sleep after two, and wound up not hearing the alarm clock.

I know this is weird, but I was practically crying by the time I got to school—not because of what was going on in my family, but because I was late. Concert Chorale had already started. We were doing *Carmina Burana*, and no one knew the piece yet, which meant it was all the more important for me to be there.

Quickly, I made my way up the shallow risers to the back of the room. Since I'd started Berkeley High in tenth grade, Mr. Seton had sat me in the top row so that my voice would carry and help everyone in front of me. I pulled out my music and sat down next to Paisley, who, without interrupting her singing, showed me the right page and measure in the next-to-last movement, "Blanziflor et Helena."

But something was off. Really off. I knew Paisley had pointed to the right spot, because the rhythms looked right, and the intervals seemed right, too. The problem was, the notes I was hearing didn't correspond with what was written. Why was I suddenly unable to read music? Why couldn't I find the right note with my voice? "What the hell—?!" I whispered to Paisley.

She pointed again.

"Those aren't the notes!" I whispered fiercely.

"Bar 110!" Mr. Seton shouted as he conducted, probably noticing my agitation and trying to help.

"He's having us read it down a whole step," Paisley answered.

"*What?* Why?" I demanded.

"It's too high for the sopranos," she whispered. "There's this high B at the end, and since it's so early in the morning, Mr. Seton said we should practice it—"

Without stopping, Mr. Seton said, "Settle down back there!" as if Paisley and I were throwing spitballs or something.

"I can't—I can't even read this!" I sputtered, and all at once, like one of those people in the movies who are about to vomit and are frantically trying to make it to the toilet, I dropped the score and bolted out of the room as if the tears were puke in my throat. I didn't grab my purse or my books, or even my protective pea coat.

I leaned against the bulletin board just outside the Concert Chorale room, crying, then slid down, not really intending to sit on the polished vinyl floor but just kind of letting it happen. Maybe everyone else in the room could sing an A and pretend it was a B, but I certainly couldn't. With the pitches not corresponding to my internal sense of the note, it was as if I'd been exposed to Kryptonite. My special powers were gone, never mind the fact that I was section leader and would likely get several of the solos in *Carmina Burana*. I cried, wiped my nose with my sleeve, and cried some more. I'd gone from being more than competent to being worse than everyone else.

"Martha?"

I looked up, startled. It was Clifton, carrying a large stack of sheet music.

"Clifton!" I scrambled up, wiped my eyes. "I was—I'm just—" *Shrug.*

"What happened? Are you okay?"

It was way too hard to explain; no one would understand. But then I remembered: Clifton Cray had perfect pitch, too. "Mr. Seton moved us down a whole step! And we're supposed to sight-read! How can I sight-read when I have to transpose every single note at the same time?"

"Oh, God, that would drive me up the wall," he commiserated.

"I *know*! It's not fair!"

"—in fact—now that I think about it, it *did* drive me up the wall. This one summer, when I went to Cazadero? I tried clarinet instead of violin, and the same thing happened to me!"

"They transposed the piece?"

"No," he explained, "it's the damned notation! So confusing! You're reading a C-natural, so you play what's *called* a C on the clarinet. But the sound is actually a concert B-flat!"

"You're kidding me." I had some vague sense of the B-flat clarinet, but had never given much thought to its notation, how confusing it would be.

"I'm *not* kidding! It's enough to give you, like—"

"A seizure!"

"Exactly," he said. "Frothing at the mouth."

Clifton Cray had suddenly grown into himself, but it was more than that. There was something so *formed* about him—confident, solid, as if he had never once experienced self-disappointment. He'd followed me around like a puppy for years. Now I realized I'd mistaken that for a permanent condition of shakiness.

"What are you doing here, anyway?" I asked, trying not to stare. I'd never noticed before that underneath Clifton's eyes, the skin was just a little darker, and that instead of making him look tired, this made his eyes look bigger and more expressive. The creases at the edges of his mouth were also a little darker than the soft, pillowy lips. "Isn't Orchestra first period?"

"Krantz sent me to give these scores to Seton," Clifton answered. "C'mon, let's go in," he coaxed, putting a hand tentatively at the small of my back. A little shiver went up my spine.

I looked up at him. "Thanks, Clifton. You really cheered me up."

"Isolating the spots!" he said, and winked.

21

ABD

By the time I got to the store after school, Hildy and Drew were already there. I stuffed my pea coat behind the counter as Hildy filled me in. My father had gone with Shalimar in the morning for a meeting with Mr. Hinge, a lawyer who specialized in something called family law.

I remembered Mr. Hinge. He was a Chesterfields smoker and a die-hard fan of the composer my father referred to as Wagner the Interminable. A history teacher of mine had said Wagner didn't like Jews and that his music was later used by Nazis to stir up anti-Semitism among the German people. Apparently this was not my father's primary objection. One time, right in front of Mr. Hinge, he said, "Isn't there some quote about Wagner's music being better than it sounds?"

"Oh, for God's sake, Jules, shut up," Mr. Hinge had retorted.

My father had started telling people that Smoke and Records would be closing soon, and he wasn't ordering new merchandise anymore. There were already a few holes where certain candy bars and a couple of cigarette brands had run out. Hildy was worried about how we could afford a lawyer, because my father owed money to people who supplied the store with stuff to sell; that was what "business debt" meant. Plus, Shalimar had told Hildy it sounded like my father would need a lawyer for more than just one conversation. Mr. Hinge thought that stopping my mother was going to take time, maybe a month or two.

Stopping my mother: it hadn't occurred to me. If Mr. Hinge could stop Willa Goldenthal, could he make her go back to the way she was before? If he could make her go back to the way she was before, could he force her to change some other things, too?

It was gloomy at the store, but somehow business went on; people kept coming in for cigarettes or an issue of *Ramparts* or Jacques Loussier doing jazz versions of Bach pieces. When I arrived, my father was pacing, clearly annoyed by one of the regulars, known in our family as "the mooch." The mooch was at it again—standing in the magazine area and leafing through the pages of the latest issue of *Playboy* in his short-sleeved seersucker shirt, not noticing the foot traffic all around him. As always, the mooch was careful to turn the pages gently so he didn't damage them. But after all these years, he'd still never even bought his cigarettes at Smoke and Records, or candy, or gum. And this time, while he was "reading," he had a bright green *RECORDS—AT A DISCOUNT!* bag lodged between his feet.

I braced myself; I just knew that any second, my father was going to let the mooch have it once and for all. Instead, my father went up and leaned strangely, quietly underneath the guy, as if he were looking at the *Playboy* upside down. I heard a *click* that sounded like a chrome cigarette lighter closing; then my father stepped away. But I still didn't understand what was happening until a second or two later.

"Hey, what the hell—*HEY!*" The mooch leaped backward and dropped the burning magazine on the floor, stomping it out, trying not to get his feet tangled up in the green *RECORDS—AT A DISCOUNT!* bag. The faint smell of singed hairs from the mooch's forearms wafted toward me as Bob Metcalf guffawed. The mooch was sweating, and his belly was heaving up and down.

"I'll show *you* the fires of passion!" my father shouted gleefully. Drew whooped with laughter, and Hildy and I looked at each other and giggled as the mooch ran out of the store with the green bag, nearly mowing down a pretty, skinny woman as she came in.

My father scooped up the ruined Playboy and bowed elaborately, as if he had just done a magic trick for the customers. There was clapping, and one guy gave a loud whistle in appreciation. Drew stood next to me and kept saying, "That was *so* cool!" over and over.

"Shalimar, you missed it!" said Hildy.

"Missed what?" The pretty, skinny woman—that was Shalimar. She turned to me. "You must be Martha!" she said, reaching out a thin hand. I could tell right away that she wasn't really my father's girlfriend. She was way too young for that, and way too neat a person. She was tall and bubbly, and she wore a long, loose, green skirt and a green-and-purple peasant blouse. She smiled all the time. She seemed very intelligent. "Nice to meet you. I've already met Hildy and Dave."

"Drew," I corrected, tousling my brother's hair.

"Drew, of course! Duh! I'm very sorry, Drew!"

"It's short for Andrew," I said. I wanted to help her.

"Right!"

I took the opportunity. "What does Shalimar mean? I've never heard it as a name. Only as a perfume, at Hink's. Which—I really like the smell," I added.

"Well, my real name is Susan, but everyone's named Susan! So I started calling myself Shalimar a few years back. In Pakistan and in India, it means 'abode of love.' My parents think I'm cracked, of course, just like they think I'm cracked for studying Indian art. They still call me Susie."

"Don't you hate that?" Hildy asked.

Shalimar shrugged. "It's just the way they are," she said. She turned and looked at me with concentration, as if I were the only person around. "I know you're wondering," she said.

What was I wondering? Why she'd have my father for a friend, I guessed.

"I'm twenty-six," she said. "I'm getting my PhD in Art History. Or maybe I should call it my ABD."

"AB—?"

"All But Dissertation. You know. I have all my other work completed. Courses, research, all that. I just have to write it now."

"Oh."

"Your father is such a sweetie."

"He is?" *Shrug.*

"He's been helping me as I write it," she went on as we kids gathered around. There was something magnetic about her. "He's really encouraging—I've never had that kind of encouragement. The last month or two, I've gotten so much done!"

Hildy nodded in agreement, catching my glance: *See? Our dad really is great.*

"I mean, it's not that I don't know what to say," Shalimar explained. "I'm writing about Amrita Sher-Gil—she's an Indian painter who led this amazing life. She was only twenty-eight when she died, but her work is just as significant as what the masters of the Bengal Renaissance accomplished. That's what I'm trying to show in my dissertation. But the thing is, I have this block. Like, writer's block. I get really tense when I actually have to sit down and do it."

"Kids! Let's go!" My father was itching to get out of there. It was really too early for dinner, but he wanted to take us to the "Human" Village, and I could definitely eat.

"Are you coming with us?" Hildy asked Shalimar.

"You go on," Shalimar said. "I think your father wants to spend some time with you. Besides, I already ate." She kissed my father on the cheek.

On the way over, my father walked ahead, his arm across Drew's shoulders. Hildy and I talked. "Shalimar seems nice," I said.

"She's really neat," Hildy agreed.

"Why did she go with him to Mr. Hinge's?"

Hildy stopped and looked at me. "Dodo! They're sleeping together!"

"What—? Are you sure? I mean, she's so young! Why would he even think of—why would he be interested in her?"

"Well, Martha, *duh*, she's a lot prettier and younger than Mom, not to mention nicer. And smarter."

"But—isn't Dad against, you know, like, graduate school and that kind of stuff?"

Hildy didn't answer. "Shalimar thinks he's really great. Maybe that's what he needs, after living with our dear mother."

"But I mean, is she—" I couldn't quite put my finger on it. "Does she, like, love all the same music that Dad does?"

"I think she likes Joni Mitchell, and Bob Dylan, and that piece *Bolero* by Ravel. Oh, and the Brandenburg Concertos."

"Concerti," I sighed. I might as well stop trying to understand. I was the one who loved Beethoven string quartets, and the Bach unaccompanied cello suites performed by Rostropovich, and the Barber Concerto for Orchestra—and my father still didn't like me. When he was singing along at the end of the last movement of the St. Matthew's Passion—praying, almost, savoring that long, exquisite, dissonant B natural just before the piece ends—I understood that he couldn't be disturbed. And now he chose to spend time with someone who didn't recognize how irritating *Bolero* is? Seriously, this is the kind of crap I had to deal with.

Mr. Hinge had told my father not to fight with my mother over her plans. My mother sounded "emotionally unstable" to Mr. Hinge, and if provoked, she might do something even crazier. Mr. Hinge had also said I was considered old enough, legally, to have a say in where I lived.

In a back booth at Human Village, Drew and I sat on one side and shared an order of pot stickers. Hildy, sitting next to my father, had a bowl of won ton soup. My father ignored a large plate of fried rice and tried to explain what Mr. Hinge had said. I'd never seen him try so hard to imagine what it would be like to be us kids. I could practically see the gears inside his head grinding with the effort. Or maybe the gears inside his heart.

Apparently, I didn't have to call any of the people on my mother's list, and besides, my father had given the list to Mr. Hinge, so he didn't even have it anymore. Mr. Hinge said that for now, I could stay with a friend. As we sat there, I allowed myself to relax, a little, into my father's reassurance. Stephanie had told me Sylvia said I was welcome to move in with them whenever I wanted. I'd started to adjust to that idea, even though I kept having flashes of worry because Sylvia wasn't on my mother's list. I'd always tried so hard to give my mother no reason ever to be angry with me. It felt very weird that I was now being told by my father—and by a lawyer—to do something my mother would be furious about.

"What about me?" Drew wanted to know.

My father picked up his chopsticks and poked at the fried rice, the little watery cubes of carrots, the withered peas. "So listen, son, I think you might like that farm—"

"Why can't I stay with you?"

"—it could be an adventure for you. And it'll be temporary, anyway."

"Dad, how do you know that?" I couldn't help asking.

"Just sit tight, all of you! It'll all work out."

"Stop saying that!" I cried. When I was worried about a test in school, he was always saying *it'll all work out.* And I would say *yeah, it works out because I study!* I was sick of it.

My father shot me a glance, the one that said *how dare you judge me?*

Shrug. Shrug.

"Stop that shrugging now!" he said.

"Dad, she can't help it," Hildy said.

My father sighed very slowly, put down his chopsticks. "Son, I can't really do anything. Not just yet. I'm working on it."

Drew was silent. We all were. Then Drew started to talk, but we could barely hear him. "Two. Three. Five. Seven. Eleven—"

"Drew, what are you saying?" Hildy said.

"—Nineteen. Twenty-three." Drew was louder now. "Twenty-nine. Thirty-one—"

"He's reciting the primes," I said. "Drewy, stop it now." I jiggled his arm.

"Stop it," my father said.

"—Fifty-three. Fifty-nine. Sixty-one. Sixty-seven. Seventy-one—"

My father pounded his fist on the table so loudly that we all jumped. I looked at him, ready to glare, but there were tears in his eyes. "Son, stop it now," he said thickly. "I'm doing the best I can. Eat, now."

No one ate.

"I said *eat!*"

We were all crying. I pulled my left sleeve down, not wanting the cut to show, and put my arm around Drew, kissed the top of his head. Tears ran down my face. I needed to blow my nose, and as I reached for a napkin from the chrome holder and caught sight of the red menus stacked upright against the wall with *Hunan Village* printed in large gold fake-Chinese letters, I realized something. We Goldenthals were crying because grief was part of the *Hunan* condition.

I started to laugh, and I couldn't stop. I laughed so hard that I couldn't talk, even though everyone was demanding to know what was so funny. My father and Hildy got mad at me, but at least Drew started eating again. Then he said, "Shitballs! I'm full."

I kept expecting my mother to ask me about the list or my phone calls, but she didn't. She didn't seem to care that Hildy was staying with my father, either. She was busy putting things in boxes and making arrangements on the phone, and wasn't spending any extra time in bed, as far as I could tell. Drew dragged a heavy old army-green sleeping bag with a plaid flannel lining out of his closet and set up camp on the floor of my room. My mother didn't even seem to care about that. She just called it Drew's "camping trip."

In the evenings after I read to him, Drew fell asleep, and I did more homework and packing, as quietly as I could. Sometimes I lay in my bed and wept, my face itching as the tears rolled down into my ears. Sniffing would have been noisy, and blowing my nose would have been worse. I kept a roll of toilet paper behind my pillow and tried to blot the flow silently.

Of course there was nowhere to put the used tissue. When I grew up, I was going to have a wastebasket in every single room, even closets, and pretty pastel-blue and pink and yellow boxes of Kleenex everywhere so that even if you were crying, at least there was something to cheer you up a little. But for now, I wound up shoving the balled-up wads up my nightgown sleeves, just like my mother. I hated her with every cell in my body. In the mornings, the only thing that got me out of bed was that I knew if I missed school or was late, she'd never write me a note.

22

hinge

The landlord had extended the lease for an extra couple of weeks, but there was still a lot of merchandise to deal with. For now, my father was selling popular items like magazines and candy at the regular price. Other stock, like imported pipes and loose tobacco, would have to be sold at cost, or at a loss. At least the unopened cartons of cigarettes and the boxes of twenty-four candy bars could be returned to the suppliers for full credit.

The distributors wouldn't take back very many of the LPs. Mr. Lucas had agreed to buy up some of the inventory, but there were a lot of leftovers. Mr. Lucas didn't have room for everything, partly because he carried a lot more pop than my father.

My father said he'd be damned if he was going to offer even his pop records to those cretins at *RECORDS—AT A DISCOUNT!* He'd sooner move every single leftover LP up to his apartment and start selling the records at the flea market. He'd sooner let his kids open the shrink-wrap and listen to whatever they wanted. Whatever *we* wanted.

There was something disorienting about my father's sudden permission, and Hildy and I both ignored it without even discussing it. All the Beatles records we'd ever dreamed of (most of them, anyway,

170

since some were sold out)? It was as weird as if my mother suddenly got us Barbies, or started keeping Nestle's Quik and fresh milk around the house. If we had a house.

Hildy and I met at Smoke and Records each afternoon, something my father seemed to expect and appreciate at the same time. There was work to do; the cartons he was packing needed to be taken up to the apartment, one at a time per person because records were so heavy. Even though we didn't talk about it, Hildy and my father and I had to be together to console ourselves about Drew, who'd been gone for nearly three weeks now.

We called Drew from the apartment every day as soon as the in-California long-distance rates went down at six o'clock, but we didn't always get to talk to him. There was just the one pay phone in the dormitory, and the line could be busy for hours, which was another reason for starting at six. Sometimes we'd get through, and whatever kid happened to answer the phone wouldn't go find Drew, or said they didn't know who he was.

With Shalimar's encouragement, my father tried calling the Plowshares office during the day, not caring that daytime long distance cost more—sometimes calling right from the store, where the call was even more expensive because rates were higher from business phones—but he didn't get far. Maybe it was Plowshares' policy not to let the kids talk to their parents very much. Or maybe my mother had warned them not to allow contact between my father and Drew, Jules being a very sick person and a highly damaging male role model, blah blah blah.

My father's studio was already jam-packed with LPs, but Hildy and I kept making trips, and if Shalimar was around, she helped, too. When we got inside the apartment, we'd take the records out of the cartons and stack them on top of the bookcases as high as we could. The clutter didn't bother my father; he just didn't want us putting the records anywhere near sunlight or the radiator, or anyplace where they might be tripped on. Once we were done, we'd bring the empty cartons back down to the store to be refilled.

Hildy and I sorted through the records, making room in the front closet for our finds. While she set aside Beatles and Simon & Garfunkel albums, I found other treasures, like Prokofiev's Symphony #5, the one whose second movement opened with that violin and clarinet dialogue they used as an introduction to the nighttime news. Finally, I had a copy.

Sometimes we'd open a box to find awful surprises—Herb Alpert and the Tijuana Brass; a Lesley Gore album with "It's My Party" on it; an album by Perry Como, whom my father had always called Perry Coma because he was about as musically engaging as general anesthesia.

The few times I got to talk to Drew before taking the bus back to Stephanie's, he sounded like a smaller version of himself. He didn't like it at Plowshares. Most of the kids there were older than he was. He was trying to be brave, but I could tell he was scared, and I was glad he had some street smarts.

"I'm telling you, it's the other way!" my father grumbled as we rode north in the cab along Shattuck. We were going to see Mr. Hinge and had taken a cab so we wouldn't be at the mercy of the bus schedule.

"It's not," Hildy assured him. "Mr. Hinge said Shattuck at Hearst, across from Oscar's. I wrote it down right here on this piece of paper."

"Bullshit!" My father clutched the carton of Chesterfields he'd brought for Mr. Hinge. "It's south of University," he insisted. "We've overshot!"

"Dad, calm down," I put in, worried about what the cab driver thought of us and wondering why Hildy, as usual, didn't seem embarrassed. According to Hildy, my father and Shalimar smoked grass every night after the phone call to Drew. Sometimes Hildy joined them. Hildy said in my father's case, grass was a good idea, because it made him a lot calmer. Too bad the pot had apparently worn off.

"Look, Dad, there's Oscar's," Hildy soothed. "Mr. Hinge said it was a brown-shingle with a bright green door. See it?"

My father folded a couple of bills from his pocket and handed them to the driver as the cab stopped. In spite of myself, I suddenly felt a wave of pity for my father. Just his folding the money with such self-assurance when we didn't have any—it was almost dignified the way he did it, hurriedly, as if it were just part of being a man, as if nothing could be more obvious, when things were completely falling apart, than going to a lawyer with his daughters and taking a taxi instead of a bus. I was glad I was still a kid for now. I didn't have to figure out what to do with plaid tobacco pouches or Italian operas that no one wanted. I didn't have to find lawyers or figure out how much to tip cab drivers.

We were a few minutes late, but it didn't seem to matter because Mr. Hinge was on the phone when we got there. There was barely room for the three of us in his airless office. My father took one dark wood chair with a curved back and Hildy and I shared the other one. The armrest kept poking into my back.

The place smelled of stale cigarettes and dirty socks and was paneled in fake dark wood that buckled out from the wall in certain spots. It was hard to picture Mr. Hinge getting excited over the thick sounds of Wagner. The office was more the workspace you'd imagine for a jazz sort of person.

Mr. Hinge got off the phone and stood up, greeting us with a gruff "Hello" and not asking us what our names were. His white Oxford shirt was tucked in diagonally across his fat belly, and the last button wasn't fastened. My father handed him the carton of Chesterfields. Mr. Hinge grunted his thanks and put the smokes in a drawer. He sat down and lit a Chesterfield from an open pack, exhaled, and rested the cigarette in an indented corner of a huge, filthy glass ashtray that was already full of butts. My father lit a Sherman.

"You told me Plowshares was a farm," was the first thing Mr. Hinge said. He sounded angry.

My father shrank back a little. "Some farm in Fresno that's also a school, is what Willa said."

Mr. Hinge's glasses were perched on top of his head, and he pulled them down onto his nose. He started looking under a stack of papers for something, then under another stack. He stood up again, turned around, and found a pad of yellow lined paper with writing on it, on top of a dusty, faded pile of magazines behind him that was so tall, it looked like it was about to fall over.

"My mother put Drew there because it's a place for rebellious kids," Hildy put in. "Which is completely unfair. He's not—"

"Simmer down, now," my father said to Hildy. Lawyers charged a lot of money.

"But Dad, Mr. Hinge needs to know that Drew is a good boy!"

"Now, you told me your son was eleven," Mr. Hinge said.

"I know," Hildy said. "It's ridiculous, but my mother—"

"Jules, you didn't have to sign anything?"

"Sign what?"

"Papers. When you put your son in there."

"I *didn't* put my son in there," my father said, flicking his ashes into the tray. "I told you, Willa took him. Whatever papers needed to be filled out, I assume she took care of all that. Look, I admit it. Forms are just—not my thing."

Mr. Hinge let out a long sigh. The yellowed slatted window blinds were aimed downward. Somehow, the sunlight showing the dust on their rounded surfaces made me want to cry.

"Plowshares—Jules, I don't know how to tell you this."

"What?" Hildy and I said at the same time.

"Spit it out, Hinge," my father said.

"Plowshares is—they do have a farm there. But mainly, it's a facility for wards of the state." Mr. Hinge stubbed out his cigarette. He didn't look at any of us.

Hildy said, "Wards of the—what does that mean?"

"It's a place for juvenile delinquents in California whose parents aren't in the picture," Mr. Hinge answered quietly, "or who have no parents."

"But Drew *has* parents! *Two* of them," I said. *Shrug.*

"And he's *not* a juvenile delinquent!" Hildy put in. "He just likes to multiply numbers. I mean, he might've stolen some stuff, plus he sold the answers—"

I elbowed Hildy.

"What?" Hildy said to me. "The lawyer needs to know everything. And he has to keep our secrets, dummy."

"Pipe down, girls," my father said.

"In any case," Mr. Hinge went on, "this seems like an inappropriate placement, maybe even an illegal one."

"Illegal?" my father said. The ashes of his cigarette were about to fall off.

"Typically the kids are older. They have criminal records. They're drinking, they're in gangs, armed robbery, that kind of thing."

Suddenly, my father had had enough. He got up, stubbed out his cigarette. "I'm getting him the hell *outta* there."

Mr. Hinge boomed, "*Siddown*, Jules."

Slowly, my father sat back down.

"Listen to me," the lawyer commanded. "You let me work on getting your son out of there. *You* work on finding a job."

"Dad is losing his lease," Hildy said.

"I know that," Mr. Hinge said.

"And he has business debt," Hildy added.

Mr. Hinge looked at my father. "How much?"

"Around twelve thousand," my father said, his head down. "And I'm—well, I'm a little behind at the apartment."

Mr. Hinge gave a long sigh. "This'll be a challenge, that's for sure."

"Getting Drew out, you mean?" I asked. "What does that have to do with money?"

"Getting custody," Mr. Hinge said.

"*Custody!*" Hildy and I exclaimed.

My father didn't look as surprised as I would have thought.

"But I thought men couldn't get custody," I said. I realized I'd been thinking we were going to the lawyer to get him to force my mother to be a mother—even though she'd been in New York for several weeks now and our house was occupied by other people, strangers. Aside from one phone call I'd made to my grandparents' apartment from my father's place, to make sure my mother had arrived safely, I hadn't talked to her. I was imagining we'd explain the situation to Mr. Hinge, and he'd force my mother to come back and rent an apartment somewhere, and Drew would come home, and things wouldn't be so different from how they were before, and I could apply to college without so much disruption in my life.

"It's true that it's rare for the court to award custody to a father," Mr. Hinge answered. "But in cases where the mother is unfit, it does happen. And, of course, in cases of desertion," he added.

Unfit. Desertion. The words were so stark that I found them strangely soothing. But looking over at Hildy, I saw only grief.

"Lemme find out what the court is willing to do on an emergency basis," Mr. Hinge said. "That eviction paper will be helpful."

"Eviction? I'm only a little behind at the apartment. The landlord hasn't even—"

"No, no, no. The list of names that Willa gave your daughter, and that you passed on to me."

Mr. Hinge didn't look at me or Hildy, but my heart skipped a beat. *Shrug.* Somehow I'd known that in giving the list of names to my father, I was telling on my mother. There was something thrilling about it.

"You get a job, Jules," Mr. Hinge went on. "I don't care what it is. Just line something up for when the shop closes, to show that you can get some income going. Don't worry about your debts for now. We may have to look into bankruptcy."

Wait, I could help with this! I could quit my job with Mr. Lucas, but first I'd ask him, beg him, to employ my father instead. I could make the case, I was sure of it: whatever knowledge I brought to On Record, my father would bring a thousand times more. Of course, I'd have to talk to my father about behaving better, because—well, he just had to. "Dad? I could—"

"And Jules—lose the girlfriend," Mr. Hinge boomed.

"Shalimar?" Hildy said.

"It'll look better to the court if there's no confusion about your commitment as a father, and nothing inappropriate going on. It'll send a clearer message. Do you understand me, Jules?"

"Fine," my father nodded briskly. "But Hinge—" he paused. "You'll call the place for me? I can't seem to get—"

"Obviously!" Mr. Hinge exclaimed. "That's what I'm here for. I'll let them know there's a custody dispute brewing. And that there's a question as to the legality of the placement."

My father bolted up, ready to leave. "Look, Hinge," he said. It was almost a whine. "You get him the hell out of there. I don't care what it takes." Then he bent his head and talked in a softer voice. "I'm just not sure how I'm going to be able—"

"By the way, Jules," Mr. Hinge interrupted loudly, "I've never been happy with that Furtwangler recording of the *Ring Cycle* you sold me. The sound just isn't that great."

"What?" My father paused. "Jesus Christ! I *told* you, if it's acoustics you're after, the Sir Georg Solti is far superior."

"I know, I know. I should've listened to you."

"I still have the Solti," my father said, "with Birgit Nilsson as Brunnhilde. I'll put it aside, damn you. Since you seem to require bombastic excess in a listening experience."

"Fine."

"Tell you what," my father went on. "I'll throw in the Guarneri's complete Beethoven string quartets and any Schubert lieder I still have. Plus, I've got David Oistrakh's rendition of the Brahms violin sonatas. It wouldn't kill you to broaden your taste to include *actual* genius, you know, Hinge."

"Go to hell, Jules."

23

hink's

After the meeting with Mr. Hinge, I didn't feel like returning to the store with my father and Hildy. I'd left my school stuff there, thinking I'd go back after the appointment, but I suddenly couldn't stand my life, its endless rotation of math assignments, Latin quizzes, physics labs, Concert Chorale sectionals, shifts at On Record, and then the college forms I was supposed to pick up at the Berkeley High counseling center and start filling out. I somehow felt these things kept me afloat. They didn't.

I didn't want to eat out with my father and Hildy, spend money we didn't have. I didn't want to hear those brainwashed, bald-headed guys next to the food carts on campus chanting *Hare Krishna, Hare Rama, Krishna Krishna, Hare Hare* over and over again in their peach togas. I didn't want to see Shalimar. I didn't want to try calling Drew. I was tired of remembering where my things were, and I was tired of keeping going no matter what. Sometimes I forgot that I was tired, but today I felt it in my body. It was as if I were on my feet all the time, had been for weeks and months, and kept looking around for somewhere to sit or lie down, and there was never anything, so I kept going, because I just wasn't the type of person to sit right down on the ground to rest. Or lie there.

I could skip Smoke and Records, retrieve my school stuff tomorrow. My toothbrush and clean clothes were at Stephanie's, and she'd have the Latin book. We could finish the leftover spaghetti that Sylvia had made last night. We could drill each other on vocab and the passages from Virgil, with that weirdo Helvetica rubbing against our ankles with her grey body. We could talk about how Declan had gotten suspended again. I never seemed to get around to telling Stephanie about my "having feelings" for Clifton, if that was even the phrase for it. It was easier just to be one more girl who was pining over Declan Wilder.

There was a southbound 51 waiting right on the corner of University and Shattuck. Before he and Hildy hopped on, my father gave me change for the bus to Stephanie's.

If I took the 67 back to my old house, would the Cal students let me in? Would they believe me, that I lived there? I could prove it. I could tell them about the hidden cubbyhole in the kitchen pantry, or about the small opening at the back of my closet that linked my room to Hildy's. If I showed it to them—told them about how I'd passed notes and a sandwich to Hildy through that opening one time when my mother had banished her to her room—would they let me stay with them? There must be a quilt lying around in the linen chest. I could bring it into the bathroom and sleep in the tub, which would only be a problem if someone had to use the bathroom during the night. Or, I could sleep in the pantry. Or the living room. I could take the quilt onto the front porch and sleep out there. Maybe the Cal students would give me the car keys and I could sleep in the station wagon. I knew how to be nice. I knew how to convince people I was trustworthy and would be okay in a pantry or on the back seat of a car. I knew how to sit on only half a chair at a dinner table, or in a lawyer's office, to prove I could make do with less than other people.

I wandered south on Shattuck toward Hink's. I needed to pee, but besides that, there was something grand and predictable about

Hink's, an oasis of calm, that always lured me. Underneath the covered walkway in front, I walked across the elegant marble tiles next to the display windows. The blond hardwood floors just inside creaked familiarly as I walked past the ladies' makeup and perfume counters. As always, a melodious bell chimed an F-sharp every now and then—who knew why? To me, Hink's was a soothing riddle, changing whenever I needed it to be different, knowable when I needed familiar.

It wasn't true what people said, that you *knew* your downtown department store, or your house, or the back of your hand. There were always unexpected angles and perspectives, so many that it would be impossible in one lifetime to experience them all. However long I walked around Hink's, there would always be spots I didn't know, patterns too intricate to be memorized.

I made my way up the wide wooden steps toward the ladies' room, which was tucked behind a luxurious burgundy velvet curtain on the mezzanine. The stairs were kind of shallow, yet it seemed, in a weirdly pleasant way, as if I could lose my balance. At the landing halfway up, I turned around and scanned the store, taking in the lingerie, the women's coats, the makeup counter in the front, the drinking fountain at the bottom of the stairs, the girls' clothing racks. The heads: long blond hair, black Afros, grey curls. Women, waiting to talk to salesgirls or looking down at price tags.

While I was upstairs, I went to the employment window and asked for a job application. They weren't looking for anyone, but I sat down on a creaky green leather club chair and filled the form out anyway. I shrugged a few times when I turned it in, and I could see the lady noticing and deciding not to say anything. Downstairs again, I got a drink from the water fountain and approached the hat department at the west end of the store, where there was an exit. Against the sunlight that streamed in through the glass door, all the hats on display looked black. When I went back out onto the glaring, sunlit street it was kind of a shock to my senses, and I squinted my way up toward the bus stop.

When I got to Stephanie's, I wasn't ready to talk. So I started in about how incredibly senseless a punishment it was that Declan Wilder, who loved to cut school, had been forbidden to attend for a few days. Then I said I thought Declan's girlfriend Raquel was materialistic. She acted like she was so great, but had a whole bunch of those colorful gauzy Indian cotton blouses, which she wore without a bra. Probably deep down, I said, Raquel was using her clothes to compensate for not having substance as a human being, which was ironic, since didn't Declan Wilder seem like the type who would see right through that?

"What he sees right through is her blouse," Stephanie said.

We made a batch of oatmeal cookies and added so many chocolate chips that there was hardly any batter in between. Sylvia didn't approve of sugar, yet she kept chocolate chips and other cookie ingredients around as if they were an ordinary household supply you had to have on hand. It never made any sense to me, but I loved Sylvia for it.

Helvetica jumped onto the kitchen counter, we shooed her off, and she jumped back up again. I couldn't look at her anymore without the name getting scrambled up in my head as *HE EVIL CAT*, even though the whole reason Helvetica was evil was because of her being a "she." It was creepy, the way she couldn't quite settle into the beanbag chair where she slept in the corner of Brett's room, the sound of the little beans inside crunching under her paws when she moved around in the middle of the night. My third morning at Stephanie's, I'd found a dead mouse in one of the creases. At least none of its tiny limbs was missing.

Stephanie and I had the spaghetti while Sylvia was at her poetry workshop, and during the ads on *The Partridge Family* and *Love, American Style*, we quizzed each other on vocab. Sylvia never bugged us about homework or bedtime or how many cookies we ate, though she did say, when she came in from her workshop, that she was surprised we'd want to fill our brains with the inanities of commercial television when there were such great programs on KQED. Stephanie flared her nostrils at me, since this was the exact kind of remark that made her hate her mother. I rolled my eyes in sympathy and smiled.

Later, Stephanie and I put on flannel nightgowns and brushed our teeth. I didn't really have a good nightgown, so I always wore one of Stephanie's. I loved how the elastic in the wrists wasn't all worn out. You could hike up the sleeves and brush your teeth, so even if water and toothpaste dribbled down your wrist toward your elbow, your sleeves wouldn't get icky.

"So—are you worried about your solos?" Stephanie asked. I could tell she was dying to know about the lawyer appointment but didn't want to push. She was sitting on the edge of her twin bed next to me, putting her long hair into one thick side braid so it would be wavy tomorrow.

"Nah, not really," I said. "It's funny, I just kind of open my mouth and the sound comes out. I don't even shrug when I'm singing."

"You never told me that!"

"Yeah! I mean, sometimes it happens before, or after, but when I'm actually singing, it's like—that's the main thing my body is doing."

"Well, that just proves it's good for you," Stephanie declared. "I'll come to the concert!" She was about to fasten her braid with a purple ponytail holder.

"My dad is gonna try to get custody of us," I blurted.

"*What?*" She turned to face me.

"The lawyer said."

"Why didn't you *tell* me?" She tied the end of her braid. "Martha. Your mom will never let your dad get custody."

"I know, she'll have a conniption, but the decision isn't up to her. The lawyer said she should never have put Drew in Plowshares, that

she might have done something illegal because that's the wrong place
for him. It's more, like, for juvenile delinquents."

"Jesus! Did she know that when she put him in there?"

"No idea. But she might be in trouble for it, plus for the list of
names she gave me. Which—I gave that to my dad, and then he gave
it to the lawyer."

"You mean it's, like, evidence?"

"I guess. The lawyer is going to set up a court thing."

"Is your mom gonna come back for that?"

"I'm sure she will." She'd relish the chance to make my father look
bad however she could.

"I mean, where would your dad put you, anyway? Isn't his apartment just a studio?" Stephanie shook her head. "Martha, there's no
way they're giving him custody!"

"I know, Steph, don't have a spaz."

"Well, you're welcome to stay here. For as long as you want."

"Thanks." I wished I could stay right in Stephanie's room with her,
even though it would be cramped in her bed. Stephanie's things were
pink and purple and orange. The nightgowns were thick and freshly
laundered, and there were so many of them that they spilled out of
her bureau drawer. Stephanie now had Brett's fish tank in her room,
and it looked cheerful in there. The shutters on the windows were
white, and the floor was painted a dark rose color. It was the kind
of place that protected you, with things whose main purpose was to
be pleasant, things like sunlight and cozy flowery sheets and a full-
length mirror so you could see what you looked like when you got
dressed in the morning and change your mind about what to wear if
you wanted.

Eventually I went in to Brett's room and turned on the nightlight,
got in bed and listened to Helvetica settling in. No matter how hot it
was during these fall days, there was always an edge of chill at night.
I tried not to think about the draft that came in through the opening

at the bottom of the doors leading out to Brett's porch, which was probably how the mouse had gotten in. I tried to ignore the lump in my throat. I didn't like Brett's drab green walls, the dark wood cabinets with black pulls, the navy plaid sheets. I couldn't even listen to music, because he'd brought his turntable and speakers with him to Humboldt State. We still had Stephanie's record player, but Brett had taken a lot of the records.

What was my mother going to do when she found out that, because of me, my father's lawyer had evidence against her? And what about Plowshares? She'd be furious about being "undermined" in what she thought was right for Drew. She'd say that she had insight, and the whole rest of the world wasn't psychologically sophisticated. And if I didn't see things her way, she'd hate me even more than she already did.

As I lay on Brett's pillow, it was Hildy I ached for. I missed the way when we were younger, she would read and read, not caring that her hair was messy or plastered to her head. It never bothered her that when she gave her attention over to a book, there was a whole world that she *wasn't* paying attention to: how did she feel safe doing that? I missed the candy and gum stashes she'd always kept in her room at home, wrappers strewn all over her bed. I missed her knowing everything better than I did. I missed how she would straighten out my blouse sometimes, or my hair, saying, "Here, Marth, lemme fix your perceptions! They're so lopsided!"

24

c**o**urt

With all the foot traffic in and out of the store, someone was bound to be looking for a violin. Mine had been sitting in the back of my closet for years, and my mother hadn't even noticed that I'd left with it. My father tried to talk me out of selling it. He said I might want to play again someday. I told him no, and a few days later, he got sixty dollars for it at the flea market. He didn't thank me.

A professor in the English department wanted to get rid of his spare car, an old turquoise Plymouth automatic with gears you changed by pushing these neat rectangular buttons on the dashboard. My father gave the professor all the remaining Bach cantatas and Handel oratorios, two or three dozen jazz records, and the big speaker he'd used the day that Nazi riot had been brewing across the street. I worried about my father's getting a car prematurely. If he was thinking we'd need it to pick up Drew, shouldn't he have waited, instead of maybe jinxing the whole thing?

Shalimar still hung around the store, but she didn't visit the apartment anymore except to help us bring cartons up. She told me and Hildy she was "on a roll" with her writing. I didn't know what she meant, since I didn't realize writing required luck, but Shalimar seemed happy. She was maybe a third of the way done with her dissertation on Amrita Sher-Gil. It was all because of my father, she said.

My father talked with the record distributors, but no one knew of any work. He went to Prufrock and Cody's and Moe's and all the other bookstores. Nobody was hiring. Part of the problem was that fall quarter had started, and students already had their jobs for the year. As the days passed and my father still didn't have work, I was glad we had the Plymouth, because he could take records down to the flea market and sell them there. But the warm weather we were having could warp the records if they were left in the sun, and especially if they sat in a hot car for storage. And then once it started raining, the flea market would close. In any case, it wouldn't be the kind of steady income Mr. Hinge had in mind.

I had decided to talk with Mr. Lucas before sitting my father down. I wanted to be able to present it to my father as a done deal—I'd gotten him a job, but he *had* to get along and do things Mr. Lucas's way. And I'd only tell Hildy once I'd accomplished the task.

"Mr. Lucas?" I began, at the beginning of my next shift. "Um, I was thinking—see, the thing is, my father really has to get a job, because—"

"He lost his lease," Mr. Lucas finished for me. He was counting bills from the register and filling out a bank deposit form. "Terrible thing."

"Right. So, um, I was wondering, wouldn't it be better to have him work here instead of me?"

"What's that, now?"

"My father. He needs a job." *Shrug.* "I was thinking—maybe he could take over my shifts? And maybe, um, a few more hours? He could help you organize the classical section!"

Mr. Lucas looked up with a strange expression, his pen stuck in mid-air. Then I realized he was trying not to smile. "Martha, uh, that probably wouldn't work out so well. Your dad likes things his way, and—"

"I know, I know, but—"

"Besides, I can't lose you," he added. "You're smart, and you learn quickly. You don't give me any crap. You're reliable. You try to be friendly. I like how you handle the customers. You just need a little self-confidence, is all."

"Oh!" I wasn't expecting a review of my performance. *Shrug.*

"Your father is used to having his own place, and—"

"Mr. Lucas, it's really nice of you to say those things about me. So, thank you! But—listen, I know my dad is kind of difficult, but—he's changed!" I said wildly.

"You know who *is* looking, though? The manager over at *RECORDS—AT A DISCOUNT!*"

"Oh! But I don't think—"

"They need someone to work evenings."

This wasn't what I was hoping to present to my father, but it was something. I knew he wouldn't thank me. Hildy did, though.

Smoke and Records shut its doors about a week after our meeting with Mr. Hinge. The landlord was going to put a Doughnut Central in there, one of those awful chain stores, but construction wasn't ready to start, so the place was locked up for now, and dark. It was too bad Drew wasn't there to see the way the shop looked just before it closed, because I knew Hildy and I would never be able to describe it with the impact it deserved. Drew would have been fascinated by the ripped out cabinets left at weird angles in the abandoned space, the deep wooden cubicles where all the candy bars had been, the huge gap left by the Coca-Cola machine, and the way the vinyl tiles underneath where it had been were a better color because they hadn't been worn down for all those years.

The Coke machine: as a little kid, Drew had asked dozens of times for orange soda. He was more interested in the purchase itself than in the "spicy bubbles" that made his throat sting. Hildy would lift Drew up, his head bobbing, his canvas PF Flyers kicking with excitement, his fingers trembling as he struggled to deposit the dime into the oversized red refrigerator. We'd all watch the red and white cup drop, followed by five or six little blobs of ice and, finally, the whoosh of brightly colored liquid that magically stopped just as the froth seemed about to spill over. "Use two hands, Drew," we'd remind him. "Careful!"

Now a few of the vinyl squares were broken or missing back there, leaving dusty, dried up black tar in a squiggly pattern in their place. Drew would have wanted to see how the whole store looked all cleared out, the tree house finally uncluttered, the cash registers empty and open. Maybe he'd be back soon. Maybe the court could make a special case for Drew to live with my father, even though no one's ever heard of a father's getting custody, let alone *my* father. Maybe I could relax into staying with Stephanie, "live a little," as she would put it, and my mother would be forced by the court to send Sylvia money for my rent and food.

On Friday, I took the day off from school to go to court with Hildy and my father. I didn't want to get behind, but I knew I was going to have to run interference when my mother got there. She'd for sure start bitching at me about how I'd been brainwashed along with Hildy and Drew, or worse, make a big fat public scene. In spite of everything, I stood the best chance of smoothing things out.

It was hard to picture my mother with a lawyer. All I could imagine was her tearfully telling the judge that she'd done the healthiest possible thing for me and Drew. If the judge didn't immediately grasp how brilliant and sophisticated her solution was, my mother wouldn't hesitate to shriek at him that his perceptions were lopsided, or demand to know why he couldn't see through Jules Goldenthal's psychologically seductive bullshit, blah, blah, blah.

But for some reason, neither my father nor Hildy seemed worried about my mother's presence, and as the minutes passed, then an hour, I realized she wasn't going to show up. Maybe my father and Hildy had already known. It made me kind of mad to think I was missing school for no good reason when I could've taken the Trig practice test and gone to my Physics lab, but I didn't share my resentment with Hildy. We sat quietly outside the judge's chambers. She twirled her hair and read *The Brothers Karamazov* while I alternated between my Virgil translation and the UC application forms I'd picked up at school.

Mid-morning, a social worker came out and asked if we wanted to go in and talk to the judge. Hildy went, but I didn't want to; even in my mother's absence I was scared of her. If I told the judge that my father was a hitter—though now not really a hitter anymore, but only because he was a pothead—it still wouldn't change my disloyalty. I know this sounds nuts, but I really felt like my just existing in this situation was a betrayal of my mother. Let Hildy be the one to tell the judge how awful my mother was.

Later, my father met with the social worker privately, and Mr. Hinge came out to talk to me and Hildy. His hair was combed. He was wearing a tan corduroy suit and a green paisley tie, and he looked much more like a lawyer. If I mentally squinted, I could almost imagine the Wagner making sense.

My father, Mr. Hinge said, had been awarded sole custody of me and Drew, effective immediately.

I don't know what I was expecting, but this wasn't it.

25

laundry land

I slept at Stephanie's that night. My father's apartment wasn't set up yet, plus there was no time to drive to Fresno; my father had a shift at *RECORDS—AT A DISCOUNT!*, and since he'd just started working there, he couldn't get out of it. None of us had planned for what happened: it was the opposite of my father's having gotten the Plymouth. Stephanie and I watched TV and made popcorn. I told Stephanie I'd still stay with her often. I made it sound like I was being forced by the court to go live with my father. This probably sounds stupid, which is why I couldn't quite say it to Stephanie, but with Drew coming home to my father and Hildy visiting often, I wanted to be part of my family again.

The next morning, when my father came to pick me up to go to Fresno, Shalimar was with him in the front seat in a long lavender dress and white sandals. She had a flowery silk scarf tied in a band around her forehead with the ends dangling at the back. I wasn't happy to see Shalimar, and the shrug happened four times in a row. I was afraid the court would somehow find out about her hanging around with us, and we'd be in trouble.

Hildy had taken the day off from Gabel. In the back seat, she reached out to touch pinkies, and I touched back and was able to relax a little. Shalimar was pretty and smiley, and everyone around her seemed to be having a better life just because she was there. We rolled down the windows. It was a warm day. Shalimar's hair blew in the wind, and she kept using her long, thin fingers to catch the ends and hold them down before forgetting and letting her hair go again.

Hildy had called Plowshares to ask for directions, writing them down on a piece of binder paper. My father was remarkably calm under her navigation, and four hours later, we were driving on a side road, past a huge overgrown garden behind a chain-link fence. As we pulled into the unpaved parking lot, the tires made a satisfying *crunch* on the gravel. It was the sound of our having arrived where we were going, and our having every right to be there.

We walked toward the main bungalow, hot gravel under our feet. Shalimar was getting tiny grey rocks in her sandals and falling behind, but no one waited for her. We needed to get to the office so Hildy could pull the court documents out of her purse. Then Hildy and I, and Shalimar, would need to try to keep my father from blowing up if it took the Plowshares people too long to produce Drew.

I was just thinking that the office could say the papers we had weren't the right papers, or that Drew wasn't there, when suddenly, there he was in his faded blue jeans and sweatshirt, grinning, waving a little uncertainly, but walking toward us, slowly at first and then fast, grey dust kicking up in the sunlight. Hildy ran up to him and hugged him close, and my father and I quickly followed. We were in a bundle, the four of us, hanging on for dear life.

Drew wasn't taller; if anything, he looked littler than I remembered, but at the same time, he seemed more grown up. He smiled again briefly and kept hugging us, but he didn't say much. His hair was dusty and he smelled like dirt. There was grime underneath his fingernails.

A tall, thin man came out of the bungalow and down the rickety wooden steps, carrying one brown grocery bag and one white shopping bag with handles. Two blond teenage boys, about Hildy's and my age, followed. They were both wearing white T-shirts, and might have been brothers. The older one was in brown corduroy cut-offs and looked mean. The younger one kept using the back of his hand to scratch his nose.

The man handed the bags to my father; they were Drew's things. He introduced himself as the director of Plowshares and smiled, showing teeth that had that overly white look of dentures. He was tan, his jeans were faded and dirty, and his slick dark hair was parted on the side and carefully combed.

"Well now, we really enjoyed having young Andrew here," the man said in a nasal tone that I could tell rubbed my father the wrong way. "Cute kid, and darned smart, too."

"Yeah, too bad he's leaving," the older of the two boys sneered. "He was just getting used to it, right, buddy?" He took a step toward Drew, and Drew moved away. The boy had a familiar lemony smell that I remembered from when Hildy and I used to go in and sniff the fragrance samples at Rexall. Vitalis hair tonic, that was it.

"Come on now, Jimmy, that's enough," the man said.

My father had handed the bags to me and Hildy. "Get in the car, kids," he said, not taking his eyes off the man. Shalimar had come up and was standing right next to my father. She slipped her arm in his. Drew and Hildy and I turned to leave, with Drew in the middle, but my father stayed put. I felt the familiar jelly in my gut, the certainty that he was about to start ranting or hitting. But when I looked back, Shalimar was pulling him gently toward the car. My father opened the trunk with the key, and we put the bags in. Drew climbed in back and sat between me and Hildy.

My father pushed the rectangular "reverse" button and backed out of the lot. As soon as we passed the garden, away from the gravel dust, we all rolled down the windows and kept them down all the way to the Foster's Freeze we'd seen near the highway exit.

Hildy and I kept holding out our pinkies to Drew, and he touched back, but he didn't smile. When we parked, Drew asked my father to open the trunk of the car. He got his sleeping bag out and, without a word, fed it into the big garbage bin at the back of the Foster's Freeze even though he was barely tall enough to reach the lid. We all just let him.

My father ordered burgers for all of us except Shalimar, who wasn't hungry. While he was at the counter, the rest of us sat down at an outdoor table and waited. No one said anything. Had Drew been beaten up by that older boy? Locked in a closet in the dark by the man? Why had Drew thrown away the sleeping bag? Usually I was able to imagine the worst, but this time it was as if my brain shut down. Drew had wet the bed, that was all. He was embarrassed, that had to be it.

A kind of quietness had settled over us, and I didn't dare break it. All I could think about was how much I hated my mother.

Soon my father brought over a chocolate milkshake and a Coke for all of us to share, a Tab for Shalimar, and a paper-lined red plastic oval basket with French fries in it. Our burgers came. Hildy told Drew about my father's job at *RECORDS—AT A DISCOUNT!* and how we were calling it *RAAD.* "Mom didn't even show up in court," I put in. Then Hildy told Drew he was going to get to go to Washington Elementary now instead of Cragmont, because Washington was closer to the apartment.

Drew didn't like Cragmont, especially since he had a horrible teacher this year, but I was worried that he might be unhappy about changing schools. His friends would still be at Cragmont, and next year, they'd be going to King Jr. High while Drew would be at Willard. "Washington is right across the street from Berkeley High," I said, removing a wilted pickle slice from my burger. "I can ride the bus with you this year. Or we can walk down together."

"Billions of blistering blue barnacles!" Drew responded, like

Captain Haddock from the *Tintin* books. Hildy and I exchanged glances. Drew wasn't normally a sarcastic kid.

Hildy said, "Tomorrow, we can go up to Smoke and Records so you can see what it looks like all dark and boarded up!"

After lunch, my father quietly drove. Now and then Shalimar would reach out for his hand and hold it for a while, until he let go to put it back on the steering wheel.

Once we were in Oakland, we stopped at Cost Plus and picked up three narrow foldable futons and three decorative pillows to sleep on. I was going to ask about sheets and pillowcases, but decided not to, and I suddenly realized it was a relief not having to use those kinds of things anymore. Besides, when my father pulled a five dollar bill and some change out of one pocket and had to go digging for more money in the other, it stabbed at my heart, even though the other pocket turned out to have tens and twenties in it and my father peeled bills off as if everything were okay. Hildy and Drew didn't seem concerned, but tears filled my eyes.

"Can we do laundry?" Drew asked as we pulled out of the Cost Plus parking lot.

Shalimar offered to get us started at Laundry Land on Telegraph while my father and Hildy went to Park & Shop for some groceries. Drew wanted to carry both of his bags of clothing, but Shalimar gently took the white bag from him, and as we walked into the crowded storefront, I tried to joke with Drew the way I would've joked with Stephanie and Brett about how pretentious the name "Laundry Land" was. "The Laaand of Laaaundry," I intoned, "is ruled by King Klothing and Queen Quilt. And there's a mean old hag who hides in the back. Letitia the Livid Laundress!" *Willa the wantonly wicked wolverine.* But Drew just held his bag close to his chest.

Drew and I did laundry at home, but we didn't know how to use coin-operated washing machines and dryers, or which soap to get or how much to use. We'd only been at the Laundromat when my father did his wash, and we'd spent our time gliding those cheerful baskets on wheels across the floor until he yelled at us to stop.

I liked Laundry Land, with its cute little dollhouse-sized boxes of detergent and the reassuring smell of clean, warm clothing as it came out of the dryer. Today, though, the row of white washing machines seemed intimidating, as if daring us to be serious about laundry for once. The coin slots looked like some kind of orthodontic nightmare, their tubs holding weirdly small loads while inexplicably, the huge burnt-orange dryers looked like they could hold four loads. There were instructions on the wall about how to be considerate in a Laundromat, and there was information on the side of an empty little detergent box sitting on a counter, but there was no guidance on how to actually accomplish the task. Laundry Land was a place for people who already knew what they were doing.

Drew wanted extra detergent. Shalimar handed me the bag and went to get the soap, and Drew and I found two available washers not far from each other. Drew emptied his bag into one of them and I started emptying out mine. A quarter, a nickel and two pennies rained down into the tub. So did a crushed Marlboro wrapper and an orange packet of Zig Zag papers. Drew's clothing smelled like dirt, sweat, cigarettes, marijuana, and Vitalis.

I had just fished the change, Zig Zag papers, and cigarette wrapper out of the tub and put it all into the pocket of my jeans when Shalimar returned with the soap. She seemed to know exactly what to do: double detergent, extra rinse cycle. It would take longer, she explained, but not as long as doing the same load twice, not as much running back and forth to Laundry Land, and not as expensive, either.

Back at the apartment with my father and Hildy, I had no chance to tell Hildy about the rolling papers or the cigarette pack, or the smells of marijuana and Vitalis. We unloaded the groceries, putting even the dry stuff like crackers into the fridge because of the bugs.

I teared up when I saw that every single item my father and Hildy had chosen was something we liked. London Broil steaks, Cheerios and a quart of whole milk, Nestle's Quik powder, four bananas, sliced jack cheese and a roll of liverwurst, a loaf of sliced sourdough, Best Foods mayonnaise and a pound of butter, Oreos, Cracker Barrel cheddar cheese and a box of Triscuits, cottage cheese and a large bag of Fritos, two cans of Heinz beans, two Jiffy Pops, Svenhard's bear claws for breakfast. Oh, and those pink-and-white-frosted Circus Animals made by Mother's Cookies, as if nothing in the world could be more obvious than that a mother makes cookies for her kids. There was also a bottle of Wishbone salad dressing—the one thing my mother had always bought that I liked—and a head of iceberg lettuce.

Iceberg: my mother said it had no food value. It was like eating water, she said.

26

creature comforts

By this time of day, the conga drumming in lower Sproul Plaza was beginning to die down, but you could still hear the Hare Krishnas chanting up near the food carts. My father had to be at *RAAD* soon, and he was anxious to get going on rearranging the apartment. I hadn't even thought about how to divide the space for the three of us, but my father had a plan. He had a dozen or more bookshelves that were two and a half feet wide by two feet tall, with a shelf dividing the bottom twelve inches from the top twelve inches—perfect for records. His idea was to stack the record shelves on top of each other and use them as partitions, with him and Drew on one side and me on the other (Hildy sleeping on my side when she came over). For once I was glad we had too many records.

"But Dad, what if there's an earthquake?" Hildy wanted to know.

"We won't stack 'em high," my father answered. "Just two shelves tall. Here, I'll show you." He started pulling records off the shelves so the bookcases would be easier to move, and we took the albums out of his hands eight or ten at a time, piling them temporarily on the kitchen table next to a clock radio and a big glass jar that held change, nails, rubber bands, and a couple of Lindy ballpoint pens. Shalimar kicked off her white sandals. She worked better barefoot, she said.

Soon my father had placed one bookshelf on top of another, in the middle of the floor, and Hildy and Shalimar and Drew started bringing the records back. My father didn't seem to care what order the records were in.

"But it's only four feet high," I pointed out. It wasn't much privacy.

"Simmer down, now," my father said. "Only your head will show."

"But, Dad, it isn't—"

"I told you, settle down!" It was the first time he'd raised his voice in days. "I know you miss your creature comforts," he accused.

Tears pooled in my eyes. I didn't know what a creature comfort was, just that I was hated for caring about the wrong things. Hildy looked like she thought I was being mean, and I didn't want to do anything that might upset Drew, so I swallowed hard. "Dad, that's not what I—"

"*You're* the problem here," my father said. "You're a paint-by-numbers person. The minute some creativity is required, some flexibility—you get uptight."

"Jules!" Shalimar said, laughing, as if my father had just come up with some hilarious witticism. *Shrug. Shrug.* I concentrated as hard as I could on not crying. Shalimar, Hildy, Drew—none of them found my father's assessment of me to be in need of correction.

I'd like to tell you I knew they were all full of crap. But I didn't. I still don't. Because—it's not that easy to believe in yourself when you're the only one in your family who does. So here's what I figured: even an uptight, uncreative person with a stupid shrug has a right to do well in school and apply to college.

Shalimar glanced at her watch. "Jules, do you want me to stay for a while and help the kids set up?"

My father didn't say no. "Make yourselves something for dinner," he barked.

"Dad, don't you want to take a sandwich or something?" Hildy asked. "Your shift doesn't end 'til eleven."

"Nah!" He waved his hand downward and turned to leave. He nearly tripped on Shalimar's sandals on the way out, but instead of throwing a shit fit, he just kicked the shoes gently aside.

"What are creature comforts?" Drew asked, after my father had gone.

"It means comforts," Hildy said.

"But then why is the word *creature* in there?" I added, trying to act normal, and wanting to keep the conversation going, since it was the first one Drew had started all day.

"Yeah, it makes no sense," Drew agreed. "Martha isn't a creature."

"Yes she is," Hildy said. "Everyone is."

"Maybe 'creature comforts' is related to the idea of a 'creature of habit,'" Shalimar suggested. "Like, you're accustomed to certain comfy things."

"Martha," Hildy said, "if this is gonna work, you need to stop taking Dad so seriously."

"Huh?" No matter how hard I tried, I never seemed to be able to figure out what I was doing wrong or how to change it. *Stop taking Dad so seriously*: it was as confusing as that line from my eighth-grade history textbook. *The general determined that the most effective course of action was to cut through and subdue the rebellion.*

What I wanted was to have a nervous breakdown. In nervous breakdowns, people stopped caring about their Latin translations or college applications or even their little brothers; they stopped functioning altogether. They were found in the gutter, rocking back and forth, singing a tune from *Guys and Dolls.* How did they do it? How did they feel entitled?

Shalimar patted Drew's shoulder. "Wouldn't you like a shower, sweetie?"

"Ten thousand thundering typhoons!" Drew exclaimed, and headed for the bathroom.

"Oh wait, the clothes!" Hildy remembered. "I'll go down and

move them to the dryer." She went into the kitchen and started grabbing coins from the jar.

With Drew in the shower, Shalimar and I were alone with the records and shelves. Her face brightened as she recognized one of the albums. "It's more fun doing work when there's music on, don't you think?" She put on *Any Day Now* by Joan Baez, and "Love Minus Zero" came through the speakers. She cranked up the volume and sang along. It didn't surprise me that she had a confident, pretty voice.

"It's hard getting used to a new place to live," she said, after the song was over. "A new situation."

"Yeah."

She looked straight into my face as "North Country Blues" came on. It was a sad song. "You know your father loves you very much," she said a little loudly, over the music.

"Oh, I know," said, my voice wavering. "He just doesn't like me." I grabbed a stack of records from the kitchen table.

"Martha, that's not true, not at all! He talks about you kids all the time. You're all he cares about."

You kids. Not *you, Martha.* Did Shalimar think I didn't notice?

But Shalimar was so lovely and so nice, she had to be right. And that meant I was wrong. My father had fought for us. He wanted us to have yummy food. I really couldn't see how he liked me, but then, I didn't like him, either.

Maybe part of the problem was that some of my mother had rubbed off on me. Maybe I had somehow gotten more of her personality than the others had. Maybe it was like those news stories about hungry toddlers in ghettoes who chew at the windows, and the windows have lead paint on them that poisons the children gradually, makes them lose the ability to learn, so that by the time they start school, they're already behind.

Shalimar and I managed to double the length of the partition. She turned the record over, and "Love is Just a Four-Letter Word" was playing when Drew came out of the bathroom, wrapped in a grayed-out white towel. I was just noticing the dirt still under his nails when Hildy got back.

Hildy and Drew and I were hungry, and Shalimar wanted to keep working on the partition, so we went into the kitchen and dipped Fritos in cottage cheese until the cottage cheese was gone and soggy little yellow bits of corn chips sat at the bottom of the waxy container. Hildy and I shared a banana. Drew wanted his own. We didn't bother to sit down.

After the Joan Baez album was over, Shalimar put it away and turned the stereo off. "Do you guys like this album? I mean, do you want me to put it someplace where you'll be able to find it?"

"Wait!" I said. "We have those records we put aside, remember, Hildy?" I trotted over and retrieved the Beatles albums and the Simon and Garfunkel from the floor of the front closet, and we put them together with the Joan Baez record at the far right end of the partition so we'd know where they were. I had stashed a few of my own favorite records in the front closet, too, but left them there for now: Volume I of the Bach unaccompanied violin partitas and sonatas performed by Henryk Szeryng, Bach's *Italian* concerto and other keyboard works, a record of Debussy piano works, Bach's *Magnificat*, and the Prokofiev symphony I'd found before. "Look, Drew!" I showed him the pop records. "And we can use the stereo whenever we want. Dad said!" A little smile flickered across his face.

We all worked until there were eight bookcases, four and four. We'd set the records up to face my father and Drew's side of the partition, so Hildy's and my side faced the backs of the shelves instead of the colorful album spines. We draped a paisley Indian cotton bedspread on top of the shelves to cover our side, holding it in place with a few stacks of dusty books. The wood showed for a few feet at the end of the partition, but it wasn't bad.

Shalimar was putting her sandals back on so she could get back to her apartment and her dissertation. She offered to walk me down to Laundry Land on the way. She chatted about how Amrita Sher-Gil's mother had been Hungarian, how Amrita Sher-Gil had studied at École des Beaux-Arts, how Amrita Sher-Gil's 1932 painting *Young Girls* had won a gold medal at the Grand Salon. When we got to Laundry Land, Shalimar turned to me and looked straight into my eyes. "Listen, Martha, I know you feel hurt by your mom," she said.

"Oh. Well, it's—"

"I just want to say that deep down, she loves you, Martha. Mothers always love their daughters. It's a very special relationship, trust me."

I nodded, trying to act mature.

"They say we choose our parents. Karmically, I mean. So we can learn the lessons we're here to learn in this lifetime. It's pointless to worry, because everything works out just as it's supposed to."

I hadn't chosen well, and it was my own goddamned fault. I hadn't learned enough in my previous lifetimes. *Shrug.*

I wanted to hate Shalimar, I really did. The problem was, she seemed like the kind of person who understood suffering. If she didn't understand mine, couldn't it be because my unhappiness wasn't that deep or important? At least, not compared to real problems in the world, like in India, where that woman artist was from? Or compared to what Drew had just been through? *You're the problem,* I told myself. *You're the person to hate.*

"Okay, well, see you soon, Martha!" Shalimar turned around and left.

Hildy had told me she'd put both loads of laundry into one dryer. I got the clothes out and started folding. A lot of Drew's socks were in bad shape, the white T-shirts were all grayish, and I couldn't help noticing there were stains in his underwear, sealed into the fabric by the heat of the washer and dryer. Had Drew been so scared at Plowshares that he'd gotten diarrhea? I winced.

We'd thrown Drew's shopping bags away, because they were

filthy, but someone had left a huge white plastic bag on one of the Formica countertops. It looked clean. I put Drew's things in there and started walking back up Telegraph toward the apartment, the bundle slung over my shoulder vagabond-style. I was thinking of taking the Durant-to-Bancroft alleyway next to Kip's so I wouldn't have to pass by *RAAD* and feel like I should go in and say hi to my father. But it was getting dark, and the alley might be creepy, so I stayed on Telegraph. Luckily, at the moment I was passing by, my father was doing a crossword puzzle, and he didn't look up.

27

brainwashed

In the evenings, after his shift, my father liked to go for a ride in the Plymouth to "unlax"— his word for "relax" that I'd never heard anyone else use and that probably wasn't a real word, just one more stupid thing about him. He'd drive to Hildy's place in Oakland to pick her up, drive around with her for a while, and be back in time for the eleven o'clock news.

"I mean, I'm right there, and he goes and gets Hildy," I complained to Stephanie as we walked across the courtyard at Berkeley High on our way to Latin. "He doesn't even pretend to want to spend time with me. If Hildy can't go, he visits Shalimar instead of taking the drive."

"Wait, I thought he wasn't supposed to have a girlfriend."

"I know, but Shalimar doesn't come over to the apartment. And she needs help with her dissertation."

"That's a funny word for her private parts," Stephanie snorted.

As we went up the steps to the "C" building, Stephanie said hi to two boys from her history class. I saw Clifton coming down the stairs and onto the courtyard, talking to Giselle, the cellist he'd started dating. Clifton and I waved at each other. I thought of shouting, "Isolating the spots!" but decided not to. Actually, I hate to admit this, but it pissed me off that Clifton had gotten a girlfriend about a minute and a half after finally having his growth spurt. A girlfriend who was my age. I kind of wished he'd stayed short so that no one else would notice what a great person he was.

"Steph, you think I should call my mom?"

"What? Why?" She held the door open for me.

"I dunno, to say hi? Check if she's okay?" It had been a week and a half since the custody hearing. No one at court had said they'd been in touch with my mother, but someone had to have contacted her to tell her that she'd lost. Now that I thought about it, of all the weird stuff I'd been through lately, maybe the weirdest was that such a huge thing had happened in our family, and I hadn't heard my mother screaming and crying about it.

"Well, she hasn't called you," Stephanie said as we started down the long hallway toward the language classrooms.

"No, but Stephanie, she can't."

"Why not?"

"Because I'm at my dad's and she doesn't want to talk to him! *Duh*."

"Martha, she didn't call when you were staying at my house, either."

"That's because she didn't approve of my being there."

"I swear, she always has an excuse! If she cared about you, she'd call."

"She can't," I repeated. "My dad says I should call her. But that's probably just him thinking he's so great because he's capable of being nicer than she is—"

"Yeah, when he's not hitting you."

"—when really, it's just another way of his acting like nothing bad has happened and I have no right to complain."

"Why can't Hildy or Drew call your mom?" We sat down next to each other in the Latin classroom.

"C'mon, I'm the only possibility. And I don't really even want my family there when I call her, and the apartment is small, so where would I go to talk? Plus, I don't want to run up my dad's phone bill." I knew my father wouldn't care about the bill. Maybe I could find a time when everyone was going out, and say I needed quiet for a history assignment or something, and then tell my father about the call afterwards. I knew he'd be glad, not angry about the cost.

"Look, why don't you come over after school and call your mom from my house? That way, you'd get it out of your system. And I can be right there with you when you're talking to her."

"Really, Steph? I could do that?"

"Dummy! You shouldn't've moved out of my house in the first place."

"I had to. The court said." I swallowed the lie. "If I call, I'll have to wait for the long-distance rates to go down."

"So? Stay for dinner."

"I think to call New York, the rates go down at five. And don't worry, I'd pay your mom back."

Mrs. Fry rushed in, dressed in her usual plaid suit and pumps. "*Discipuli*? Page two-twenty of your texts. *Celeriter!*"

"Grandma?" My heart was beating fast. At the last minute, I'd told Stephanie I wanted privacy, and had gone into Sylvia's study alone. I was sitting in an uncomfortable desk chair, but it didn't look like the telephone cord was long enough for me to move over to the low couch at the other side of the room.

"Yes? Who is this?"

"It's Martha. Your granddaughter." I shifted my weight on the chair.

"Oh. Well, you must be calling for your mother. Hang on a minute." The receiver knocked loudly as she put it down.

"Wait, Grandma?" I thought it would be more polite if I asked how she was, but I was too late, and she was probably drunk by now anyway. I'd only met my grandmother a few times, and it wasn't easy to get her attention. Mostly she lectured me and Hildy and Drew about how we should try harder with my mother. By now, she was probably as mad at us as my mother was. The *clunk* of the receiver echoed in my ears.

"*Gladys!*" my grandmother shouted, no doubt irking my mother by using her birth name, maybe because she was too drunk to remember the name Willa. I was hoping she'd just tell my mother, "phone," but I heard a brief muffled back-and-forth.

My heart kept beating, too fast. My mother would demand to know whether I was wearing undershirts. I'd feel compelled to be truthful. She'd yell, *Are you crazy? It's freezing!* even though it was still Indian summer here in Berkeley.

My mother picked up the receiver. "Yes?"

"Mom? It's Martha."

"Well, hello, Martha. What is it?"

"I—I'm just calling—"

"Why *are* you calling?"

I couldn't remember. "Um, just to tell you—I'm working on my college applications," I blurted.

"Well, good for you."

Wait, she didn't care if I went to college? "And just to see if you're, you know, okay," I added. "Like, so much has happened, and I've been kind of worried, and we haven't talked, so I thought I'd say hello—"

"Well, hello then, and goodbye."

"Wait! Mom—"

"What *is* it?"

"I just—" I remembered in a flood how many times I'd thought about this conversation, how I'd envisioned it as a chance to scream at her. "I just wanted to make sure you're okay!" I shouted. "We're all okay here, and—"

"Martha, I really don't have the patience for this neurotic shit of yours."

"Neurotic—?"

"I've had my bellyful of your goddamned anxiety! Look, I don't need you to explain. You couldn't handle the conflict. So you made your choice."

"What? Mom, that's not what happened! You're the one who—"

"I let go for *you*! Don't you understand? The conflict, the having to choose, was *killing* you—"

"Mom! What was killing me was, you *made* me choose!"

"—and it was killing *me*."

"Wait, which is it?" I yelled. "You wanted to save me, or you wanted to save yourself?"

"I did what I had to do to survive, Martha. To *survive*."

"What about *my* survival?" I shrieked. "What about *Drew's*? Do you even care what it was *like* for him in that place?"

"I've had enough of this, Martha. I see Jules has brainwashed you, too, with his lopsided perceptions. Goodbye!" The phone clicked.

"Mom?" I cried, ridiculously, before hanging up.

I swallowed. I stood up. The door of Sylvia's study made a cardboard-ish sound brushing against the carpet as I opened it. Helvetica was waiting right outside as if she'd been eavesdropping. "Steph?" I called, my voice wavering.

Stephanie came out of her room into the hallway. "That was quick."

"Yeah, I probably owe you about fifteen cents."

"How'd it go?" Stephanie put her arm around my shoulder.

"I *knew* she'd say my father had brainwashed me. I just knew it." I had to feel there was something I'd been able to anticipate.

"Oh, Martha."

"She's so goddamned predictable. Vicious bitch."

"You know," Stephanie said, "that should be a medical condition in my dad's DSM book. Vicious Bitch Syndrome!"

I laughed so hard, I knocked Stephanie's arm off my shoulder. "We finally have a diagnosis!" I shouted gleefully.

"The heartbreak of VBS," Stephanie intoned. "If caught early, this condition can be treated. But most people are too embarrassed to discuss it with their doctor."

"No, wait! Most VBS sufferers don't even know they're sick."

"Right." Stephanie adopted the doctor voice again. "Fortunately, the disease is not painful to the VBS sufferer."

"Sure does stink for those around her!" We laughed and laughed, until I was crying. I cried for a while, and Stephanie comforted me, and then we diagnosed my father.

Fucking Idiot Disorder—FID for short.

28

no singing,
no humming,
no conducting

My father held on to the job at *RAAD* for a month and a half, which, realistically, was longer than any of us thought he'd be able to stand it. The manager, whom my father called simply "the guy," was a complete ignoramus, my father said—the type of anal retentive who had a cheap ballpoint pen installed on a chain behind the counter so it'd never disappear. The guy was in his late twenties, and was only in the business because his uncle owned several *RAAD* stores around the Bay Area. The uncle was an ignoramus, too, my father said: that was why the so-called classical sections of all the *RAAD* stores were stocked with dreck like *Tchaikovsky's Greatest Hits*, Bach works performed on a synthesizer, mediocre Haydn symphonies— and Mozart flute quartets, which, let's face it, there's no way anyone would purchase unless they were hell-bent on finding a reason to hate chamber music.

The guy was constantly opening up new pop records and playing them on the store turntable, setting my father's teeth on edge.

After a week or so, the guy would take the records to the back and put them through a shrink-wrap machine to make it look like they were fresh from the factory. A lot of classical LPs weren't shrink-wrapped (which is how my father was able to listen to so many of the records he'd stocked at the shop—and as for plastic-wrapped LPs that my father felt he just had to listen to, he could usually get a spare copy from the wholesaler). Anyway, as if it weren't immoral enough to pass floor copies off as new, the guy didn't respect LPs in the first place, dirtying them with his greasy fingers right in the middle of the tracks when my father had told him in plain English never to do that.

"But Dad, you hate pop records," Hildy pointed out. "So why do you even care?"

My father gaped at her as if to say, *That's the most moronic remark you've ever made.* Sometimes I understood my father so much better than Hildy did—not that it got me anywhere with him.

My father tried to talk the guy into revamping the classical section, or at least letting him take over the ordering. But the guy said they weren't looking to expand that section; in fact, they were consolidating it with the jazz. The guy needed my father up front. He told my father never to make any comments about the customers' taste in music. My father was to leave his crossword puzzles at home, direct people to the appropriate section, answer questions, and ring up sales. "Like a robot," my father told us, but without bitterness.

Previous customers of my father's started coming into *RAAD* to see him late in the evenings, after the guy had gone home. In between shifts, my father would scan the dimly lit apartment shelves for copies of César Franck's organ works, or Beethoven's Grosse Fugue, Opus 133, or the Isaac Stern recording of the Barber violin concerto with Leonard Bernstein conducting. Then he'd take them back to *RAAD* and sell them for cash during his shift, using bags left over from Smoke and Records. Unfortunately, the guy got wind of what was happening when a customer came in one morning to return the wrong purchase in the wrong bag—a Smoke and Records bag.

Stop or be fired, the guy told my father, and my father said fine. From then on, even when customers came in looking for things like "Raindrops Keep Fallin' on My Head," my father would send them to Mr. Lucas, who at least maintained a semblance of a classical section. And then of course, my father would entertain himself by delivering elaborate lectures to unsuspecting idiots. When one customer came in looking for Johnny Mathis, my father gushed about *Edith Mathis's* recordings of Bach cantatas and Schubert lieder, complimenting the customer on his discernment and suggesting he visit On Record for the best selection of the brilliant soprano's LPs.

Sales at *RAAD* started dipping noticeably in the evenings. We were never sure how the guy found out about the Mathis incident, but it was the last straw. "I told the guy it was an honest mistake," my father said afterwards, winking at us. "So I mixed up Mathis with Mathis! Coulda happened to anyone. Jerk." Hildy laughed, and that made Drew laugh.

But how were we going to get by on the money my father made selling records at the flea market? I didn't want to use my savings for family groceries. I knew both Hildy and Drew would spend their own money on the family, no problem, and maybe I should be ashamed that I didn't feel the same way. But my father always acted as if any generosity on my part were owed to him—the least I could do to redeem myself, since I was generally such a horrible disappointment. It didn't exactly make me want to jump in and help. Besides, I was going to need all the money I had for college. Now I just had to get in.

Fortunately, a cashier had left at Prufrock, and the next week, my father went to work there. Right off the bat, he didn't like it, starting with the fact that he had to fill out a time card. Worse, the management piped in Vivaldi all day, every day—how many times could a person be expected to tolerate *The Four Seasons*, with only Pachelbel's

Canon in D thrown in for so-called variety? Plus they kept telling him he couldn't whistle. My father *wasn't* whistling, he said: why would he whistle to the mediocre offerings piped in through the PA system? Then they said he was humming. Then they said he was conducting.

My father tried to get a job at Cody's, but they weren't hiring. Neither was Moe's. So he quit Prufrock and continued with the Saturday flea market in Berkeley. He also started driving out to some big field near the Oakland airport for the flea market they had there on Sundays.

Finally, an old customer of my father's called to tell him that KPFA needed a host for their classical music program on Sundays from six to ten a.m. My father was no morning person, but he took it. Oddly, on the day he started, someone at the station mentioned that KALX, the radio station at Cal, was also looking for an announcer to do a classical music show. That gig was from midnight to six a.m. on Thursday nights (Friday mornings, really). Both stations said he could bring his own records if he didn't see what he liked in the studio's collection.

Of course, my father had to learn the ropes of live radio, starting with the fact that singing along with the music wasn't okay, even if the microphone was off, because mistakes do happen on air. No "conducting"—there wasn't room to move around in either studio without the risk of banging into some important piece of equipment. And no humming, either: Glenn Gould may have wheezed his way through his studio sessions, but that didn't entitle a radio announcer to indulge in the kind of vocalizing the eccentric Canadian pianist had done during the recording of what was arguably the greatest Goldberg Variations rendition of all time.

At 5:55 that first morning, Drew and I dragged ourselves off our futons and huddled around the kitchen radio to hear my father's first moments on KPFA, Drew's red army blanket draped across his narrow shoulders. We put the portable heater on full-blast and leaned our elbows on the red-and-white-checked, cigarette-holed oilcloth that was sticky no matter how many times we sponged it off. A couple of noisy buses passed on Bancroft. My father had left a package of powdered sugar-covered miniature doughnuts in the fridge for us. We'd taken it out, but it was too early to eat. Drew yawned and played solitaire, his messy dark curls sticking up on one side of his head. I made hot tea. My stomach was in knots because of the early hour, plus nervousness about how my father would do.

We moved the dial until we found KPFA. Normally, since my father was a sound sleeper, Drew and I listened to KFRC or KYA while we crunched our Cheerios, even though both stations seemed to rotate only seven songs: "Imagine," "Maggie May," "Theme from Shaft," "American Pie," "Gypsies, Tramps and Thieves," "Superstar," and "Have You Seen Her." Drew and I both hated "Have You Seen Her," with its goopy narrated opening and closing. Whenever it came on, we'd try to keep straight faces as we sang along in a maximally histrionic way, substituting the word "emphysema" for "have you seen her." It was practically the only time Drew would laugh.

Actually, Drew and I kind of hated all the songs except "Maggie May" and "Theme from Shaft," and we were getting sick of those, too. The announcers on KFRC and KYA were shrill. They were always interrupting the songs with blaring ads and inane comments. Plus, they'd start playing the next song before the one that was playing was even over yet, even if the ending was the very best part and, musically, should never be interrupted. When we were little, my mother had told us that our home radio was the type that only played classical music, and we believed her for years. After that deprivation, access to AM radio was like getting to eat from our Halloween candy bags as much as we wanted: even when there was nothing good left, the idea of it never got old.

Since Plowshares, Drew hadn't initiated eye contact with me—or with anyone else, as far as I could tell. But at six o'clock, as soon as my father said "This is Classics in the Morning" in a ghostly, tentative voice and didn't introduce himself, Drew looked up at me in alarm. Then we both burst out laughing. We couldn't believe how wooden my father sounded, how scared. It was as if a whole chunk of his personality had disappeared now that you could only hear his voice. "I'm going to play Mahler's *Des Knaben Wunderhorn*," my father offered in the same hushed bland tone, like a timid schoolboy obligated to recite the Pledge of Allegiance—as if he'd never had an audience before, when in fact, he'd had his very own stage. I started laughing again, but Drew didn't join in. He opened the package of doughnuts and took one and we kept listening. Cornstarchy sugar stuck to his lips.

A guy named Bruce Rolligan, Jr., had moved into the brown-shingle with Hildy and Ann. He'd come to the Bay Area after dropping out of college somewhere in Connecticut, Hildy told us. He couldn't stand being called "junior" and he didn't really like the name Bruce in the first place, so he went by Rolly. Rolly was thinking of going back to school, but in the meantime, he was doing some carpentry work.

For months, Hildy called him "my housemate" or "Rolly," so it took a while to figure out it was really "my boyfriend." Rolly didn't come with Hildy when she visited us, because he was shy, and Hildy had never invited us over there. So we didn't actually meet Rolly until the time we drove Shalimar to the airport.

It was a drizzly December day. Hildy had said over the phone that she wanted us to stop by so she could say goodbye to Shalimar, but that the place was a mess and she'd rather we not come in. My father left the motor and the windshield wipers running and pulled up on the curb while Drew ran in to get Hildy. It took longer than we thought, and my father started hyperventilating. The wipers whined.

"Jules," Shalimar said, and my father turned toward her as she pulled a little gold charm out of her wallet. It was on a gold chain. "I was going to give this to you when I handed in my dissertation."

My father turned off the motor. "I can't take this," he said thickly.

"Of course you can!" Shalimar laughed. Then she turned around to me. "It's my Phi Beta Kappa key. Don't you think your dad should have it?"

I didn't know. Was it something having to do with a sorority?

"Phi Beta Kappa is an honors society," Shalimar explained. "If you do well in college, in the liberal arts, you get elected to it." She turned to my father again. "You know I would have been stuck forever if not for you."

"You get that goddamned dissertation *written*, goddamn it!" my father shouted. I expected Shalimar to at least wince, but she just leaned over quietly and put the necklace in his plaid shirt pocket as Hildy was coming out of the house, leading Rolly by the hand while Drew trotted around the car and got in next to me.

Rolly was very tall and very big, with granny glasses and a long beard and wavy light brown hair almost down to his waist. It would have been tempting to call him jolly, except he wasn't.

"You just met Drew," Hildy said, "and this is my sister, Martha. And this is Shalimar. And that's my father, Jules!" she pointed. Shalimar and I had rolled down our windows so we could say hello, and the drizzle was getting on us. Rolly nodded and waved and said, "Hey man," without coming any closer. I could tell he wanted to get back inside.

Hildy let go of Rolly's hand and walked up to the car, leaning in to kiss Shalimar on her bony cheek. "We're gonna miss you," she said, and Shalimar smiled warmly. Then Hildy threw kisses to my father, me, and Drew while Rolly waited, his glasses getting sprinkles on them. Hildy's glasses, too. My father waved, almost a dismissal, and turned the motor back on. We headed for the highway entrance to get to the airport.

Shalimar was sick. It was something called anorexia nervosa, where girls or women thought they were too fat and starved themselves on purpose. It was psychological, so they wouldn't listen when you told them they weren't fat. Shalimar's clothes had gotten even baggier, and her heart had become weak. Once recently, she'd wound up in Cowell Hospital on campus. Today was the first time I'd heard her mention her dissertation in a few months. She still smiled a lot, but her eyes were bulgy, because even her head was kind of skinny. She was going back home to St. Louis so her parents could take care of her.

29

unlaxing

Drew had never been the type to get into fights, but now if anyone messed with him, even a kid who was taller or who outweighed him, he'd go after them with his fists. He'd come home with sore knuckles, not to mention a black eye or badly kicked shins or a bloody nose. He never complained, of course, but I begged him to settle his fights over poker. He kept fighting, *due to his unhealthy identification with his sick role model, Jules Goldenthal!* Clearly not due to his outrageous recent incarceration in a shit-hole.

Drew kept using those wordy curses like Captain Haddock, plus he'd started making up his own. *Millions of maximally moronic muttonheads! Quadrillions of queerly quiescent quagmires!* Normally when people swear, it's a way to connect with the other person—a way of emphasizing that whatever it is you're saying, you really mean it. But Drew's elaborate curses had the opposite feel. It was as if he were pushing you away, as if he had a *private* private joke, and didn't give a damn that you didn't get it.

Sometimes my father would get calls from the principal about Drew's cutting class, or from the school counselor about the urgent need for Drew to see a psychiatrist, or from teachers reporting that

Drew didn't listen, that he was always "somewhere else," that he had unmet potential, stuff like that.

It didn't seem to occur to my father to hit Drew or even yell at him about messing up in school. "This is pure horseshit," my father would tell the school. Then he'd start in about how if "you people" had anything remotely interesting to offer to an imaginative math genius, Drew wouldn't have these so-called problems in the first place.

As for pot, my father knew Drew was "experimenting." It was normal, he said. It was the human condition. He even pretended not to know about the stash that Drew kept in the partition, in the back of the shelf that had the pop records Drew and I liked, where the records jutted out a little from having the plastic bag behind them. What my father probably didn't realize was that every day on his way to school, Drew was taking a quick detour up into People's Park to get high instead of walking straight down Telegraph to get to Willard. In the afternoons, on his way home, Drew repeated the detour in reverse.

I wouldn't have known about Drew's circuitous route to and from school if not for a bloated, sweaty-palmed boy in my Israeli Folk Dance class at Berkeley High. Stephanie, Paisley, and I all needed two semesters of PE credit senior year. When we found out Israeli Folk Dance had been approved as a way to fulfill the requirement, we were happy to sign up. So were the non-athletic kids from all the other grades, which didn't include Clifton, since he'd gone out for track, or Declan, since he didn't seem to give a damn what the requirements were for graduation.

"Isn't that your little brother I keep seeing at People's Park?" the boy said to me after class one morning. We'd ended with a line dance, and I'd been next to him. His hands were cold and clammy.

I peered at him. "How do you know my brother?"

"Drew, right?"

"But you're a tenth grader, and he's in seventh, so how—"

I felt Stephanie grabbing me by the arm and dragging me away. "Dodo!" she said, as we left the Community Theater foyer where our dance class was held. "He's talking about the pot smokers up at People's Park."

"Wait, I thought they smoked in *Provo* Park!"

Stephanie gave a long sigh. "Martha, I hate to be the one to break it to you, but—Drew must be smoking pot on the way to school. A lot of the kids that live near People's Park do that. And on the way home, too. Didn't you know?"

There was something about me that was just hopelessly stupid. I was used to thinking it was because I was only in fourth grade, or only in ninth grade, or only in eleventh. But I was a senior now, and I was turning out to be one of those people who *don't* learn as they grew older. I'd heard the tiny crinkle of Drew's plastic bag behind the partition every morning, and I still hadn't figured it out. I just thought Drew was checking the bag or something.

As much as Drew hid his pot habit from my father, my father hid his from Drew. Stephanie had a theory about why they kept up the charade. She said it was like if you feel comfortable getting undressed in front of your best friend, and you also feel comfortable getting undressed in front of your cousin, that didn't necessarily mean you'd feel comfortable getting undressed in front of those two people at the same time. We couldn't figure out why that was true. It just was.

"You ready?" My father shouted to me from the kitchen.

"Hang on—just a few more minutes," I answered from my futon. I could hear him jiggling his keys against the box of Shermans in his pocket while *Lost in Space* blared on the little black-and-white TV.

I was writing a paper for Independent Study, the eight a.m. English class you could enroll in if you'd gotten good grades in English all through high school. You didn't have to show up, which was nice, since you could sleep late, but Paisley and I both found the policy kind of bullshitty, because the teacher didn't really teach us anything. I wished I'd decided to take honors English with Stephanie instead.

The independent study assignment was to do a twenty-five-page report on literature, music, dance, or art, whichever you cared about the most. You had to make sure your thinking was original, and back up your points with rigorous analysis. Paisley and I both chose music, but that was where the similarity ended. She was writing about musical instruments and notation during the Renaissance period. I decided to write about how classical composers could sometimes be disappointing in what they did with their ideas.

Like, I think the best part of the entire Mozart *Requiem* is during the "Confutatis" movement, when the sopranos and altos come in singing *voca me* in harmony, with total serenity and quietness, kind of as a counterbalance to the basses and tenors' turmoil in the previous bars, where they're singing *confutatis maledictis*, about bad guys getting rebuked. I've always felt let down that the women's part of the *voca me* doesn't last longer. So I wrote about how fleeting that theme is.

Then I added that I felt the same disappointment in Verdi's *Otello*, where the most transcendent moment, which Mr. Lucas said was called the kiss motif, evaporates way too quickly. Which was why, I said, Leonard Bernstein had to steal Verdi's basic idea and run with it in "I Have a Love" from *West Side Story*.

I was pretty sure my thinking was original. The problem was, I didn't know what else to write in the paper. I supposed I could discuss all the pieces that I loved because the best parts *were* allowed to blossom fully. But there were so many, I didn't know where to start. Maybe with examples of Mozart and Verdi that are more satisfying? Or, conversely, with examples of composers beating their ideas half to death, as in *Bolero*? Or maybe with Brahms or Mahler or Bach, where you never felt let down, either by over-development or under-development? What would make the best argument?

It was only because I was stuck that I pulled out the UC application. I'd already filled out the easy parts, but I'd been avoiding the required essays, especially the one at the end. *Lastly, have you faced any unusual personal circumstances that you would like the admissions committee to know about in considering your application?*

Everything I thought of seemed impossible to write about. My shrug. My father's hitting. All the fights when I was growing up. My mother's hatred of everyone in the family except me. My mother's hatred of me. My father's hatred of me. My father's pot smoking—which was obviously way better than his hitting.

But then, maybe I could write about things that were more like events, rather than things that were just always true in our family. *Custody case*, I wrote on a piece of binder paper. *Going to live with Dad. Smoke and Records—losing lease.* Maybe there were tricks I could use to make my life sound interesting and unusual instead of sick and pathetic.

"C'mon, shake a leg!" My father was getting impatient, and the truth is, I was still scared of him, so I got up off the futon.

My father and I each had a reason to go for our rides. For me, it was night driving practice and a chance to pass places in Berkeley that were important to me. As for my father, I'd finally learned why his nocturnal car rides with Hildy were so "unlaxing" for him. "Unlaxing" meant getting high.

In the kitchen, Drew was sitting too close to the TV, his mouth agape. My father was across the table in his jacket, bent over the crossword puzzle with a turquoise Lindy pen that was missing the cap that most people put on the end to make sure it doesn't get lost. Underneath the folded newspaper was the UC Berkeley financial aid form, skewed to the diagonal and already a little crumpled at one edge. Somewhere in that pile, too, was my permission slip for the five-day bus tour to Los Angeles that Concert Chorale and Orchestra were taking next semester.

"Dad, I thought you were filling out the Parents' Confidential Statement."

"Petunia!" He started writing.

"I won't be able to go to Cal if you don't fill out the financial form. Also, could you try not to fold it?"

He was bent over the crossword, putting letters in the grid.

I sighed loudly. "Dad! I thought you were itching to go."

"Shitballs, I can't hear!" Drew turned the TV up.

"You're sitting too close," I told Drew.

"Alien!" my father exclaimed.

"You *guys*!" Drew whined.

"Okay, well, could you at least sign the Concert Chorale tour form? They need it early."

In truth, I was anxious about leaving my father and Drew for a few days for the Concert Chorale trip in the spring, let alone moving to campus housing next fall. I only kept pushing because it was one of those situations where you know in your bones that you'll regret it if you don't participate. Clifton was going on the trip, for one thing. So was Giselle. I couldn't miss it, because I'd almost certainly be given a solo, plus the other altos needed me. I had money saved up, so it's not as if my father could be mad about that.

My father got up, tossed the puzzle on the table, and jingled his keys, turning to leave. I pulled the Parents' Confidential Statement out from under, straightened the dog-ear, and laid it neatly on top of the crossword. Then I laid the tour permission slip on top of that, since it was easier than the financial aid application. "We'll be back soon," I told Drew. "Brush your teeth."

The Plymouth was parked a block and a half down on Bancroft, and I waited until we were close before I asked. "Dad, can I have the keys?"

"I'll drive." He started whistling from his favorite Haydn string quartet.

"No, really, I need the practice. Remember you said it's a lot trickier than day driving?"

He turned the engine over. KKHI was blasting, and he made it a little softer, pulling out into traffic. "Pure dreck," he declared as a flute was finishing up an elaborate solo with the orchestra accompanying. The announcer took over in a strange combination of mispronounced L's and a strange accent. *"That was Mozart's Flyute and Harp Concerto in C, Köechel 299. And this is KKHI, San Francisco. And Paylo Aylto. And now here's a yittyle something for you from a famous fiylm soundtrack."*

My father identified the new piece before the first measure was over. *"Alexander Nevsky.* Prokofiev. Do you know the film, by the way? An absolutely brilliant work. That battle scene later on, with the soprano in the background! My God, pure genius." He started singing along, without the words, just *ya da da.*

We were a few blocks down Oxford Street at a stop sign when he pulled the Sherman box out of his pocket, and the joint out of the Sherman box.

"Dad, *please?"*

He pulled forward and lit a match, still singing, neither of his hands on the steering wheel.

"C'mon, Dad, I thought we had a deal." I said it halfheartedly, because he'd never really agreed to it. He sucked in at the end of the joint and waved the match out and put his right hand back on the steering wheel, the joint wedged between the first two fingers. He was holding his breath. With his left hand, he opened the triangular window flap, blew smoke out of it. "Getting high makes me drive *better,"* he said, making a *whoosh* noise at the end of the sentence. "Way more instinctual—*acuity.* Want a hit?"

"I don't smoke, Dad."

"You should really try it sometime. When you're ready to stop feeling superior."

"Dad, seriously, I really need practice. You always let Hildy drive at night. You said she'd need it, remember?"

"Shhh! Listen!" He turned up the volume. "This section, oh my God. Just listen to that plaintive voice!"

"Maybe you could say stuff like that when you're announcing," I ventured. "You know, like, talk about the parts of the piece that you really like, so the audience can—Dad, watch out!" A pedestrian was about to dash into the crosswalk, but saw the car and ducked back.

"You know the story of Alexander Nevsky." My father was talking loudly; how did he expect me to listen to the soprano? "A thirteenth-century Russian prince. They made a saint out of him—he was a national hero. Basically, Eisenstein was trying to prepare Russia for Hitler. Only he couldn't say that directly, of course. . ."

When was I supposed to listen, and when was I supposed to ignore?

". . . so he made a movie about a prince's victories over the Teutonic knights of that era. That's the human condition, baby! History repeating itself. . . ."

Abruptly, he pulled over at a slight diagonal into a yellow zone. "Fine, you wanna drive?" He pressed the little rectangular Park button, left the motor running, opened the door, and began to climb out with the joint in his hand.

"No, no! You scoot over! I'll get out." I scrambled out of the passenger seat, shut the car door, and went around. It would be just our luck to have a cop pull up behind us.

In the driver's seat, I turned down the volume a little and rolled the window all the way down. "Look, Dad, I know you hate paperwork—"

"You've got plenty of time." His voice was pinched as he tried to keep the smoke in his lungs and talk at the same time. "You'll knock it out."

"But about that financial aid form—it's due the end of this month."

He exhaled irritably. "What's the big goddamned deal if you miss the deadline? So you wait awhile and go to Cal in the spring!"

"Dad, I told you about this months ago! And I'm doing all the work. All you have to do—" I knew I sounded shrill, but I was convincing myself, too. He had no idea how much the essays made me want to give up.

"You always worry, *'Am I gonna get an A?'*" he mocked. "When are you going to figure out that you always get your goddamned A?" His lips were so dry from the grass that they were sticking to his front teeth.

I wanted to say, *Why is it okay for Shalimar to get A's and even go to graduate school?* But Shalimar was still very sick, still staying with her parents, so I didn't bring it up. "Look, Dad, if you just tell me the numbers, I can fill out those financial forms. I'll put the numbers in the boxes. All you have to do is sign." Even as I said it, I knew it had to be more complicated than that. He probably didn't even know where his tax forms were.

"You know, daughter of mine," he said quietly, then paused, as if he were about to tell me something highly confidential. "If you were a real intellectual, you wouldn't need college."

Shrug. Shrug. My eyes stung and my cheeks grew hot. My father was wrong about so many things, but I couldn't deny that this was one thing he was probably right about. I wasn't a real intellectual. The truth was, I was applying to college because my friends were—a lightweight's reason, not an intellectual's. Real intellectuals loved Cody's and Moe's. What would happen in college, where the books would be harder and my trouble concentrating would probably only get worse?

"You don't tell Hildy not to take classes," I managed weakly, though I guess Hildy *was* what my father considered an intellectual. "And anyway—what about Shalimar?"

The Prokofiev had ended and a Bach cantata was on. *"Liebster Gott,"* my father pronounced, wetting his lips as we rode along. I passed the street where Paul Shapiro had lived before his family moved to Vancouver to protect Paul and his older brother from the possibility of getting drafted. I went through the tunnel and onto Solano, drove west for a while, and then began circling back near King Junior High, letting my father think I wanted to pass by Stephanie's house when really, I was passing by Clifton's and mentally waving.

"Dearest God," my father was saying. "That's what *Liebster Gott* means. Did you know the German word *liebe* comes from the same root as our word *love*?"

I tried not to sigh too loudly.

"Basically, man has a psychological need to look upon God as dear, as loving. That's the human condition, baby! Although historically, of course, this wasn't always true. You see, in pagan times. . . ."

Stephanie was applying to Stanford and Yale, plus some little college in Vermont, or maybe it was New Hampshire. She was filling out the UC application, too, but planned to check the box for Davis, UCLA, and Santa Cruz, not Berkeley. She'd become so self-confident. She even knew she wanted pre-med for a major.

We could go to Santa Cruz together, Stephanie said, be in the same dorm, ask to be roommates! Or Yale. They had a good music department there; didn't I want to apply? Didn't I want to go away, get a fresh start? Live a little? Paisley encouraged me, too. She was applying to Reed and Radcliffe as well as the UC system.

Maybe that's what gave me the stamina to keep pushing my father: that compared with other kids, I wasn't planning a radical escape. I wouldn't even be going as far away as Hildy's place in Oakland. Just across the street. I wished he could see that.

It turned out the reason my father couldn't find his tax forms was that he'd given them to Mr. Hinge. According to Mr. Hinge, since I was in my father's sole custody, we didn't have to deal with my mother's income or any of her financial information; Cal would make the decision about my financial aid based only on my father's situation. That sounded good, since my father was broke, and I didn't want to have to call my mother to talk in the first place, let alone try to get financial information from her. Money—well, that was out of the question.

I tried to attack the financial aid forms myself, but it was hopeless. "Taxable income including wages, pensions, capital gains, interest, dividends, annuities. . . ." "Non-taxable income, including workers' compensation, welfare benefits, housing and food allowances. . . ." I couldn't make sense of it, either. So my father and I kept fighting.

Thankfully, Hildy stepped in one evening after we'd had a family dinner at Human Village. Back at the apartment, she coaxed him with the kind of soothing talk I could never manage—*C'mon, Dad, it won't be that hard, we'll do it together.* With a sideways nod, she banished me to the main room, where I leaned against the wall on my futon and translated the assigned section from Book IV of *The Aeneid* while Drew sat on his futon with a well-worn copy of *Red Rackham's Treasure.*

At the kitchen table, Hildy gave my father the same kind of hand-holding that my father had apparently given Shalimar, only he kicked and screamed the whole time. "What the hell do they want from me? I don't *have* any assets!"

"It's okay, Dad," Hildy said, "that's exactly what they want to know," whereas I would have said, "Well, *duh* now, Dad, our not having money is the whole point of applying for financial aid!" When my father didn't settle down, Hildy calmly took the tax forms from him and figured out, one item at a time, which figures to put in which boxes on the Parents' Confidential Statement. I had no idea how she knew what to do. I only hoped she *did* know what to do.

I felt so relieved when everything was finished, when all the materials were safely in the mail on time, that I wasn't prepared for my own second-guessing. The counselor at school had urged me to check the boxes for more than one campus, explaining that Berkeley was accepting fewer students since campuses like Irvine and Santa Cruz had opened. I'd ignored her advice; how could I leave my father and Drew so soon after all that had happened? But with the application mailed, I worried endlessly about not getting in.

All I could do was hope, because I didn't have a backup plan. Backup plans were for people who weren't already pushing their luck just in having regular plans.

30

t°ur

In the spring, on the last night of the concert chorale tour, one of the bass players in Orchestra managed to score some big bottle of booze and was passing it around the rooftop garden of the hotel where we were all staying. A few hours before, we'd gotten the highest possible marks from the judges for our final performance, so everyone was in a good mood. I guess Mr. Seton and Mr. Krantz figured their job was basically done: somehow there was no adult supervision up on the roof.

I wouldn't have gone, but the two girls who were sharing a room with me and Paisley said everyone else was going, and apparently there was a great view up there; were we sure we didn't want to come check it out? I guess they could tell Paisley and I weren't party types. But there was something freeing about being on the tour, where our usual selves, the things we were certain about, didn't seem as certain, all the more since we were heading home on the tour bus early tomorrow morning.

By the time we got up there, a bunch of people were laughing really hard. Most of the girls had changed into jeans. The boys had loosened their bowties and put on Keds or sandals, eager to get out of their formal shoes but not bothering with a complete change of clothes. Clifton, in a plain white tee, blue jeans and *huaraches*, was the exception.

I was surprised enough that Giselle was one of the drinkers. But it turned out she was at the center of the whole scene, louder and laugh-ier than the others. She was still in her concert black skirt and white blouse, but she'd kicked off her shoes and was walking around in her black stockings, apparently not worried about getting a run or making her feet filthy on the asphalt. Her wavy long blond hair was tangled and loose—still beautiful, of course, like the flowing mane of a Botticelli goddess. Clifton, meanwhile, was quietly trying to keep the bottle away from her. You could tell he wasn't used to handling this type of situation.

"Giselle, I think you've had enough," Clifton told her softly, putting an arm around her waist and trying to lead her away.

"Oh, Clifton, for God's sake, lighten up!" Giselle responded loudly. "I mean, oops! I don't mean that literally, of course!" She started laughing hysterically at her own witticism. Besides the joke's being completely tasteless, it was also weird that she'd say something that stupid. But maybe it was one of those paradoxes: I'd noticed over the course of the tour that Giselle had this way of lording it over everyone how cool she was for dating a black guy.

Clifton put a little more muscle into trying to drag Giselle out of there. "Come on, now. That's right. You lean on me." Giselle responded by turning around and puking on the asphalt behind some planter box. Clifton rustled around for a Kleenex in his pocket and came up empty. In one quick move, he pulled off his white tee and gently wiped her mouth. I tried not to stare at his lean, muscular chest. He reached down to pick up her black high heels, then put his arm around her waist, firmly walking her into the elevator and still holding the bunched-up pukey shirt in case she needed it again on the ride down to her room.

I stayed up on the roof and talked to Paisley about what a pretty view it was, and we agreed that "sunset" wasn't a very accurate word, since the best part of any sunset was actually *after* the sun went down, when there was no glare, just a prolonged show of melty pink and orange. Slowly, the other kids started going back downstairs. The empty bottle was sitting upright on the ledge where people had been congregating. A stray black bow tie lay on the asphalt nearby. Paisley and I talked about how the performance had gone—my solo (for which she over-praised me); which parts sounded more ragged than we'd hoped; which parts we'd done really well. Then we heard the elevator door behind us, and suddenly Clifton was next to me. He'd put on a fresh black tee. *YPSO*, it said, for Young People's Symphony Orchestra.

"Clifton, hi!" I said. "Everything okay?"

"Sure." He looked confused.

"I—um, saw you earlier. Is Giselle—?" I managed.

"She's asleep."

"Oh."

"How about you?" Clifton asked.

I heard the elevator doors open, and when I turned I saw Paisley stepping inside. Were my feelings for Clifton that obvious? I'd already told Paisley I used to know him when I studied violin with his mother, but she seemed to have made her own inference. I'd have to explain to her that Clifton and I were just friends.

"I've hardly talked to you lately," he went on. "How's it going?"

Maybe it was inner exhaustion that made me want to give Clifton Cray a real answer. "Well—it's been kind of a roller coaster ride," I began, even though I couldn't think of any highs, only lows. "My father—my mom kicked me out! For basically no reason. You know, she's the one who—" I was about to tell Clifton she'd made me stop taking lessons with his mother, but how would I explain such stupidity and meanness? "And then my dad got custody!" I went on. "Because, see, my mom put Drew in this horrible school for kids whose parents are drug addicts, or in jail. So my dad got a lawyer. My mom didn't care! She didn't even show up in court."

I talked for awhile, and then Clifton put his arm around my waist and slowly drew me close and kissed me on the forehead. I gazed up at him, and we looked at each other for a moment, and then suddenly we were kissing, a long kiss, before I drew back.

"Clifton, I can't—you already have a—"

"I know," Clifton said. Then he kissed me again, and I could feel the bulge in his pants, my private parts melting, my knees going weak. He tasted salty, sweet, almondy. Like the right combination of everything. It was as if my body knew this, because it totally forgot to shrug.

We were up on the roof for a long time, talking and kissing. I asked Clifton about being bullied in seventh grade. He asked me more about my family. Finally, I confided in him about my father's hitting. Clifton winced, and then his jaw tightened, and in that moment I could tell he was never going to like my father.

The next morning, Clifton was sitting with Giselle on the bus as if nothing had changed. I caught his eye as I was taking a seat next to Paisley, diagonally across from them. Clifton looked pained, as if he felt terrible but there was nothing he could do about it; Giselle was still his girlfriend.

Then it occurred to me that maybe what I'd told him about my father had so appalled Clifton that he'd decided he couldn't have anything to do with me. For sure that's what my mother would have thought, and how did I know she wasn't right about stuff like that?

I cried over Clifton. Stephanie tried to comfort me by saying the world was a lot bigger than Berkeley High, and that in college, I'd have plenty of guys to choose from. But that only reminded me: what if college fell through? I hadn't told Stephanie that I'd stupidly only checked the box for Berkeley. Now I realized I should have explained in one of my essays about how I had family responsibilities and needed to stay in Berkeley. If I had, maybe the admissions office wouldn't think I wanted Berkeley just because it's the coolest and most prestigious of all the UCs. I'd had the chance to make my case about that, and I'd blown it. If the college thing went down in flames, it was my own damned fault.

Besides, what if I didn't get financial aid? I could keep working, use my money for tuition and books, and keep living with my father, but that wasn't exactly ideal. What if Hildy hadn't quite known what she was doing on those forms? I kept having to remind myself of her heroism in filling them out for me, all the more because she herself wasn't transferring to Cal. At least not yet, because that whole plan had slowed way down. I couldn't help blaming Rolly.

Hildy had been supporting Rolly since he'd decided that instead of being a carpenter or going back to college, he was going to write a novel. Hildy thought he was absolutely brilliant, and told him so every time he read paragraphs to her from his yellow legal pads, on which he was scribbling his masterpiece double-spaced with a blue medium-point Paper Mate while Hildy did her shifts at Gabel. Though Rolly had convinced Hildy that creating a full-length work of fiction was the equivalent of graduate school, his parents didn't see it the same way, and they'd stopped sending him any money. Rolly must've felt bad about living off Hildy, because he'd started dealing pot and also hash.

Ann had moved out. She was going to nursing school in San Francisco and needed to be in the city to make life easier, but I think she also wanted nothing to do with Rolly. She tried to get Hildy to move to SF with her, but Hildy believed in Rolly and didn't want to go. Meanwhile, Hildy had stopped taking classes for now. She was having stomachaches again, and between school and the job at Gabel, where she was now an assistant manager, it was just too much.

The worst thing, though, was that Rolly had roped Hildy into doing a hash delivery for him. He couldn't manage the delivery himself, he said, because the cops already had their eye on him. He told Hildy she'd be perfect: no one would suspect a cute young girl with granny glasses. Reluctantly, Hildy did the delivery, and immediately, Rolly talked her into doing another one. Then, thankfully, Hildy put her foot down. She made me swear I'd never tell my father.

The very next time Rolly did a pickup, he got busted. His parents were so mad at him by then that Hildy had to bail him out.

31

oddities

Weeks passed, but I couldn't seem to shake off the unexpected make-out session with Clifton and the rejection that followed so quickly. I felt hopeless about ever getting a boyfriend. I mean, if I couldn't even get Clifton, who had always wanted me, wasn't that a pretty good sign of the big fat nothing to come? I could tell Stephanie was getting sick of hearing me go on about it: whether I'd made a mistake in telling Clifton about my father; whether I was just a bit of an idiot, or a complete idiot; whether I only wanted Clifton now because he was good-looking (and what that said about me); whether I only wanted him now because he was unavailable (and what *that* said about me). At first I could barely eat, but as the weeks went by, I settled into my self-pity, thinking of the Clifton situation as the latest addition to the long list of things that were wrong with my life.

One Thursday afternoon, a refreshing idea came to me. I had the money, and there was a place a few blocks down Telegraph. So in the late afternoon, I went. The lady asked me if I was sure.

"Definitely," I said, even though my heart was racing and my stomach churned, plus I shrugged a few times. But as soon as she started, I could see that the shoulder-length cut was going to be an improvement. Which was a good thing, because just as I was leaving the salon, there was Declan Wilder, sauntering out of Moe's and heading into Cody's.

He was wearing black jeans, his black leather jacket, and a black wool beret. A walking cliché, I supposed, but then maybe I was a cliché myself, getting a new hairstyle after a painful experience with a guy. Besides, instead of wearing black leather boots, Declan was in red high-tops with white shoelaces and those big white rubber half-moons at the toe. I had to admit the whole look was pretty original.

I watched him for a moment, and then found myself crossing the street, my heart a loudspeaker in my chest. Cody's. I hated being reminded that all my efforts in school hadn't turned me into the kind of thirsty intellectual Declan would want to spend time with. Or that my father might finally stop disdaining. But my legs kept moving, and I braved the door, entered into the sanctum.

Declan was bent over the second table, turning the pages of a thick volume of art prints. I walked up slowly and stood there until he sensed my presence. "New hairstyle," he remarked by way of greeting, tipping the beret. A few of his own hairs, fine long blond strands that were the antithesis of the curly burden I'd just gotten rid of, stood up slightly, then lay flat as he replaced the cap.

"Thanks," I answered, before realizing Declan hadn't said he liked it. I reddened, willing an imaginary elephant's foot onto my shoulder—my latest technique for postponing the shrug.

He looked at me skeptically without closing the book. "So how goes it?"

"Pretty well! Still waiting to hear about college, though."

"Good for you!" He had the bemused expression of someone who thought of the Berkeley campus as a good place for rallies and a convenient corridor between Northside and Southside.

Declan wasn't graduating from Berkeley High with our class. He had a few incompletes, and didn't care about making them up, because of an apprenticeship he'd gotten with an important local photographer named Leonard something. Apparently Declan worked in the darkroom and lugged Leonard's equipment around, cameras and lights, I guessed, and in exchange, he got to use the guy's studio, somewhere below Shattuck on Southside. Plus Declan got to stay in a room at the back. I knew this because Paisley had sat next to Declan's on-and-off girlfriend Raquel in Physics senior year.

I'd just come into Cody's, but now Declan shut the book, ready to leave. "You coming?" he asked, as if we'd agreed to it—as if he knew damned well I hadn't gone in there to browse. Why was he interested, somehow, all of a sudden? It seemed to be happening to someone else. My heartbeat was loud in my ears.

Outside, he pulled a sky-blue package of Gauloises from his pocket and lit one. "So, Miss Martha," he said, inhaling sharply as he peered at me. "A café au lait, perhaps?" I nodded yes, and we crossed Telegraph and headed toward Caffé Med, Declan putting the cigarette out on the white bottom of his shoe and throwing the butt into the gutter before we went in. Where had he bought the cigarettes? Not at my father's.

At the counter, I reached into my purse, not wanting Declan to think I thought this was a date. But he ignored me and bought his espresso and my tea, and led me up to the balcony, where we found a rickety table. Then he leaned over his cup and talked about why he found black-and-white photography so compelling. "There's a certain impact you don't get with color."

"Oh." I kind of knew what he meant.

"Color always seems a little false, however good the chemicals are," he went on, lighting another Gauloise and waving the match out in the air. "It's a paradox of the trade: black-and-white is actually more natural-looking. Even our models prefer it."

Our models. His and Leonard's. I tried not to blush: somehow I understood he meant nudes. I swished my tea bag around in the leaky metal teapot and fixed my mind on how pretentious Declan Wilder was.

He leaned back, tipping the chair slightly. "How's Jules, by the way?"

"Okay. He's scraping by. Still has a stall at the flea market."

"Ah."

"Plus two radio gigs," I added, grateful for the chance to fill Declan in about a person he clearly thought of as cool—and hoping he'd forget that my father was cooler than I was.

Declan's chair clopped as he sat upright again. He eyed me narrowly. "So Miss Martha. How long have you and I known each other?"

I knew exactly how long. "Let's see." I stalled. "Ninth grade? That makes three or four years, I guess."

"Well. You've grown up nicely."

I'd grown up nicely? We were the same age. *Relax*, I told my shoulder.

"Hey, so, you want to model for me?"

"M-model?" I stammered. "Declan, in case you hadn't noticed, I'm not very—"

"My models aren't of the Hollywood ilk," Declan interrupted.

Great! Mom would approve.

"Sometimes," he went on, "it's these float-down-the-river Ophelia types I find most compelling."

Ophelia type—was that what I was? A suicide waiting to happen? Without thinking, I pulled my left sleeve down over my wrist.

Declan blew smoke up toward the ceiling, flashed the misaligned smile. "You're so earnest! And at the same time, innocent. Look, it's entirely up to you, but you should come by if you'd like. I've gotta get to the darkroom, but I should be free by six, and Leonid is out of town, so I have the studio all to myself. It's a wonderful space. Terrific natural light."

I could feel the pulse in my neck. Weren't these the things that men said when they wanted to seduce you? That their mentors (Leonids, not ordinary Leonards) were out of town? Or that their wives were? That you were earnest but also innocent, that their place had wonderful natural light? I jostled the teapot by mistake and it clanged cheaply and spun around, sending anemic lukewarm liquid across the table. *Shrug.*

I grabbed my napkin, blotting the spill as Declan watched in amusement. I felt like a fool. Why had I gone into Cody's to "run into" him there if I didn't want to have sex? Wasn't that the whole point of having a crush on someone? Besides, why shouldn't I have sex with someone like Declan? He was the type who, if I ever told him about my father's being a hitter, probably wouldn't think any less of him for it. There was something perversely relieving in that.

Hildy had lost her virginity, obviously. So had Stephanie, who'd slept with her boyfriend from camp when they were both counselors for the last two summers. My pathetic experience consisted of kisses, from Brett and then from Clifton.

So when Declan borrowed a pen at the front counter of the café and wrote Leonid's phone number and address down on a napkin, I knew I was going.

"Call me if you're interested," Declan said. "Or just stop by later," he added in a softer voice, before tipping his goddamned beret again.

I went into Dharma Bums and tried on skirts for a while, just to look at my new haircut from different angles in the rickety three-way mirror, to bask in anticipation about Declan, and to push away the question of whether Clifton would like my new hairstyle. Then I wandered up and down Telegraph, not wanting to go back to the apartment but also not wanting to seem overly eager or annoying by showing up at Declan's too soon. I stopped at a phone booth and checked in with Drew, who said my father would be home shortly. I was free.

But what if Declan was one of those guys who didn't want the burden of having sex with a virgin? Stephanie had read somewhere that a girl can become very attached to her first lover. I could promise Declan I wouldn't be that way; I could reassure him. But what if he didn't believe me? And—what if I couldn't keep my promise? I tried not to think about the fact that none of this would be a problem if it were Clifton.

I thought of calling Stephanie or Hildy to talk, but then I'd lose momentum, and besides, I had no dimes left. I figured I'd walk down to Declan's studio instead of hopping on the bus. Walking would take more time, plus it was one of those crisp, vivid spring afternoons that make you realize how overrated summer is.

What if Declan didn't believe in condoms—what if he thought they were "like taking a shower with your raincoat on," as I'd heard? Also—I didn't have any condoms. Did young women even carry condoms? Probably not. Probably the guy took care of that. What if it hurt to have sex and I said, *Ow*, and Declan laughed and told me I was too serious? What if I couldn't stop shrugging?

The studio was a run-down, one-story bungalow built on a corner lot. I walked tentatively up the front steps, the wood creaking under my weight. I knocked quietly. But there was music, Steely Dan or something, blasting from inside, and Declan didn't answer. I knocked again, more loudly this time. Why hadn't I called? No: why had he invited me to drop by if he was going to play records at a volume that guaranteed he couldn't hear the door? Goddamn him. I was about to knock again, hard, when the door opened.

"Miss Martha!" He looked like he was trying not to laugh, whether at my agitation or at the fact that I'd shown up in the first place I wasn't sure. His smooth blond hair was a little staticky, from having had the beret on earlier, I guessed. Even from the porch, the place smelled of hash, and he was drinking straight out of a bottle of Irish whiskey. He'd probably wind up with psoriasis of the liver or whatever that disease is called.

He gestured me in. "Want a swig?" he said loudly, waving the bottle.

"I should probably tell you, Declan—" I began, practically having to shout over the music. *You go back, Jack, do it again. . . .* I'd heard the song on the radio and really liked it, the haunting instrumentation and lyrics, the maracas, or maybe they were shaker gourds. Now I'd never be able to get the damned thing out of my head.

"Make yourself at home," Declan said, waving grandly behind him.

I backed off, looked around. The studio was one large main room with big windows whose thick wood trim was a dark red that was chipped in places. A lot of the room was taken up by a silver photographer's screen, with silver umbrellas clipped to tripods to direct the lighting from two huge lamps. The wood floor was painted dark blue, with the previous color, a comforting sky-blue, showing through the parts that were heavily trafficked. Kind of like my crushes, I guessed—cumulative, the past remaining visible underneath the present.

A small oval coffee table was strewn with issues of *National Geographic* and books about cameras: Canon, Polaroid, Nikon, Leica. On an overstuffed faded burgundy sofa, a huge gray cat lay sleeping in the crack between the two cushions. The sofa was covered in its hair. Every wall that had a window in it was lined with low bookshelves: art and photography books, several large atlases, and what looked to be several shelves of spy novels or maybe thrillers. The one wall with no windows was covered with black-and-white photographs. They looked pretty professional, so I guessed they were Leonid's work.

"Nice pictures," I said tentatively, walking over for a closer look as Declan watched me. The first one I saw was a nude full-body shot of a seated elderly black woman with a breast on one side and a scar on the other, from cancer surgery, I guessed. I was surprised by how serene she looked, with an almost whimsical expression on her thin face. The flat spot where the breast and nipple used to be looked so natural, the scar at a matter-of-fact diagonal, as if her chest had simply been zipped back up at an angle. Or as if that side of her body were winking at you. I didn't want to stare too long with Declan watching me, but I also didn't want him to think I was afraid to look, because then he'd see me the way my father did, as a paint-by-numbers kind of person.

I took in an image of a very fat, middle-aged nude woman who was smoking a cigarette while sitting on the ledge of the burgundy sofa, looking almost defiant. Her hair was teased, her eyeliner and mascara too heavy. Suddenly I could feel Declan's presence just behind me. Slowly, I leaned back into him, and my eyes fluttered shut. I felt him bending down to put the whiskey bottle on the floor, the hollow sound punctuating Steely Dan's lyrics. And then Declan's hands were around my waist and his breath was on my neck and he turned me around and kissed me, alcohol and tobacco and hash overlaying a distinctive bitter-sweetness. It was kind of like the smell of gasoline: you knew the fumes were toxic, but you loved it anyway. I whimpered with pleasure.

"Declan." I looked up at him. "It's just, see, I'm still—"

"Miss Martha. All this is optional. I could photograph you with clothes on. We could drink whiskey together, or smoke a little hash. We could read Rilke. I'm at your service. Or, at your—cervix," he smiled. "Whichever you prefer. And yes, I do have rubbers."

"Oh!" I stood there blushing.

"Don't you think," he confided, leaning into me, "that four years of foreplay is enough?" He picked up the bottle and offered me a swig again, but I shook my head. I didn't want to do anything that might confuse me, or make me unable to remember and savor things later.

"C'mon back," Declan said, "and I'll show you my den of iniquity." He strode through a short dark hallway, opening the beaded curtain for me and letting me in first. The beads clicked soothingly as the strands swung to rest.

Declan's room was small, and the air in there was stale. Piles of books lay on the floor: *Under the Volcano, In Cold Blood, The Armies of the Night.* There was very little room left for the large, unmade bed. Each wall was a different color: olive green, navy blue, bright orange, and hot pink, as if in mockery of my childish red-blue-green-yellow sense of order. Against the orange wall was a narrow wooden table littered with prints. "My latest forays into photo-land," Declan explained. "This is my work. The ones in the main room, of course, are Leonid's. Go ahead, have a look. See what you think."

There were two shots of Raquel, one with clothes on and one with clothes off. She had a beautiful body and for some reason didn't look show-offy in the nude the way she did in real life. There were nudes of several other girls that Declan had been involved with, two of which were taken outdoors. There were also some pictures of people I knew from school that I'd never have dreamed Declan would be interested in, like Diego someone, a black football player in our grade who had a huge Afro and shark-like teeth. In one of the photos, Diego was smiling and nude, in a he-man-type pose with his arms, but with his legs pressed together. He had pubic hair but no penis. I winced.

"That one?" Declan laughed.

I wished I had something original to say. Raquel probably would. She'd probably act as if a guy without a penis were nothing unusual and then make some joke on top of that. "What—"

Declan was merciful. "He just stuck it between his thighs."

"Oh," I said, forcing a smile. There was something about Declan's pictures that made me feel excluded, as if everyone else got the joke except me. Were they all like that? I rifled through the stack.

There seemed to be two categories: (a) people Declan was interested in, and (b) people who had something wrong with them. That studious, acne-scarred girl named Fumiko who had been in my Latin class! It was surprising enough that Declan noticed her existence, but how had he gotten her to take her clothes off? I looked back down. A girl in my Trig class who had become skinnier and skinnier over the last year or so, like Shalimar. She was wearing her glasses, but nothing else. And underneath that one, a nude of a cheerleader who sat in my homeroom class and was always smacking her gum. I'd heard she'd had to undergo an operation to remove part of her digestive system. On the cheerleader's abdomen was a strange plastic bag that seemed to be attached right to her body.

Oh, God, what was this? Giselle? Nude, on tiptoe, with one hand on top of her cello as if for balance, and the other hand waving the bow? There was nothing wrong with Giselle! She would have to be in the other category. Did Clifton know? Was the photo taken before he and Giselle were together?

There was no doubt in my mind that in order to photograph these girls, Declan had told all of them something. They had a special aura about them, or they were imperfect but also perfect, or the light was reflected so beautifully in their faces. He'd kissed them, and said he was at their cervixes, and said that *x* number of years of foreplay was enough. Doing that to a girl you wanted to sleep with—I guess that was one thing. But the idea that Declan would seek out odd girls and feature what was weird about them—now, finally, I was angry.

"You just want people who—who're damaged. Is that it?" I demanded.

"Miss Martha, don't be—"

"They're all—oddities behind what looks normal! Or—normalness behind—look, I get it, okay? I'm an oddity to you!" *Shrug.*

Declan put his hand on the jumpy shoulder. "My lady—"

"Don't *my lady* me! You think you can capture my shrug in a nude photo? You can't!"

"Miss Martha. Don't you realize? We're all oddities!" From another stack, Declan pulled out a nude self-portrait he'd taken in a mirror. This one was in color. He was wearing heavy blue eyeliner and coral lipstick. Goddamn him, he was even pretty as a girl.

I stared at the photo. The kind of person who would put on makeup and then take a picture of it and show it off—that was a person who, I knew, would never be interested in me. Declan was going to want to spend his time with people who were as brave as he was—who were willing to expose the parts of themselves that were scary, I guessed. As hard as I worked, I couldn't be like that. It was too advanced for me. It was like the infinity of books at Cody's—an equally impossible demand.

I walked past Declan back out to the main room, where I'd left my purse. He didn't try to dissuade me. He just stood at the beaded curtain, watching me with that maddening expression of amusement, the bottle in one hand. I had my kiss, and I could always come back and have sex with him if I changed my mind.

Giselle. What was I going to do about that? I'd have to think. In the meantime, Steely Dan ushered me out.

32

berkeley

A few days later, a big envelope from Cal arrived in the mail. I knew that if I'd gotten in, my father would start bitching about how I always worry for no reason, and if I'd been rejected, he'd offer me some bullshit about the human condition. If I'd gotten in but hadn't gotten financial aid, he'd probably give me a little of each. I was in no mood for any of it. So I took the envelope into the bathroom for privacy, my heart racing and my stomach roiling as I tore open the flap.

Suddenly, privacy was irrelevant. "Dad! Dad!" I shouted, flinging open the door and racing into the kitchen. "I'm accepted at Cal! *And* they're giving me money!"

My father looked up from his crossword with a mild half-smile. "Good, honey."

It wasn't exactly the full-throated congratulations I was expecting. "Dad, you understand, right? That I have the money to go? They're giving me a Regents' Scholarship of $650 per year for four years! That's gonna cover all of my tuition and registration fees. Plus they awarded me living expenses. Which means I can use it for a dorm or a co-op, plus it'll pay for my books and stuff! So—thank you for filling out those forms!"

I figured that at the very least, my father would be happy he didn't have to support me anymore. But he just gave me this baffled look, as if I'd gotten around the money obstacle using the same illegitimate trick I'd used to do well in school all along. As if Bancroft Way were some sort of picket line that I wouldn't dream of crossing if I were a moral person.

I ignored him and went and sat on my futon. The envelope was filled with papers and brochures: housing forms; pamphlets about activities and clubs; a glossy sheet about the history of the university. There were all kinds of pictures of the Campanile and Sather Gate and Sproul Plaza, landmarks so familiar that they looked almost unfamiliar on paper. There was a sheet about medical services on campus. I must have checked some box saying I was Jewish, because there was an invitation from Hillel to come enjoy free dinners on Friday nights.

I could be Jewish if I wanted. I could go to a doctor if I wanted. I could live in a dorm and hang around with other Cal students if I wanted. All of these were things I wished for Hildy and Drew. But it had been hard enough making them happen for myself.

I thought of calling my mother to tell her I was going to Cal, but I didn't want a lecture about how I wasn't getting far enough away from my sick, destructive father. On the other hand, I was worried that she'd get really upset if she somehow found out and I hadn't told her. So I wrote her a brief letter at her parents' to show I was mature. Also to show I'd be moving to student housing.

"Dear Mom," I wrote, "How are you? I'm fine. I wanted to tell you I'm starting at Cal in October. They gave me all the money I need to go, and even to live in a dorm. I hope you're okay. Love, Martha."

Graduation came, then a long summer of working for Mr. Lucas, hanging around with Stephanie and Brett and Paisley and Hildy and Drew, and trying not to roll my eyes when my father would lecture us kids about how we should really call our mother. Who, by the way, never responded to my letter.

I also spent a lot of time daydreaming about Clifton. I hadn't figured out what to do about that photo of Giselle at Declan's, so I hadn't done anything. Then toward the end of the summer, I found out that Giselle had broken up with Clifton, apparently in order to take up with his best friend, Ben, before leaving for Oberlin. I thought of calling Clifton. I wanted to call. But Mrs. Cray might answer the phone, so again, I did nothing.

In the fall, my father, Drew and I put half a dozen boxes of my stuff into the Plymouth and drove over to the women's co-op I'd been assigned to on the north side of campus. Dorm rooms were more expensive than co-op housing. So were two-person rooms at co-ops instead of the four-person suite I'd chosen. I was worried that my father would criticize me for liking creature comforts, so I purposely chose something less expensive and a little chaotic.

As we were bringing my cartons into the room I'd been assigned to, a mouse scuttled across the floor next to the molding in the front hallway. Actually—it was a pretty big mouse. I hoped my father hadn't seen. But then the roommate who had already gotten there was sullen and unfriendly, and there was something about the green, poorly lit walls and the cabbage-y, institutional smell wafting in from the kitchen that made my eyes fill with tears.

My father took one look at me and said, "You know, you don't have to move in here," and, without waiting for my response, started carrying my things back to the car. Drew followed him, a box of clothes in his bony arms, and then I brought up the rear with my blanket and pillow. I hate to admit it, but I was really relieved.

I know, I know, you're disappointed. You were hoping I'd make a clean getaway. Look, it's not so easy for people like me to escape with certainty or elegance. We limp along, or shrug along, until we can take the next clumsy step in the right direction.

Back at the apartment, of course, I had second thoughts. I steeled myself the next morning and called the housing office, and luckily, a very nice woman answered and put me on the waiting list for another co-op or a dorm. "Students change their plans sometimes," she said kindly. It wouldn't be for the fall, she said; I was too far down on the waiting list. But something might open up winter quarter.

It was finally the day I was starting my fall classes, and I'd been up most of the night tossing and turning. What if I couldn't keep up with all the reading? What if I didn't get good grades? What if there was no housing available winter quarter? What if housing was available but I got a crummy roommate? Why was my mother so mad at me? What had I done, really? It was beyond unfair. Was Drew going to be okay? Was Hildy? And then there was Clifton. I'd bought him a greeting card and was planning to send it to him, but what would I write? I didn't know how to find the words, figure out how to say, *Hello, I'm here, call me*, without quite saying it.

I dozed off around four and overslept, but luckily, my first class wasn't until ten. I sat bleary-eyed at the kitchen table in a pool of autumn sunlight, picking at a bowl of dry Cheerios and sipping hot tea while my father drank his instant coffee and pored over yesterday's newspaper. I checked my schedule again: Beginning Musicianship (though my father thought it was ridiculous for me to sign up for something so basic), Introduction to Western Music (ditto, but I was worried that I'd learned stuff from him along the way that just wasn't true), English 1a, Psychology 101, and University Chorus.

The table jiggled a little as my father got up and left the kitchen. I heard him open the door to the front closet, and figured he was rustling around for LPs to take to one of the dealers in San Francisco.

But when he came back into the kitchen, he was carrying a dusty violin case, which he shoved into my hands without comment.

"What's this—? Dad! You can't afford—" *Shrug*. I felt awful. I had more money now than he did. I was rich.

"It's in shitty shape," he interrupted. "Got it at the flea market. Needs new strings, and the—what do you call it? That piece that holds up the strings—"

"The bridge?" I got up and put the instrument on the deep ledge of the kitchen window, opened the case and took it out. My father apparently hadn't noticed that by now, I was much more of a singer than a violinist. Still, the violin was an inviting, mellow shade, and the inside of the case was crushed blue satin that had faded but that was still pretty. The bow needed to be rehaired, but I was glad to see that rosin dust had collected around the violin's *f* holes and the wide end of the fingerboard. Someone had played this instrument.

"The bridge," my father said, as if he'd come up with it on his own.

"It's okay! I think that's all very minor—"

"Take it down to Aschow," he barked, referring to the violin repair guy way down Telegraph in Oakland.

"Dad—thank you!"

"You'll get it fixed up. Isn't that teacher of yours in the Music Department over there?"

For a minute, I was annoyed that my father just assumed he knew what I wanted. But then I realized I was smiling. He was right, for a change: I *could* study with Mrs. Cray again. I'd been planning on private voice lessons, but maybe I could do both if I alternated.

I put the violin back in the case and hugged my father. Just for a second.

And then I gathered up all my stuff from the shelf above my futon: my reg packet, with the Regents' Scholarship card that would be fed into a computer, my schedule, my textbooks, and a spiral-bound Cal notebook and Lindy pen that I'd bought for the occasion. I thought of Hildy, who was so much more of a natural for this than I was. *Natural*, ha ha. I wished she and I had matching Cal notebooks that kept getting confused with each other. I wished she could show me the ropes now the way she'd tried to do when I was starting kindergarten. *Shrug.*

I thanked my father again and left the apartment. Down on the street, the fall light made everything look really vivid. I walked up Bancroft toward Telegraph, treading over those strange little frosted glass panels that were still embedded in the sidewalk even though so much else had changed.

I crossed Bancroft, leaving behind me the Doughnut Central that had replaced Smoke and Records, and leaving Cody's behind that. There were Cal students everywhere, my peers, all of us immersed in an overture of sound: Holy Hubert spouting fire and brimstone, the Hare Krishnas in their endless metal-castanet-punctuated chant, the congas thumping hollowly from Lower Sproul Plaza, the rhyming knish vendor singing *Delicious! Nutritious! Hot knishes!* over and over, a 51 bus making that loud letting-off-steam sound as it nosed into the A/C Transit stop in front of the student union building. The whole place was jumping with noise and color and vitality, and I was part of it.

acknowledgments

I am very grateful to the visionary Brooke Warner and the She Writes Press team for their exceptional professionalism and steadfast support throughout the publication process. I also want to acknowledge Julie Powers Schoerke and her team at JKS Communications for their enthusiasm about my book and their excellent follow-through.

I had many fine readers who helped me along the way. Kathleen Caldwell, Jody Cornelius, Liza Dalby, Amy Grossman Di Costanzo, Ruth Greenstein, and Elisabeth Schlessinger offered valuable feedback and cheered me on. Very special thanks to Joanne Rocklin for her thoughtful reading and generosity with her time. And heartfelt gratitude to Michele Lieban Levine, whose critical eye and friendship were, and are, godsends.

I've been working on this book for a long time. My husband, Mark Moss, always my first reader, gamely took on draft after draft, somehow able to give me a fresh perspective each time. I am deeply grateful for his loving support.

As a survivor of childhood domestic violence, I've been very glad to witness the increasing awareness of how battery at home affects children. More information is available from the Childhood Domestic Violence Association (cdv.org).

Appendix

musical references in *Shrug*
(in order of appearance)

Brahms's cello sonata opus 38

Mahler's *Des Knaben Wunderhorn*

Beatles' *Help!* album

Beatles '65

Beatles VI

Johann Strauss's waltzes

Mozart's *Eine Kleine Nachtmusik*

Debussy's "Clair de Lune"

Copland's *Fanfare for the Common Man*

Bach's *St. Matthew's Passion*

Khachaturian's violin concerto

Prokofiev's 5th symphony, *Allegro marcato*

Dobie Gray's "The 'In' Crowd"

Dobie Gray's "The 'In' Crowd," Ramsey Lewis version

Beatles' *Yesterday And Today* album

Beatles' *Revolver* album

Beatles' *Rubber Soul* album

Cole Porter's *Kiss Me, Kate*

Beethoven's 8th symphony

Beatles' "Dizzy Miss Lizzie"

Beatles' "I Saw Her Standing There"

Beatles' "You're Gonna Lose that Girl"

Beatles' *Sergeant Pepper's Lonely Hearts Club Band* album

Beatles' "You Like Me Too Much"

Beatles' "If I Needed Someone"

Beatles' "Think for Yourself"

Beatles' "Ticket to Ride"

Beatles' "And Your Bird Can Sing"

Beatles' "We Can Work it Out"

Bach's Cantata #140, *Wachet Auf*

Beatles' "Martha My Dear"

Youngbloods' "Get Together"

Beatles' "For the Benefit of Mr. Kite"

Beatles' "Strawberry Fields Forever"

Beatles' "Lucy in the Sky with Diamonds"

Richard Strauss's *Thus Spake Zarathustra*

Richard Strauss's *Don Quixote*

Richard Strauss's *Rosenkavalier* suite

Brahms' piano quintet opus 34, *Scherzo*

Franck's Prelude, Fugue and Variations for organ

Schubert's *Lieder* (songs)

Schubert's piano trio opus 100, *Andante con moto*

Irving Berlin's *White Christmas* sung by Bing Crosby

Stravinsky's *Petrushka*

Beethoven's *Archduke* trio

Bernstein's *West Side Story*

Bernstein's *Chichester Psalms*

Bernstein's *The Age of Anxiety*

Bernstein's *Trouble in Tahiti*

Orff's *Carmina Burana*, "Blanziflor et Helena"

Loussier's jazz versions of Bach pieces

Ravel's *Bolero*

Walter Gold's "It's My Party" sung by Lesley Gore

Wagner's *Ring* cycle

Beethoven's string quartets

Brahms's violin sonatas

Loesser's *Guys and Dolls*

Bob Dylan's "Love Minus Zero" sung by Joan Baez

Bob Dylan's "North Country Blues" sung by Joan Baez

Bob Dylan's "Love is Just a Four-Letter Word" sung by Joan Baez

Bach's unaccompanied violin partitas and sonatas

Bach's *Italian* concerto

Debussy's piano works

Bach's *Magnificat*

Mozart's flute quartets

Beethoven's *Grosse Fugue*, opus 133

Barber's violin concerto

Burt Bacharach's "Raindrops Keep Fallin' on my Head"

Vivaldi's *The Four Seasons*

Pachelbel's Canon in D

Bach's *Goldberg Variations* performed by Glenn Gould (1955 version)

John Lennon's "Imagine"

Rod Stewart's "Maggie May"

Isaac Hayes's "Theme from *Shaft*"

Don McLean's "American Pie"

Cher's "Gypsies, Tramps and Thieves"

Bonnie Bramlett and Leon Russell's "Superstar"

The Chi-lites' "Have You Seen Her"

Mozart's *Requiem*: "Confutatis"

Verdi's *Otello*: kiss motif

Bernstein's *West Side Story*: "I Have a Love"

Mozart's Flute and Harp concerto in C, K. 299

Prokofiev's *Alexander Nevsky*

Bach's Cantata #8, *Liebster Gott*

Steely Dan's "Do It Again"

About the Author

© Chris Loomis

Lisa Braver Moss has written for *Parents, Tikkun, Lilith,* the *Huffington Post,* and many other publications. She specializes in family issues, health, Judaism, and humor. Moss is the author of the novel *The Measure of His Grief* (Notim Press, 2010). Her nonfiction book credits include *Celebrating Family: Our Lifelong Bonds with Parents and Siblings* (Wildcat Canyon Press, 1999) and, as a coauthor, *The Mother's Companion: A Comforting Guide to the Early Years of Motherhood* (Council Oak Books, 2001). She is also the coauthor of *Celebrating Brit Shalom* (Notim Press, 2015), the first-ever book of ceremonies and music for Jewish families opting out of circumcision. Moss, a survivor of childhood domestic violence, grew up in Berkeley and lives in nearby Piedmont with her husband. They have two grown sons.

SELECTED TITLES FROM SHE WRITES PRESS

She Writes Press is an independent publishing company founded to serve women writers everywhere. Visit us at www.shewritespress.com.

Cleans Up Nicely by Linda Dahl. $16.95, 978-1-938314-38-4
The story of one gifted young woman's path from self-destruction to self-knowledge, set in mid-1970s Manhattan.

How to Grow an Addict by J.A. Wright. $16.95, 978-1-63152-991-7
Raised by an abusive father, a detached mother, and a loving aunt and uncle, Randall Grange is built for addiction. By twenty-three, she knows that together, pills and booze have the power to cure just about any problem she could possibly have . . . right?

I Like You Like This by Heather Cumiskey. $16.95, 978-1631522925
When social outcast Hannah captures the attention of a handsome and mysterious boy who also happens to be her school's resident drug dealer, her life takes an unexpected detour into a dangerous and seductive world—and she is forced to reexamine what she believes about herself and the people she trusts the most.

The Rooms Are Filled by Jessica Null Vealitzek. $16.95, 978-1-938314-58-2
The coming-of-age story of two outcasts—a nine-year-old boy who just lost his father, and a closeted young woman—brought together by circumstance.

Arboria Park by Kate Tyler Wall. $16.95, 978-1631521676
Stacy Halloran's life has always been centered around her beloved neighborhood, a 1950s-era housing development called Arboria Park—so when a massive highway project threaten the Park in the 2000s, she steps up to the task of trying to save it.

Beautiful Garbage by Jill DiDonato. $16.95, 978-1-938314-01-8
Talented but troubled young artist Jodi Plum leaves suburbia for the excitement of the city—and is soon swept up in the sexual politics and downtown art scene of 1980s New York.